NO MAN'S LAND

Beltran's big hand snaked out and wrapped around Frank's right wrist, pushing the gun away from him. He gave it a stout yank and both men fell back to the ground.

Frank expected Swan to shoot him at any moment. His strength was failing. He knew he couldn't hold on to the gun forever.

A sudden thud rocked both men. For an instant, Frank thought it was the Ranger. Then he saw Velda, her flimsy gown gathered up at her hips, rear back and kick Beltran again in the head.

The outlaw's eyes went wide and his grip loosened enough for Frank to pull his arm free. Beltran was only momentarily stunned and moved toward Frank again, a deadly look of determination in his dark eyes.

The gunfighter shoved the revolver toward the only target that wouldn't endanger the Ranger, and shot Beltran through the neck.

His spine shattered, the outlaw went instantly rigid. He sputtered and gurgled, trying to talk, but his voice box had been torn away, leaving behind only a mass of blood and gore.

Frank realized he was no longer a threat and rolled quickly to get a shot at Swan.

The outlaw leader had vanished.

BOOK YOUR PLACE ON OUR WEBSITE AND MAKE THE READING CONNECTION!

We've created a customized website just for our very special readers, where you can get the inside scoop on everything that's going on with Zebra, Pinnacle and Kensington books.

When you come online, you'll have the exciting opportunity to:

- View covers of upcoming books

- Read sample chapters

- Learn about our future publishing schedule (listed by publication month *and author*)

- Find out when your favorite authors will be visiting a city near you

- Search for and order backlist books from our online catalog

- Check out author bios and background information

- Send e-mail to your favorite authors

- Meet the Kensington staff online

- Join us in weekly chats with authors, readers and other guests

- Get writing guidelines

- AND MUCH MORE!

Visit our website at
http://www.kensingtonbooks.com

WILLIAM W. JOHNSTONE

THE LAST GUNFIGHTER
NO MAN'S LAND

PINNACLE BOOKS
Kensington Publishing Corp.
http://www.kensingtonbooks.com

PINNACLE BOOKS are published by

Kensington Publishing Corp.
850 Third Avenue
New York, NY 10022

All Kensington Titles, Imprints, and Distributed Lines are available at special quantity discounts for bulk purchases for sales promotions, premiums, fund-raising, and educational or institutional use. Special book excerpts or customized printings can also be created to fit specific needs. For details, write or phone the office of the Kensington special sales manager: Kensington Publishing Corp., 850 Third Avenue, New York, NY 10022, attn: Special Sales Department, Phone: 1-800-221-2647.

First Pinnacle Printing: March 2004

10 9 8 7 6 5 4 3 2 1

Printed in the United States of America

I feel an army in my fist.

—Johann Christoph Friedrich von Schiller

Chapter 1

Frank heard the wagons long before they came into view, and he smelled them before he heard them. The odor of soap and other fancy stinkum hit his nose hard in contrast to the periodic whiff of cottonwood on the windswept Kansas plains. Dog, the scruffy cur that sat by his side, smelled it too and whined softly, looking up at his master. Soap meant women, and more often than not, women meant trouble.

Frank sat on the knife ridge overlooking what passed for a trail, and watched the slow procession of wagons struggle single-file out of a low draw to the east. Five big, fine Conestoga prairie schooners, each pulled by six of the most handsome mules Frank had ever seen. Stout, red Missouri mules. A lone rider, likely the wagon master, rode scout about a hundred yards ahead of the lead team.

Five mounted men flanked the train, three on one side of the wagons, two on the other. Each man carried a rifle across the pommel of his saddle, ready for use.

When the lead rider drew within hailing distance, Frank lifted his rains and urged Stormy, his big Appaloosa, down the incline to intercept him. Rocks and loose gravel skittered around the horse's hooves as they slid down the hillside.

The scout spotted Frank and lifted his left arm, halting the train. His right hand dropped to the butt of his pistol.

Frank reined up, raised his hands, and smiled. "No need for that, friend," he called. "I mean you no harm."

"State your business," the scout shouted back, a little

louder than Frank thought necessary. He was no more than twenty yards away.

"Just some company on the trail. Maybe some coffee and a speck of conversation when you decide to make camp for the evening."

"You alone?" The wagon master surveyed the open ridge-line above them, shielding his narrow eyes with the flat of his hand.

Frank shrugged. "I am what you see, friend."

"Look at the dog, Mama." A girl of five or six with blond braids stuck her head out of the canvas flap on the lead wagon.

"Does he bite?" another called from the driver's seat of the next wagon in line. This one was older, well into her teens, with frizzled red hair the color of a carrot.

Dog sat on his haunches beside Stormy, studying the girls. He didn't move.

"Only bites if you try and do him harm," Frank called out, tipping his hat to the young ladies. "Told you there were women out here," he whispered under his breath to Dog.

"We're about to find a place to make camp," the wagon master said, trotting up next to Frank. "You familiar with this country?"

"Not too much. Been heading west for the better part of a week, staying out of the strip."

The wagon master turned in the saddle to look around him. "We're out of the strip, I think."

Frank nodded. "By about ten miles, I'd say."

"Good. That's a blessing anyhow. You got a name?"

"I do." Frank smiled and watched for a change in expression. "Frank Morgan."

The wagon master looked like somebody had pulled the plug and drained all the color out of him. He took a deep breath to steady himself. When he finally found his voice, he shouted back to the train. "We got Frank Morgan here paying us a visit!"

That got everyone's attention. Those in the wagons nearest the two men sat and stared in silence at the West's most
famous gunfighter.

"I'm not on the prod for anyone," Frank told the other
man, hoping to settle his nerves a little. "I'm just drifting,
seeing the country."

"You plannin' on riding along with us, Mr. Morgan?"

Frank shrugged. "Unless you have an objection." There
was something about the wagon boss that didn't fit with his
smile. He looked Frank over like he was sizing him up for a
fight. His left eyebrow was crooked and white as a sheet. A
thin scar ran up through the middle of it, crossed his forehead, and disappeared again under his hat. It made the man
look like he was in a state of a perpetual scowl.

"You'd be welcome." The man held out a hand. "Steve
Wilson."

Frank shook the friendship hand, and then fell in beside
the other man on point as the wagons began to lumber along
behind them again.

"Fine-looking wagons," Frank remarked. He began the
sizing-up process he did when he met anyone new: height,
weight, skill with a horse, nerve, demeanor, and the small,
almost imperceptible things that you didn't see unless you
were watching carefully—it was what had kept him alive for
so long. This Wilson character seemed mighty preoccupied
with something.

"Huh?" Wilson finally said.

"The wagons," Frank repeated. "With the West building
up since the war and the railroads coming in all over, I don't
see wagons as much as I used to. These look to be good
ones."

"Aren't they, though," Wilson said snapping out of his stupor. "All of them special built in Indiana for this trip.
They've served us well. Got us this far without too much
trouble."

"Where you headed?"

"Colorado. In another week or so we'll turn north some and then it's on to our new home."

"Farmers?" Frank caught Wilson staring at the Colt Peacemaker on his hip.

Wilson nodded. "You bet. And we're good farmers too. It's in our blood. It's just getting too crowded back in Indiana. We all wanted some space where we could stretch out some. Build a place to call our own."

Frank looked at the man's hands. They were strong hands, but didn't have the calluses he'd expect of a farmer. Wilson had been on the trail a while, though, so Frank dismissed the notion that the man might be lying.

"Yeah, I know what you mean," Frank said. "I'm partial to the wide-open spaces myself."

"That's a fine lookin' horse you're ridin', Mr. Morgan. I don't believe I ever seen one quite like it."

"Appaloosa, Mr. Wilson. Nez Percé Indians breed them."

Wilson shook his head. "Beautiful animal. Very striking."

They rode on for a few hundred yards without speaking. Only the creak of the wagons and groan of saddle leather broke the silence. As they topped a small rise, Frank pointed to a hollow below them.

"Looks like a nice little creek down there, Mr. Wilson. Plenty of firewood, forage for the stock, good spot for a camp, wouldn't you say?"

"Looks good to me too, Mr. Morgan. I'll ride back and tell the others."

"Before you do, Mr. Wilson, I'd like to propose a suggestion."

"Certainly."

The man tensed and seemed to hold his breath at what might be in store. Frank couldn't be certain, but it almost looked like the man was getting ready to draw his gun.

"Let's you and me drop this *mister* business before we wear each other out. I'm Frank and you're Steve. What do you say?"

The wagon master relaxed and gave a nervous chuckle. "Sounds good to me, Frank. You got a deal."

Wilson spun his horse and trotted back over the ridge to bring up the wagons.

"What do you think, Dog?" Frank said as the other man rode out of sight. "Am I getting too jumpy or is that man hiding something?"

A few minutes later, Frank squatted by the creek and watched as Wilson positioned the wagons on a flat in a tight circle. The man appeared to know his business, Frank thought. Maybe he was just what he said he was.

The men in the group tended to the stock, while women drew water from the creek for cooking and drinking. Once the huge oak barrels on each wagon were filled, the children led the horses and mules down to drink. Frank helped gather wood for the cook fire, ignoring the surprised looks he received from the men. The women thanked him in hushed tones, and the children followed him around, the young boys trying to emulate his walk.

Once the stock was settled and the firewood was gathered, the women dragged out camp ovens and busied themselves with their mixing, stirring, and kneading. Rich smells of meat and gravy filled the still air as the men sat down to cups of fresh-brewed coffee and conversation.

Wilson introduced the families in turn: Able and Carolyn Brandon and their three children, two girls in their teens and a boy of about ten, each with freckles and frizzy carrot-colored hair, just like their mother. Weldon Freeman and his wife Paula, with three blond girls that stair-stepped from five to thirteen. Randall and Judith Fossman were the oldest couple, with two boys in their teens and twin fifteen-year-old girls. Harry and Betty Ellington had a boy and a girl, neither over ten years old. A sour-looking fellow named Virgil Carpenter and his family rounded out the group. He had two daughters and his wife's name was Dixie.

"My mother liked the name Dixie," Mrs. Carpenter explained with an easy smile, green eyes sparkling in the fire light.

"Well, I don't," Virgil said, spitting on the ground. "The word leaves a bad taste in my mouth. I call her by her middle name—Lou. Guess it comes from my time in the damn war. I was just a boy really, but I killed me my share of them damn stinkin' Rebs." Carpenter took a sip of his coffee and eyed Frank over the rim of his cup. "You fight in the war, Morgan?"

Frank nodded. "Yes, I did." He took Mrs. Carpenter's hand gently and shook it. "And I believe I'll call you Dixie." Before Carpenter could say anything else, Frank looked over at Mr. Brandon. "Y'all have some fine-looking mules, Able. Are they plow-broke?"

"Well, I . . . suppose they are. I mean . . . of course they're plow-broke."

Silence fell around the camp for a few moments. The women whispered among themselves.

"I suppose we should level with you, Frank," Wilson finally said. "You're a smart enough man to figure out ain't.a one of us know anything about farming."

"Wilson . . ." Weldon Freeman cocked his head to one side and gave the wagon master a tight-jawed look.

The wagon master waved him off. "Oh, it's all right. I know a bit more about the famous Mr. Morgan than you folks. Read a long article about him in the St. Louis paper a while back. Seems he's a rich man. Got more money than all of us put together. He's got no need to steal from us. Isn't that right, Frank?"

Frank nodded and took a swallow of coffee. "I reckon I'm worth considerable, for a fact."

Betty Ellington smoothed her apron out in her lap and began to fuss with her daughter's braids. "If you have so much money, why are you out here? Don't you have a real home?"

Frank grinned. Something that seemed so simple to him was always so hard for others to understand. "I have all this." He waved his hands at the sky and plains around them.

"But don't you want more?" Judith Fossman asked.

"I have a nice little place in the mountains west of here," Frank replied. "I reckon I'll retire there someday. Maybe raise cattle and a few horses. But that's years down the road."

"So for now you just . . . drift?" Dixie Carpenter said.

Frank said, "I enjoy life."

"And take a life occasionally, so I hear," Randall Fossman said without any detectable note of malice in his statement.

"When I'm pushed." Frank turned to the wagon master. "So, if I may be so bold, if you're not going to Colorado to farm, what are you folks up to?"

Wilson leaned in close, his voice almost a whisper. "We're going to hunt for gold."

"Gold?"

"Yes, sir," Able Brandon said. "Gold. In the Sangre de Cristo mountains west of Canyon City. According to Mr. Wilson, only a few people know about it. We plan to be among the first to stake our claims."

"I suppose that could be gold country, but it's also Ute country," Frank reminded them.

"Oh." Wilson waved his hand at the thought. "I hear tell the Utes aren't much of a problem to go fussin' over anymore. Besides, these folks are plenty capable. They can handle themselves very well."

"I see," Frank said, carefully studying the wagon master. The nagging feeling that something about Steve Wilson didn't ring true tugged at Frank again, but he let his suspicion slide for the moment. He sat quietly, drank his coffee, and listened to the others talk about their hopes for gold. The longer they talked, the more Frank wanted to know about Steve Wilson. He was beginning to take on the slimy air of a snake-oil salesman, and Frank wondered how much these poor folks had paid for his services.

"I know of a way that will take days off your trip," Frank offered finally. "If you're interested, that is."

"Oh, I don't think so," Wilson said, a little too quickly to suit Frank. "I know this way. I think it would be best to stick with the route we planned."

Frank shrugged. "Just a thought. Say, this is mighty good coffee. Mind if I have another cup?"

"Certainly, Mr. Morgan," Dixie said, leaning forward to fill his from the big camp pot.

"Much obliged, ma'am. I'm a coffee-drinkin' man, for a fact."

The woman smiled, her roundish face reflecting the firelight. She'd taken off her bonnet after sundown, and her auburn hair hung in loose locks around her cheeks. Her skin was pinked with the color of health. Though her eldest daughter was nearly grown, Dixie Carpenter retained the shapely figure of a much younger woman. Frank found himself wondering if sour old Virgil even noticed her figure anymore. He had yet to see the man smile.

Frank leaned back against a water barrel and listened. He was conscious of Dixie's eyes occasionally touching him, too often to be an accident. At first he made a few feeble attempts to avoid her gaze, but finally gave into it completely. There were questions on her face, and if Frank surmised correctly, a number of silent promises.

No one else appeared to notice the silent conversation. Frank bit his lip and tried to shake off the feelings that seized him. She was another man's wife. This could lead to nothing but trouble.

Able Brandon's voice rescued Frank from his own thoughts. "You plan on riding along with us for a ways, Mr. Morgan?"

"No." Frank said suddenly, surprising even himself. He watched to see Dixie's reaction. "I don't believe I'd better.

Think I'll pull out come morning. But I want to warn you folks to stay out of the strip just south of us. It's a mean place full of all sorts of lowlifes."

"I plan to steer well clear of No Man's Land," Wilson said quickly. "Don't worry about us in that regard."

"I thought you were going to ride with us for a time, Mr. Morgan," Dixie said. She didn't look him in the eye.

"Oh, I changed my mind, Mrs. Carpenter," Frank said with a tired sigh. "That's the beauty of riding alone. A man can shift directions like the wind." He cut his eyes to Wilson. A look of relief had washed across the wagon master's drawn face and his bent, snowy eyebrow had come down some.

Something was definitely wrong here, Frank thought. Very wrong.

The next morning, just before dawn, as Frank knelt rolling up his blankets, Dixie Carpenter slipped through the mist beside the cottonwoods where he had camped.

"Mrs. Carpenter." He gave a smiling nod. "You're up awfully early."

"You said you were a coffee-drinking man. I hated for you to slip off without one last cup." The sun was not yet up, but she seemed to radiate light. "Sorry, it's a little strong, warmed up from last night."

Frank took the offered cup and sipped it. "It's wonderful and much appreciated. As is the company." He met the woman's eyes in the darkness. "Something on your mind, Mrs. Carpenter?"

"I thought you were going to call me Dixie." Her eyes held a hint of mischief.

"I did say that, for a fact." Frank chuckled. "So, Dixie, what besides your good manners and desire to serve me coffee brings you out so early this morning?"

"I don't trust that Mr. Wilson," the woman said bluntly.

Frank raised a brow at that and cocked back his hat. "What does your husband think about him?"

Dixie scoffed. "Virgil is basically a good man, but he's no smarter that this tree stump. Wilson has him completely hoodwinked. He thinks the man hung the moon and stars, but I know different."

Frank said nothing about his own concerns. "What makes you so suspicious?"

Dixie hesitated for a few seconds. "He's . . . well, devious, Mr. Morgan."

"Devious?"

"When I asked about other groups he's guided west, he became defensive, almost surly. I don't know how to explain it. He's . . . oily is the best word I can think of."

Frank nodded and drained the last of his coffee. "He won't give you a straight answer?"

"No. He says everyone he's taken west is likely spread all over and he doesn't know where they are."

"Spread out could well be true."

"I know it could, but I still don't trust him. We're carrying a lot of money, Mr. Morgan." Her eyes narrowed, and she wrung her hands in front of her. "All of us are. We sold everything we had to come on this trip, and some of us took sizable sums from the bank. I'm not ashamed to admit it. I'm frightened something is going to happen."

Before Frank could reply, Steve Wilson's voice cut the early morning air.

"Who's out there? That you, Morgan?" The voice was stronger than it was the day before—and Dixie was right, there was something oily about it.

Wilson sauntered into view out of the fog, and raised an eyebrow when he saw Dixie. "This sort of thing could lead to trouble, Morgan. She's a married woman."

"Mrs. Carpenter was kind enough to bring me a cup of coffee before I pulled out. Nothing to get knotted up over."

"Then I beg pardon . . . from both of you. I was wrong in assuming the worst."

Dixie took the cup and held out her hand. "I'm glad we met, Mr. Morgan. I hope you find whatever it is you're seeking."

Frank gently took the hand. "Thank you, ma'am. You and the others have a safe journey."

Dixie disappeared into the early morning shadows.

"So, Morgan, you're pulling out then?"

"That I am." Frank lifted the stirrup leather to tighten the cinch on his saddle. He turned his back on Wilson. "Right now, as a matter of fact."

"Maybe we'll meet again." Wilson's voice had an edge to it.

Frank picked up each of Stormy's feet to check for stones. "I'd count on it, Mr. Wilson."

"What's that supposed to mean?"

Frank turned and smiled. "Means we're heading the same direction but taking two different trails to get there. Nothing more."

Wilson grunted, then turned and walked away without another word.

Frank patted his horse on the neck and swung into the saddle. "Something about that fellow makes the hairs on the back of my neck stand up." He looked down at Dog. "What do you think?"

Dog growled, low in his throat.

"That's what I thought," Frank said, lifting his reins. "All right, boy, let's travel."

Chapter 2

Three days after Frank Morgan drifted away from the wagon train, Dixie Carpenter slapped the thick leather reins and whistled to start the mules. The terrain had changed little in the ensuing days.

Virgil and the other men rode out to the sides of the wagons scouting for game and signs of trouble. Wilson spent all his time out front. The train rumbled along at an agonizingly slow pace, creeping up low hills and slipping down shallow valleys that all melted into one long red and gray formless plain.

At least the men got to look at something different. Dixie and the other women didn't get to see much except the back end of the mules. The shorter wheel animal nearest her reminded her of Virgil. It was strong enough, but endowed with a permanent scowl and more than content to do nothing but follow in the traces behind the others. He put his back into it when he absolutely had to, but never seemed to get excited about much of anything.

The lead mule on the right was a big red beast with a kind face and a soft eye. This particular mule had a look that seemed to always wander along the horizon, looking for adventure. It pulled with a vengeance when in harness, and ate and played with gusto when turned out at the end of the day. This mule reminded her of Frank Morgan.

No matter how hard she fought the thought, ever since he'd ridden away on his beautiful spotted horse, she'd felt as if a part of her was missing. Of course, she knew it was a stupid notion, but no matter how she tried to busy her mind, it always returned to thoughts of the handsome drifter.

He was tall with strong shoulders, and had just enough gray in his dark hair to give him the dignified look of a man who knew things—a man who'd been places besides Indiana and this barren plain. But it was more than that. None of the men in the group were ugly. Each was strong, and capable in his own way. Even Mr. Wilson, with his funny pale eyebrow, was not completely unattractive. But Frank Morgan had a way about him that made all the others sit up and take notice. The men were all a little afraid of him and the women were curious about him. And it wasn't just his name either. Dixie had heard the name of the famous gunfighter, but dime novels weren't on her reading list and she had no more than a passing knowledge of him. But there was a presence that followed the man wherever he went, a stoic strength that comforted and frightened at the same time.

"Everything all right, Dixie?" The wagon master trotted up next to her wagon and reined in his horse to match her speed. Dixie. That was a switch. He'd never been so bold before as to call her by her first name.

"Everything's fine, Mr. Wilson." She stared straight into his eyes. "Why do you ask?"

He didn't flinch. "I don't know. You seem sort of preoccupied since your friend left. That's all." There was something different about him. It was as if all his manners and social pretence had dissolved as soon as Frank Morgan had ridden away.

"I was under the impression he was a friend to all of us, Mr. Wilson."

"That's a fact," the man said with a hint of a sneer. "I guess he is. More to some than others, I would wager. Well, good day to you then." He put the spurs to his horse and trotted back to take the lead.

Dixie shivered in spite of the intense sun that beat down

on the desolate plain before the wagon train. The wagon master was up to no good. None of the men appeared to notice it, but in the days since Frank had gone, there was a bounce to Wilson's step—as if he knew something was about to happen. When she tried to bring it up with Virgil, he'd dismissed her concerns. But the women could see it. They could tell something had changed. Wilson was cocky, and outspoken with the children, and bossy—even sometimes flirtatious with the women when none of their husbands were around.

That very morning, Carolyn Brandon had taken a tumble off her wagon when her mules shied at a rattlesnake. All the men had been off hunting, and Wilson was alone with the train. Dixie was in the wagon directly behind, and had heard her scream.

By the time she'd gotten back to the poor woman, Wilson was off his horse, standing over her, staring down and grinning like the lecher Dixie know he was. Carolyn's dress had caught on the brake handle and a good deal of it had ripped away, leaving her stripped down to her flannels.

When Dixie had shooed the man away, he'd just glared at her and gotten back on his horse, smiling and taking his own sweet time about it.

Something bad was about to happen. Dixie Carpenter just knew it. Steve Wilson was up to something. She couldn't put her finger on it, but she knew it surely as she knew she could trust the handsome drifter. She could feel it, deep in her soul.

The auburn-haired woman shielded her eyes with an open hand and searched the horizon. She knew the odds were against it, but hoped against hope that she might spot a lone rider on an Appaloosa horse.

"Frank Morgan," she whispered to herself. "Where are you when I need you?"

Chapter 3

Frank stayed about five miles north of the wagon train, paralleling their route. Occasionally, after topping a low hill, he could just make out the dust kicked up by the mules and the wheels of the heavy wagons. It was slow going, for the train could only make eight miles a day—and that was if everything went right.

On the fourth morning out, just before dawn, Frank lay in his bedroll trying to chase thoughts of Dixie Carpenter from his mind. Dog sat up suddenly. Faint popping sounds carried in on the morning breeze. Gunfire? Frank lay still for several minutes, straining to hear anything that might tell him what was happening. Nothing.

The sun was pinking the eastern sky when he slipped out of his blankets, put on his hat, and tugged on his boots. He stood up, buckling his gun belt around a narrow waist. He built a small sage fire to boil water and make coffee. He looked over at Dog. The big cur sat on his haunches, ears pricked, staring to the south.

"So, I did hear something, eh, boy?"

A short time later, Frank dumped coffee in the pot of boiling water, then added a bit of cold water to settle the grounds. While he was waiting, he sliced some bacon and laid the thick strips in a small frying pan. He had some pan bread left over from his supper.

Dog suddenly left the clearing in a burst of energy, and returned a few minutes later with a jackrabbit in his mouth.

"So we both have breakfast, eh, boy?" Frank said. "You want me to cook that thing?"

Dog gave him low look and clamped his mouth down tighter on the rabbit. He trotted over the edge of camp, flopped down, and proceeded to dine.

"Didn't think so," Frank said.

Smiling, he poured his coffee and then rolled a cigarette. He leaned back against his saddle and decided that when he had good daylight, he'd ride south a ways and take a look at things. Satisfy his curiosity about the shots. They were probably nothing; maybe he'd just dreamed them. Frank often dreamt of gunfire.

Frank found the wagon tracks and followed them west for a mile. Buzzards circled on the heated morning air over the rise ahead of him. Frank set his jaw and urged Stormy into a quick trot. He shook his head sadly when he topped the rise.

A large party of men, twenty or so judging by the tracks, had jumped the train as they camped for the night. The wagons and livestock were gone.

It didn't take Frank long to discover the bodies. The dead had been piled up in a dry creek bed, and one wall of sand and dirt had been caved in over them. He prodded the pile with a stick and discovered it was only the men and boys. The kids had all been shot in the head—the poor little ten-year-old Brandon boy looked like he was sleeping. The men had suffered various wounds. The body of Steve Wilson was nowhere to be found.

Frank covered the bodies again and marked the mass grave with a large mound of rocks. He stood for a moment, grimly considering the scene before him. He'd been right not to trust the wagon master, Steve Wilson, but he'd never expected him to be up to something like this. Any outlaw that would do such a thing to helpless children needed to be hunted down and killed.

The women were gone.

"Some of them are just babies," Frank muttered to himself. "Dammit!" He spit in the dirt. He didn't want to admit it, but he worried the most about Dixie.

Frank calmed down a bit and made a small, smokeless fire for coffee while he began to work out a plan. It would be no problem tracking the outlaws. The heavy prairie schooners left ruts deep enough to plant corn. Even a city slicker could follow them.

He smoked a cigarette and drank a couple cups of coffee, letting his rage boil down to a mentally manageable level. What kind of a man was this Steve Wilson? What kind of a human being would travel a thousand miles with people—men, women, and children—get to know them, share their food, enjoy their hospitality, and then coolly and dispassionately kill them? It would take some sort of inhuman creature. A monster.

Thinking about it made his anger return, and he felt the bitter taste of bile in the back of his throat. He fought the feelings, pushing them back. He wanted the hot coals he felt banked for the job ahead. He didn't need a white-hot rage riding on his shoulders. It got in the way of clear thinking.

He finished the coffee, carefully put out the fire, then tightened Stormy's cinch. He looked down at Dog.

"Let's go save us some women, boy."

Dog growled, low in his throat.

Frank kept Stormy at a ground eating dog-trot, and he made much better time than the outlaws with the wagons. It took him only a few miles before he could smell the dust kicked up by the caravan. After the attack, the killers had taken the wagons hard left, and Frank figured they were now well into the desolate strip of lawless territory known as No Man's Land.

Frank halted below the crest of a long rise, ground-tied

Stormy, and looped the packhorse's lead to a shrubby bit of sage. He took out his binoculars to study the situation.

The wagons were stopped all in a straight line. Outlaws sprawled all over the place, sleeping, drinking, and playing cards. A trickle of a stream ran nearby, but it was awfully early to set up a camp. They appeared to be waiting for something—or somebody.

The horses were all on one picket line strung between two of the wagons. The big chestnut Wilson had been riding was nowhere to be found.

At first Frank couldn't figure out where the women were, but a man in a scruffy gray hat walked around one of the wagons and lowered the tailgate. He motioned with his hand, and women and girls began to climb to the ground. Frank counted them, trying to remember how many daughters everyone had. As near as he could figure, they were all accounted for. His hopes rose when he saw Dixie jump down from the wagon. Her hat was off and her auburn hair shined in the sun.

Frank studied the group through his long lenses, and could see the girls and Mrs. Fossman were crying uncontrollably. The man in the gray slouch hat sneered and used his boot to shove the women out into the brush. At first Frank thought the women were done for, and held his breath. But the outlaws didn't do anything but push the women around. One slapped the youngest Brandon girl, knocking her to the ground.

Frank backed away from his vantage point and rolled over on his back, looking at Dog. "We can't do anything until dark, boy," he muttered. "Hell, I'm not even certain I can do anything then. But I aim to do something, even if it's wrong."

Mounting up again, Frank made a wide circle, ending up about a mile from the outlaw camp, in a little draw. He cleaned his guns twice, and every hour shimmied up the edge and removed his hat to check on the situation.

The outlaws seemed to be in no hurry to move. Frank wondered about that. What were they waiting for? What did they have planned for the women and girls? Sell them, no doubt. But to whom? Comancheros? Not this far north. Other outlaws in No Man's Land? Now that was certainly a possibility. Maybe that's where Wilson had gone. To fetch those that wanted to look over the merchandise.

Frank shook his head. Wilson was as sorry as they came. He'd met bad men before, too many of them to count—men who would kill a man for a nickel and laugh about it in front of his kids. Life came cheap to such men, and cheapened their own worth in the bargain. The more they gave up their value for life, the more worthless they became. Wilson was one of those men. One of the worst—worthless as dung in the street.

As he lay in the little draw, Frank witnessed something that shook him down to his boots. Judith Fossman seemed to be in a heated argument with one of the outlaws. The man had shoved one of her girls and Judith, her mother's rage ignited, slapped him hard across the face. The man backed away a step, put his hand to his jaw, them calmly pulled his pistol and shot her. He showed no more emotion than if he'd been at the supper table and asked someone to pass the beans.

"Dear Lord," Frank muttered. He watched the Fossman girls run to where their mother lay and throw themselves on the lifeless body.

The outlaw scum jerked the girls to their feet and shoved them back toward the wagon. Other outlaws gathered around and laughed, pointing at the dead woman. Some of the men began to tease the killer and gesture to edge of the camp. Halfheartedly, he grabbed the dead woman by the arms, dragged her out of the camp, and dumped her unceremoniously in a shallow ditch.

"Whatever you plan to do, Frank," The Drifter muttered to himself, "it has to be tonight. You can't allow this to go on."

Chapter 4

Dixie Carpenter sat on a sack of mule oats, a prisoner in the back of her own wagon. Her two girls, Laura and Faith, were about the same age as the Fossman twins. They had their mother's fortitude, but the death of their father had been devastating. The killers hadn't made them watch, but they hadn't warned them to look away either.

No one had dared speak when the outlaws had stopped and marched all the men and boys out into the little clearing beyond the line of bushes. Even after the kidnapping, and the cruel shooting of Able Brandon, who'd tried to stop the evil men, even after that, the women had not dared to think their husbands, fathers, their brothers and sons would be marched off and shot.

Dixie wept when she thought about it, wept for the unspeakable cruelty of it all—and the uncertainty of her own daughters' future.

Everyone had suffered a loss. The wagon train had melded into a tight-knit family over the hundreds of miles they traveled together. Grown men had become uncles and friends, and boys had become brothers and sons to each of the women and girls.

For the first little while, Dixie had felt nothing but shock. Pure miserable grief had followed, and she had cried just as hard as all the other women. Now, in the back of her wagon, watching her daughters and wondering what would become of them, she just felt hollow—without hope.

After their mother's murder, the Fossman girls had been told to shut up and ride in Dixie's wagon. Now the poor girls had no mother to look after and console them. To their credit, Dixie's girls dried their own tears and worked to cheer up the newly orphaned twins.

Virgil's death had been a hard thing to take. They were not the happiest of all couples, but in Dixie's mind marriage wasn't all about bliss and happiness. It was about raising a family and building something good. Now any hope of that was gone.

The brutality of her husband's murder, and all the killings, had taken its toll on each of the women. Judith Fossman had gone mad immediately. She had moaned and sobbed and shrieked at her tormentors, until they'd finally decided she wasn't worth the trouble or the price they might get for her.

Poor Carolyn Brandon, who'd watched not only her husband, but her ten-year-old son, murdered on the desolate Kansas prairie, hadn't spoken a word since the incident.

Paula Freeman wept and tried to console her three daughters at the loss of the father, who'd doted on all four of them like they were his prize, golden-haired jewels.

Dixie just felt hollow. The fact that she'd lost a husband didn't bother her as badly as the girls losing a father. That damned Frank Morgan kept popping into her mind.

For the better part of the morning after the killings, she'd cursed the famous gunfighter for leaving them to fall prey to such a slaughter. But the more she heard Wilson gloat over his victory, the more she was glad Morgan had moved on. There were too many of them, and they'd struck with such speed and force that even Morgan would have surely fallen to their bullets.

Harry Ellington had killed two of the outlaws. For his bravery, he'd been left to die slowly with the other dead, shot in the belly.

Dixie had no idea why they'd stopped. Wilson had ridden off shortly after the ambush, and she assumed they were waiting for him. It was miserably hot and stuffy under the canvas awning of the wagon. The sun beat down unmercifully and shone through in dozens of tiny nicks and holes in the gray covering. Some of the holes were from outlaw bullets.

Dixie tried to occupy her mind by imagining what she might do to Wilson if she ever had the chance. She felt sorry for Carolyn and Betty, who'd lost husbands and sons. For the first time in her life, Dixie Carpenter found herself glad her own son had died of influenza as a small child and been spared from this senseless slaughter. She tried to think back on her departed husband, but on each attempt, Frank Morgan's face came drifting into her thoughts.

She wondered where he'd gone. Wondered where he was right now. He was fond of her. A woman could tell these things. There'd been a look in his steel-gray eyes that said he was put on earth to take care of things—maybe even take care of her.

The rumble of distant thunder shook her from her thoughts. It was noticeably darker outside, and a cool breath of wind drifted in through the back flap. There was a muddy smell of rain on it. She chanced a peek outside, and saw outlaws checking the picket ropes and their horses in advance of the approaching storm.

A white squall line moved in front of a black cloud to the northwest, kicking up a column of dust in front of it. Lightning rent the gunmetal sky and sent the smell of sulfur ahead on the wind. Thunder shook the ground and the wagons with it, and all the killers looked up at the approaching storm at the same time.

Instantly, Dixie felt a calm come over her as if she'd been enveloped by a warm quilt. Morgan was coming for her. She knew it. He had to be, for he was their only hope. She looked at the rank killers out with their horses, and smiled at the thought of what the gunfighter would do to them when he came.

Chapter 5

Frank watched from his hiding spot in the low draw as a lone rider appeared just after noon. He'd wanted it to be Steve Wilson so he could take care of everything in one fell swoop. No such luck. Frank figured as much. Wilson was the type to let others do his dirty work.

Within minutes of the new arrival, the outlaws had their cinches tightened and the mules re-harnessed. They looked to be making for a stand of cottonwoods about two miles away. Cottonwoods generally meant water and with the approaching storm, the train might have to hole up for a while.

Dixie and the rest of the women had been herded back inside the wagons shortly after the Fossman woman was killed. Frank hadn't seen Dixie since.

He stayed well back, to keep from being spotted, but the outlaws looked to be a lot more worried about the storm ahead of them than anyone who might be on their trail.

It took the better part of an hour for them to reach the line of trees. Frank left Stormy and the packhorse tied to an abandoned wagon wheel, and ran forward a quarter mile at a half crouch to watch the outlaws make camp.

He was pleased to see they circled the wagons, for although it made a neat fortress against marauding Indians, it would also group most of his entire quarry together making his job a little easier. He doubted they would even post much of a guard.

From the snake-level vantage point of his belly, Frank

could see the women had been allowed out of the wagons again. The wind was in his face, and occasionally he could hear the gruff barks and shouts of the outlaws as they harassed and cajoled the prisoners into making a hasty supper before the rain got to them.

Frank estimated there were seventeen men. Some of them moved with the cocksure swagger of boys in their teens; others moseyed like they had a few years' experience. Frank made it a point to watch where the older men spent their time, planning to spend his first rounds on them. With any luck, he could spook some of the boys and run them off.

He'd been motionless for so long, forming the battle plan in his head, that Frank didn't notice the ambling coyote until it was almost on top of him. Rolling onto his side, the gunfighter hissed between his teeth. The poor animal, startled out of his skin, nearly turned inside out trying to turn and run the opposite way. Dog gave chase, but luckily the hapless coyote turned away from the wagons. Luckily for Frank, that is. With Dog after him, the coyote didn't stand a chance.

Frank made his way back to his horses and prepared for an attack at nightfall. He didn't so much have a concrete set of plans as an attitude. He'd ride in slowly, loaded for bear, and see what transpired. After what he'd seen, he didn't intend to give any quarter, and that made his job a heck of a lot easier.

If he had any kind of a plan it all, it was only a vague one, and it involved saving Dixie Carpenter if there was any way at all to get it done.

By and large, outlaws were an easy bunch to spook in the dark. They lived a life that had them constantly looking over their shoulders, constantly on guard. It was a tiresome existence, and made them prone to jerking the trigger instead of taking careful aim.

The rain started about dark. Huge drops at first, far apart enough that a body could ride between them if he took the time. They were warm, and Frank wouldn't have minded getting a little wet if they hadn't stung so hard each time they struck. Stormy pinned his ears back in annoyance, but pushed along into the storm as Frank pointed him in a wide circle so he could approach the wagon camp from the north, along the swollen creek.

About two hundred yards away, he dismounted in the trees and made ready for his assault. First he changed into a pair of moccasins so he could move more quietly and with greater speed. He tucked his boots into the pannier on the packsaddle and took out his two spare."45 Colts. Each was well oiled for storage. He wiped off some of the excess grease as he loaded each firearm, shielding them from the rain with his body. He hung one of the side arms in a holster in on his left side, in front of his razor-sharp sheath knife. The other he hung around the horn of Stormy's saddle, securing the holster with a leather whang in case things turned rodeo.

He left the 44-40 rifle tucked in its scabbard in the saddle. It might come in handy if he got pinned down, but Frank didn't intend to let that happen. Instead, he got the double-barreled coach gun out of the packsaddle. He cracked it open to make certain each tube was free of any blockage, dropped in two paper shells of buckshot, and snapped it shut with a quick flick of his wrist. The sound of the street-cannon clicking shut made his heart feel good. It was the perfect weapon for wanton killing, and Frank intended to give no quarter. He dropped a handful of extra shotgun rounds into the pocket of his hip-length leather coat. He'd save as many of the women as he could, but only the outlaws who ran stood a chance of getting out of this alive.

Frank had heard of killers and rapists going free back East after slick-talking shyster lawyers pleaded their cases for them with half-truths and twisted facts. There was no room for that here. If there was any pleading to be done for these men, it was going to have to be outside the gates of hell, because they'd never have time to see the inside of a courtroom.

Stormy was as good as they came when on the attack. The stout Appy was brazen in the face of gunfire and went boldly wherever Frank pointed him.

Two hours after dark, the rain fell in sheets. Frank, drawing his leather coat up around him, moved on the horse like a ghost through the wind-whipped cottonwoods. Lightning periodically flashed across the plain. At each strike, Frank memorized the scene before him and made ready for his attack. So far as he could tell, there was only one guard, sitting with a piece of canvas pulled up over his face. The rest of the men had taken shelter in the wagons, leaving the women crowded into one.

Lantern light and cigarette smoke poured from the three wagons where the men joked and played cards. The women's wagon was dark and quiet.

They were making this much too easy.

The wind slashed at the trees and the wind blew rain with such a fury, Frank was able to ride to within feet of the dejected canvas-covered guard. A flash of lightning split the darkness, and the gunfighter coughed quietly under his breath, causing the guard to turn and face the gaping barrels of the 12-gauge.

The outlaw's head evaporated like an exploding melon. The shotgun's roar mingled with a roll of earth-shaking thunder.

Frank dismounted before the body hit the ground, his eyes on the lighted wagons. He snapped open the Greener's breech and dropped two fresh rounds into the tubes.

He threw Stormy's reins around the back wheel of the dark wagon, and poked his head under the flap, his finger to his lips. Both the Fossman girls screamed when they saw him, in spite of his warning. Dixie lit a match and held it up in tiny fingers, looking at him with pleading green eyes. Frank couldn't remember ever wishing a match would burn forever.

"I knew you'd come back," she said when the wagon was dark again.

"You bet." Frank tried to hush the girls. "Quiet now and we can all get out of this alive." He handed Dixie the dead guard's rifle. "You know how to use one of these?"

Dixie nodded in the darkness. "I do."

"Good. Stay tough. When the shooting starts . . . "

"Ferg, everything okay?" One of the other outlaws had come to investigate. No doubt because of the Fossman twins' screaming.

Frank put a finger to his lips again and handed the shotgun to a trembling Paula Freeman. His knife hissed from the scabbard at his side. "Around here, checking on the prisoners," he mumbled.

"Huh? Ferg, what the hell you doin' . . . " The outlaw's face widened in fear and his hat blew off as he walked into Morgan's blade.

It was Judith Fossman's killer.

Frank pushed the knife in sharp edge up, and drew the surprised man to him, ripping up through gut and lung. "Little tougher when it's not a helpless woman, isn't it, partner?" Frank whispered in the dying man's ear. He lowered the body to the ground.

He poked his head back inside the wagon flap. "Are all you women accounted for?"

Paula nodded and handed back the shotgun as if it might bite her. She was definitely out of her element.

"Good," Frank said. "That makes my job a heck of a lot easier."

"What job is that?" a wide-eyed Brandon girl asked.

"Slaughter," Frank whispered to the frightened redhead. "I intend to kill every last one of these murdering scum."

A murmur went through the dark wagon.

"Good," Betty Ellington said.

* * *

The way the wagons were circled, Frank was able to position himself halfway in between the two that looked to hold the largest number of outlaws. He slogged up in the mud and measured the distance, then took four extra shells out of his pocket for the shotgun. Two he put in his left hand, two he held in his teeth.

Taking a deep breath, he aimed at the wagon to his left about a foot above the sideboard. He had the element of surprise on his side, and he figured he could get four shots off before he had to face anyone.

Fire spit from the short-barreled Greener. Frank shot one barrel at a time, spinning to put one round into each of the two wagons to throw them into pandemonium before reloading to repeat the process. He was able to use up all six rounds before wounded and frightened outlaws began to fall and swarm out of the canvas like bees.

"It's a posse," one of the younger kidnappers shouted above the storm and gunfire. Frank dropped the shotgun and cut him down with a round from his .45 as the man started for the horses.

"Posse my ass," one of the older men shouted. "It's Morgan come back for the women just like Wilson said he would. Somebody locate that son of a bitch and kill him."

Frank rolled under a wagon full of dead outlaws as a volley of gunfire kicked up the mud at his feet. Evidently, two or three of the older men had been sleeping in one of the dark wagons away from their more boisterous partners. Frank thanked his lucky stars he'd picked the right wagon to look for the women.

One of the gunmen came rushing around the wagon to the same side as Frank. He was obviously confused by the gunfire and storm. Frank gave the surprised man a smile and drilled him in the belly. The outlaw flailed frantically in the mud, crying out in pain. Another quick shot shut him up for good.

Rifle fire erupted to his right, and Frank realized Dixie

had found a clear shot. Horses squealed in the darkness and hoofbeats echoed through the wind as the remaining outlaws fled into the night.

After a few minutes, Frank climbed to his feet and counted the dead and wounded men. If his original estimate was correct, three had gotten away. Fourteen men lay in various stages of dying and death in and out of the tattered wagons.

Once he felt certain the kidnappers had truly run off, he went to check on the women.

"Hello, the wagon," he called out well in advance so Dixie didn't shoot him in the darkness. "It's me, Morgan."

Dixie stuck her head out the canvas. "Is it over?"

Frank nodded. "For now. Three slipped away, but I don't think they'll be back until they get some help. Do you ladies think you could help me get these mules harnessed? I believe we should put a little distance between us and this place just to be on the safe side."

All the women nodded, looking relieved to have something productive to do.

In less than an hour, the four wagons with intact canvas were hitched and eight outlaw horses were tied to the tailgates, their saddles and other tack stowed inside out of the weather.

Mrs. Freeman sat in the driver's seat of the last wagon in line. "What about the wounded?" She looked down at Frank and Dixie, who stood beside him. "I can still hear them moaning."

"They'll soon be quiet enough," Frank told her before he turned to Dixie. "We were lucky here. Very lucky. But his isn't over. They'll likely be back, this time in force."

"They'll not take us again," Betty Ellington said, patting the shotgun on the seat beside her. "I'll shoot my own daughter before I let her fall into the hands of those . . . " She began to sob.

Dixie reached up and put a hand on the woman's knee. "Hush now. Don't speak of such things. Mr. Morgan has a plan. It won't come to that."

A minute later, nearer Dixie's wagon, she turned and looked Frank in the eye. "You do have a plan, don't you, Frank?"

He nodded. Then he did something he rarely did. He lied. "A plan? You bet."

Three of the wounded outlaws were still alive and propped up against one of the wagons.

"If I had time, I'd hang you proper, boys. But trees are in short supply out here," Frank said, squatting beside the youngest-looking of the bunch. "I reckon there's a slim chance some of you might survive your wounds, and I'm willin' to trade you that chance for some information."

"That's a piss-poor excuse for a trade," an older outlaw with a bloody hand over a hole in his belly groaned from where he lay against a wagon wheel.

Frank gave a solemn nod. "Well, sir. You're a piss-poor excuse for a human being, so it all evens out. The way y'all treated those women . . . I ought to plug each of you right now—or let the woman have a go at you. The way I see it, it's not just Indian women who got a knack for slowly hurtin' a man. It's women in general—especially women who've been wronged."

"I never laid a hand on them women," the boy moaned at Frank's feet. "We was under orders not to touch 'em. Swan said they was worth too much money to spoil 'em."

"Who's Swan?" Frank kicked at the young outlaw to keep his attention.

"Shut up, Bobby," the gut-shot outlaw coughed. "You fool kid."

"Are you . . . Frank Morgan?" the third outlaw asked. He was a bald man and though the rain had stopped, drops of sweat and water rolled down into his squinting eyes. A crackling wheeze escaped his bullet-riddled chest as he spoke.

Frank touched the brim of his hat. "That's my name."

"Who's with you?"

"Just me, boys."

"I thought it was you. . . ." The bald man gasped before closing his eyes for the last time.

Frank turned his attention back to the boy. "Who's Swan? And where's Wilson? When is he coming back?"

The young outlaw's face twisted in pain as he spoke. He wouldn't last long. "He's a right powerful man, Mr. Morgan. He's got money, and plenty of men to back his play. They got a place not far from—"

"Shut the hell up, Bobby." The gut-shot outlaw kicked out and connected with the boy's ribs. Both men cried out in pain, but the boy fell silent.

Alone now, the older outlaw glared at Frank. "Bobby was right about one thing, you son of a bitch. Swan has a bucketful of men to back his play. That I know for certain. He'll hunt you down wherever you go, you can count on that. And when he catches up to you, he's gonna rain down on you like hellfire."

"Hellfire, sir, is something about which you will soon be intimately acquainted." Frank rose and turned to walk away.

"You aim to just leave me here?" The outlaw hacked up a mouthful of blood and spit it into the muck.

"I tried to trade with you." Frank said. "If all you can talk is trash, go talk it to the devil."

Frank climbed into the lead wagon and sat on the springy wooden seat beside Dixie. "You ladies got everything you need?"

"I think so," she said. "If we left anything behind, they can have it." She turned to face him and took a deep breath. "Frank, did you find Virgil?"

Frank slapped the mules with the leather reins to get them started. He nodded, staring straight ahead. "I did. Found all of them—and the Fossman woman."

The wagon lurched forward as the mules dug into the mud. "I want to turn us north and get us as far out of No Man's Land as I can before Wilson gathers his forces. We need to get to a town. Dodge isn't too far. I know people there. We can re-outfit and you ladies can decide what you're going to do."

Dixie suddenly burst into tears, burying her face against the sleeve of Frank's coat. "They just killed them, Frank. Herded them out into the open and shot them all—even little Timmy Brandon. I don't think Carolyn will ever be the same. None of us will." Her words gushed out as if keeping them bottled up might kill her. "They were going to sell us, Frank. They were taking us to some town where they planned to sell us all, even the baby girls."

Frank drove on through the mist, relying on the mules' night vision to steer them clear of obstacles. Soon he was keenly aware of Dixie sleeping against his shoulder. He smelled the rain on her skin and the fragrance of the soap she'd used to wash her hair, felt the rise and fall of her chest as she sobbed in her sleep.

Three hours later, he rolled to a stop. Afraid they might break a wheel if they kept going, he pitched a quick camp. They were all exhausted, and the country was getting too rough to go on in the dark. He made a quick fire for a pot of coffee, and let Dixie and the others sleep.

The rain had turned to a heavy mist, and the coffee warmed his body and spirits. Alone with his thoughts, Frank sipped the hot brew and mentally prepared himself for the attack he felt sure would come. Huddling under a makeshift canvas, he checked the rounds in his shotgun, petted Dog, and waited for the dawn.

Chapter 6

The idiot Finch kid came sliding into camp, drenched to the skin like he'd fallen in a river. Ephraim Swan heard the muffled voices outside his tent and pulled his boots on. He had given strict orders no one was to leave the women until he returned. With Frank Morgan on the prowl, it was impossible to predict what might happen.

"I'm cold, Ephraim. Where are you goin'?"

Swan turned to the skinny little redhead in the bedroll next to him and held up an open hand. She was no more than seventeen, and groggy from the Chinese drugs he'd given her. "You stay there, Carmen, and shut your mouth. I got some business to take care of and then I'll be back and warm you up proper."

He pushed the tent flap aside and pulled his oilskin duster up around his shoulders to ward off the heavy mist. He hadn't bothered with a shirt, and a trickle of rainwater ran down the small of his back and made him even more irritable than he already was.

"What in the hell are you doin' here?" he spit at the Finch kid. "The buyers won't be here to talk to me till tomorrow. I told Spence you should all stay with the wagons until I got back."

"Spence is dead, Mr. Swan." The frightened kid chewed on his lower lip enough to make it bleed. He had his hat in his hands, and rain plastered his blond hair to a freckled face. "They're all dead except Gibson and Farmer. I think they ran off right after the shooting started. I thought maybe they might beat me back here."

"Dead? Ran off? Who was doing any shootin'?" Swan doubled his fist and swore. His snow-white eyebrow crept up his forehead in frustration. "Slow the hell down and tell me what happened. Are the women dead?"

Finch shook his head. "Not as far as I know, sir. It was all out of nowhere—like the pure fury of hell. A posse swept down on us not more'n a couple hours ago." The boy's eyes were still wide with the terror he'd seen during the attack. "They didn't ask no questions or even give us a chance to give up. They just started shootin'. I was in one of the wagons. I heard a noise and when I looked out, I watched 'em blow Will Pascoe's head off with a shotgun. People were dyin' all around me, but somehow I made it to the horses and got away."

The breeze kicked up a little and Swan could smell urine. The idiot kid had not only abandoned his post, but had pissed himself in the process.

"Let me see your pistol, you gutless little puke," Swan snapped. "Did you even shoot back at the posse?"

Finch handed over his gun and nodded quickly, his head bobbing up and down like he had palsy. "Yes, sir, Mr. Swan. Sure I did, but there wasn't much to shoot at. It was dark and they was everywhere. All I could ever see was fire and smoke and rain."

The revolver had indeed been fired four times. Swan emptied the spent rounds into the mud and held out his hand until the boy gave him four fresh ones with trembling fingers.

"Calm down and listen to me, Finch." Swan put a hand on the kid's shivering shoulder. "I stand to lose a lot of money if anything happens to those females. They got their life savings hidden in the wagons, and I got an interested party who will pay handsomely for fresh women. I need you to think back and tell me which way the posse came from. How many were there and what was the last thing you saw them do?"

Swan was having a difficult time believing a posse would

just happen on a wagon train of kidnapped women and shoot it out with his men without asking a few questions about identity. His gut told him different. This whole thing smelled like Frank Morgan.

Finch's voice broke as he tried to speak, and he cast his wide eyes this way and that, as if looking for a place to run. "I . . . I don't know how many there were. Ten, maybe a dozen. Like I said, they came on us after it got dark in the middle of a gully-washer. With all the thunder and lightning it was hard to tell how many of 'em there was for certain."

"But you came back to tell me, while Gibson and Farmer ran away for their lives? You just wanted to let me know something happened. Didn't you?" Swan's hand still rested on the kid's shoulder.

Finch's sallow face brightened at the thought that he might have done something good. He looked at the small crowd of Swan's other men who had gathered around, their own slickers drawn tight to their necks from the cold rain and the tension in the air. The boy swallowed and started to stand a little straighter.

"Yes, sir, Mr. Swan. I did. I came back to report to you what happened."

"But think now. You don't remember any more?"

The kid shook his head. Rainwater dripped off his nose. "No, sir."

"All right then." Swan's voice was calm, even soothing. He smiled and tilted his head toward one of the far tents. "You go and get dried off and get yourself something to eat."

The boy nodded and turned to go. He stopped and turned back. "Oh, my pistol," he said.

"Here," Swan said softly, and shot him in the face.

The horses along the picket line a few yards away snorted and stomped at the shot, and several men poked their heads out of their own tents to see what had happened. When they saw Ephraim Swan standing in the rain with a gun in his hand, they wisely got out of his sight.

"I reckon Gibson and Farmer were the smart ones," Swan mumbled to himself, before handing the smoking pistol over to the stoic outlaw who stood beside him.

Swan looked down at the body and watched it twitch in the mud. "I can abide a man who gets run off by a posse. I can even abide a man who gets himself shot up by Frank Morgan. But I can't abide a man who'd piss himself in the middle of a fight."

He strode back to his tent, then turned and looked at the other outlaws. "I want the men ready to go first thing in the morning. Those wagons can't have traveled far in this weather. That wasn't no damned posse that took those women back from us. It was that son of a bitch Frank Morgan. I don't care how fast he is, I aim to get back what's mine."

The other man grunted and slogged away through the mud. Swan had no doubt the men would be up and ready before he was. He kept them in lots of money, liquor, and women for very little work—and every so often he killed one of the weak to show them all he was a serious man.

Inside the tent, he threw the wet oilskin over a small wooden traveling chest and climbed back into the blankets next to Carmen. The Chinese herbs he'd given the girl to smoke had made her groggy, and her head lolled back and forth when he tried to wake her up. She smacked her lips and mumbled something in her sleep.

"Stupid whore." He slapped her hard across the face to bring her out of her doze. His hand left a pink imprint across her pale cheek. He slapped her again to make sure she was awake. She flinched and batted her foggy eyes at him, then smiled.

Swan stared at his groggy bedmate in disgust. It was no wonder his buyer was willing to pay for fresh meat—women who a man didn't have to slap to get them going—women who still had some fire left in their eyes.

Tomorrow, he'd ride back with his men, kill that meddling fool Frank Morgan, and get those women back.

Chapter 7

Dixie drifted in on the mist in with a cup of coffee about four o'clock the next morning. She carried a rifle in her free hand.

"Thanks." Frank sipped the hot drink and smiled at her company. "What's got you up so early?"

"I came to give you a break from watch. You'd better get some sleep, Frank Morgan. If what you say is true, come tomorrow we are going to need you awake and ready."

Frank gave her a weary nod. "I'm afraid I'm still too wound up to sleep, but I'll try to get a catnap if I can." He stared into the cup for a long moment, then looked up at his visitor. "Mind if I ask you something?"

"Not at all, Frank. Ask me anything you want. Were it not for you, none of us would be around."

"What do you plan to do from here on out?"

Dixie shrugged. "Go forward, I guess. Just like Virgil planned. We sold everything we had back home in Indiana. The girls and I have nothing left to go back to." She clutched the rifle to her chest as if she had a sudden chill. "Why do you ask?"

Frank ignored her question. "What will you do when you get there? Hunt for gold?"

"In Colorado? Oh, heavens, no. Gold hunting was Virgil's job. I'm not too old yet. I suppose I could learn to do a number of things." She winked. "Paula Freeman's a schoolteacher and I'm every bit as smart as she is. I could always be a matronly widowed schoolmarm."

She took a seat under the canvas shelter next to him, and they sat in silence for a few minutes. Rain dripped of the edge of the makeshift tent. Horses and mules milled about in the predawn darkness, snorting for their morning feed.

At length, Frank stood and gave a yawning stretch. "Dixie, you may be a lot of things. But a widow is something that will not suit you for long."

Before she could say anything, Frank tipped his wet hat and walked to an empty wagon. To his surprise, he fell quickly into a dreamless sleep.

Four hours later, he woke with the smell of coffee and bacon in his nose. He sat up, rubbed a calloused hand across his face, and groaned. Dog, lying a few feet away, chewed on a soup bone and gave him a scolding look for sleeping in so late.

The rain had stopped and the sun was well up, but everyone was still asleep except Dixie, who stooped over a fire, stirring a pan of bacon with an iron fork.

She brushed a lock of auburn hair out of her green eyes and looked up at him.

"Thought I could make myself useful while I stood watch." An errant dab of flour decorated the tip of her button nose.

Frank couldn't help but notice the pink glow in her cheeks. "Why Mrs. Carpenter, considering the circumstances, you look the picture of health."

"Well, that's just what every woman wants to hear in the morning, Frank. 'Dixie, you're not as sickly as I thought you might be.'"

"I mean you look radiant. Happy." He searched his brain for the right word. "Corn-fed."

She threw her oven mitt at him and stuck out her bottom lip in a mock pout. "Where I come from, corn-fed means fat."

Frank looked at Dog, who offered no help. "Out here, certain things are important in a woman." Frank said. "Sturdy health and having a little meat on the bones are traits to be envied for certain." He scratched his head and tried to smooth down his wayward hair. "Though I reckon next time I'll just say you're beautiful and stop it right there."

Betty Ellington's six-year-old daughter Sara rescued him. She walked up to Frank's wagon, dragging a quilt, and held her hands up for him to take her. He squirmed and looked over at Dixie.

"She trusts you, Frank. Pick her up and hold her for a few minutes." Dixie dabbed a tear out of her eye. "The poor child deserves to feel safe for a few minutes." She sniffed and turned back to her bacon and biscuits. "Just don't call her corn-fed and you'll be all right."

Frank hoisted the tiny girl up into the wagon beside him. She didn't say a word, but seemed content to sit in his lap and lean her small head against his chest. He could feel her heart beating. She trembled like a frightened bird. He couldn't help but imagine what Wilson and his men had had in store for this innocent little one. Bile rose and burned the back of his throat. His stomach churned, but he tried to keep his outward composure so as not to alarm the girl. He rocked her gently and vowed to get her safely out of this awful place.

Two hours later saw everyone loaded, hitched, and on the trail. Frank rode Stormy out on point. He entertained the thought of riding some more with Dixie, but decided against it. She was too recently widowed, too emotionally raw. His feelings were too strong for her; he couldn't hide them. It was best to give her a little time.

By three in the afternoon they were well out of the desolate strip known as No Man's Land. They'd had such a late start, they didn't stop for lunch but kept pushing, hoping to put as much distance between the plodding wagons and Steve Wilson's gang as possible before making camp.

Frank checked each wagon, asking if the women were all right. They all nodded in turn. The only two of the ragtag group who ever had much talk in them now were Frank and Dixie. He rode by her wagon in silence for a time, scanning the country, listening to her cluck and scold the mules. She had no idea what a commodity she was in country like this. The low sun cast an orange shadow across her face and hair. The auburn locks mixed with the dark, shadowed highlights and made a radiant show of color. It reminded him of a brindle bull he'd once had, and though he'd always thought the bull particularly handsome, he decided to keep the comparison to himself.

"I'm going to hang back for a few miles," he said at length. He didn't want to make another social blunder, so he kept his words all business. "You take the wagons up over that little ridge ahead there. I'll scoot up there first to make sure nothing is going to bite you on the other side, then I'll work my way back to see who's following us. You stay with the wagons."

Dixie smiled and nodded. "You know best, Frank."

He turned Stormy to ride away, but she caught him. "Oh, and Frank, don't worry. I've had three babies. I suppose there are worse things to be called than corn-fed."

The gunfighter tipped his hat, put the spurs to Stormy, and whistled for Dog to follow. His mind was awhirl and he needed some male companionship.

The terrain was a series of one grassy rise after another, and Frank watched the last wagon disappear over a long mound to the northwest. He left his horse in the draw and worked his way up on the ridge to the south. Flat on his belly, he used his field glasses to scan the prairie on their muddy back trail.

"Damn," he hissed into the wet clay, spitting a fleck of muddy grass stem out of his mouth. "Wilson, you sure know how to build an army."

A large cadre of riders kicked up turf along the wagon track. He played the binoculars back and forth until he found the face he was looking for—Steve Wilson.

The outlaw rode to the far left of the group, on a nimble sorrel that looked like it might be a thoroughbred. Frank didn't recognize any of the other men, but two fellows out front looked haggard, as if they'd been riding all night. He pegged them for escapees from his ambush.

He counted nineteen men. All riding with a vengeance. There was no way he could take them all, not even from his position on the high ground. But he could kill Steve Wilson. That might be enough to confuse the gang—cut off the head of the snake, leave them leaderless.

Frank smiled as the outlaws came into range, and adjusted the elevation on the Creedmore ladder sights of his rifle.

"Just a few yards more . . . " he whispered against the wooden cheek-piece.

But Wilson had a bit of the curly wolf in him. Just before he came into range, he slowed the tall sorrel to let the rest of his gang rumble past him. Once they realized he'd stopped, the others reined up as well, circling their leader, milling about in the sparse grass.

Wilson spun on his thoroughbred, pointing up the track where the wagons had disappeared. Three of the men peeled off from the main group and took off at the lope to reconnoiter. Their route would bring them within in fifty yards of Frank's spot. Except for the short-stemmed buffalo grass, he had no cover.

"Dammit," Frank muttered. "How am I gonna kill you, Wilson, if you stand back and let your boys do all the dirty work?"

He swung both legs around to half-turn his body and get a better shot at the three approaching riders. He was still invisible to Wilson and the others, but if they all decided to rush him at once, things were bound to get hot.

"Turkey-shoot time, I reckon." Frank lowered the sliding

V on his sights, readjusting for the closer range, and followed the first of the three galloping outlaws with his rifle barrel. Methodically, he squeezed the first round, knowing it would hit its mark without looking, then swung his aim to the right as he ejected the empty brass and levered in another. He squeezed the trigger again and the trailing rider tumbled backward, head over horse butt, to the ground. The middle rider, all alone now and in the open, tried to turn his horse and race back to his companions. Frank never gave him the chance.

All three rider-less mounts, tired from the hard push, dropped their heads to their dead riders, sniffed them, and commenced to graze on what little of the tough grass they could find on the prairie.

Frank turned his attention back to the now-smaller army of outlaws, pushing three fresh rounds into the magazine of his Winchester as he did. It would be suicide for Wilson to charge the hill, but Frank had come across plenty of suicidal leaders before, especially those willing to let their men do the lion's share of the dying.

Laying the rifle on the ground beside him, Frank picked up the field glasses again. Wilson studied the plain around him. He had a spyglass of his own, but the setting sun was in the outlaw's eyes and made it difficult for him to get anything but a glare. Frank was sure the man had a pretty fair idea of where the shots had come from, though, so he pushed himself back from the lip of the hill, then sprinted to Stormy, and loped along the draw to get a new vantage point, a few hundred yards to the north of the wagon track.

When he poked his head up again with the glasses, the outlaws were on the move. As Frank suspected, they were doing just what he would do if he were them—trying to flank him.

Wilson and a small contingent of three riders stayed back, just out of rifle range, while the rest of the crew split off into two groups of six, riding to the north and south. If they figured out where he was and rushed him all at once, Frank was done for.

The riders heading north were well within rifle range, but if he shot, he'd give away his position. He thought about hopping on Stormy and trying for a better fighting place. Trouble was, there wasn't one.

That fact alone had haunted him more than any other since he'd rescued the women. It was one thing to sneak up on a band of killers in the rain at the darkest hour of night. Defending anything once you held it on such a wide-open plain—especially as one man—that was nigh unto impossible.

But Frank thrived on impossible tasks. Besides that, he didn't have a running bone in his body.

"If this turns out like I fear it might"—Frank looked at the cur dog on the ground next to him—"you take care of your old bones."

Dog whined and backed down the hillside a few inches as if he knew what was coming.

The gunfighter picked the lead northern rider, vowing as he did to save at least one bullet for Steve Wilson before the fight was over. As he aimed, he took into the account the stiff evening breeze that whirred in his ears, and made ready to start the fight.

The crack of a distant rifle sounded over his right shoulder, and he glanced to see one of the southern riders tumble off his horse. The man stood, clutching his arm, then fell to his knees. The sound of another round reached Frank after the first bullet had done its work.

Willing to take help from wherever it came, Frank spun and began to pluck northern riders from their horses. He took out three of them before the others could scurry out of range and lope back to their boss. Four outlaws returned from their foray to the south. A look through the field glasses revealed one of their horses was limping from a bullet wound in the shoulder.

Wilson played his spyglass back and forth along the horizon. The big man seemed to shake with hatred as he sat in the saddle.

"You know it's me, don't you, you worthless son of a bitch?" Frank watched the gang turn, Wilson in the lead during the retreat, and lope back the way they'd come. Before they were out of sight, the man on the wounded horse slid to the ground, shot his mount with no more care than if he were pitching a stone, then climbed on behind another outlaw and disappeared over the long hill.

"Wilson—or whatever your name really is, you are gonna rue the day you ever even heard my name," Frank said, pushing himself back from the crest of bunchgrass. "But first, I reckon I should go see who just saved my hide."

Ephraim Swan jerked on the reins and slid his sorrel thoroughbred to a sliding halt in the mud. He let fly a string of stinging epithets that caused the rest of his men to hunt for an escape path. He'd run across Gibson and Farmer earlier that day, tracking the wagon train and trying to figure out a way to get the women back. That alone had saved their worthless lives.

Now he was down by eight men and the same number of horses. Some of the horses might wander back, but he could ill afford to lose eight more gun-handlers. Morgan had already killed twelve of them, thirteen if Swan counted the Finch kid—whose death Swan ultimately pinned on Morgan's actions anyway. That left a total of twenty-one men—a mighty tall order even for a man with Frank Morgan's reputation. Some of the women must have been helping him.

Beyond the losses, Briscoe was wounded in the thigh and Farmer in the shoulder. Swan was sure both men knew the consequences if they slowed down.

All the surviving men milled around their leader waiting for an order. He could see the anger and fear on their faces, but at least none of them had pissed their pants.

"We're gonna have to rethink this, boys." Swan twirled his jigging horse, inwardly chiding himself for trading for such a hot-blooded animal. The horse stretched its mouth and fought the bit. "He's got some of the women shooting at us too, but I don't think they'll be much of a problem once he's gone. They still got a long ways to go. They're bound to make a slip."

Swan surveyed the group of mounted men. Each of them was toughened by weeks on the trail and had a hard enough look to frighten most civilized humans. But he doubted any one of them could handle a man like Frank Morgan—from what Swan had heard of the man, he was a long way from being civilized. No, Swan would need more than he had if he wanted to take back his women.

So far the odds had been in Morgan's favor. There had to be a way to tip those odds. Swan's released the pressure on his thoroughbred's mouth, and the horse immediately calmed. The outlaw smiled to himself. He knew what it would take to stack the odds against the famous gunfighter. Odds were nothing more than numbers, after all—and with the profit Swan would make if he got back the wagons and the women, he could afford to invest a little money to up the numbers.

"Spread the word, boys, to all those you know that I got ten thousand dollars to anyone who can bring me proof they killed Frank Morgan. I don't care how it's done. I just want him dead."

Chapter 8

By the time Frank worked his way back to the wagon track, he saw Dixie making her way toward him on a big paint horse that had belonged to one of the kidnappers he'd killed. She was wearing her blue gingham dress, a gray cooking apron, and a smile that covered her entire face.

Frank's jaw dropped. "What were you thinking?"

The smile disappeared. "Is that anyway to treat a fellow combatant?"

He let out a low sigh as she drew up next to him and they rode stirrup-to-stirrup. The rising prairie wind blew a lock of hair across her flushed face, and whipped her billowing skirts around enough to give her paint the jitters.

"How about this then?" Frank hung his head. "I'm much obliged to you for saving my worthless neck."

Dixie sniffed. Tears formed in her reddening eyes, the gravity of the fight finally catching up to her. "That'll do," she said.

Over a hot supper of chili and cornbread, the little group celebrated the day's victory. In a country as hard as this, Frank reminded them, surviving another day was something to be thankful for. All of them knew firsthand what a hard country it was.

"Are you ladies certain you want to continue in this venture?"

"We have nothing to go back to, Mr. Morgan." Betty Ellington ran a brush through little Sara's hair. The poor woman had already cried herself dry. "Wilson came into our little town back into Indiana and convinced our husbands to sell everything we had to give us a stake out here. He got them all whipped up into a frothy fever about the prospect of gold. I told Harry I didn't trust the man, but he was blinded by the thought of riches. Now we're stuck between a place we used to call home—where everything that was once ours has been sold off—and a fearsome place we've never been where we have nothing."

"Indiana is just too full of memories." Paula shrugged and poked a stick at the fire. "Memories of our husbands and our sons. It would be too painful. I'll never go back. I can teach school and every one of us has experience working in shops or sewing. If we pooled our money we could start any number of different kinds of businesses."

"Once you get settled, you can sell these mules and get a handsome sum of money," Frank said. "They are magnificent animals."

"As much as we paid for them, they ought to be. Wilson found them for us and recommended them to our husbands." Paula poked at the fire as if she were poking Wilson in the eye.

"How much further to Denver, Frank?" Dixie sat down on the quilt next to him. She was close enough he could smell her hair again.

"A good ways still. Weeks depending on the weather and how well the stock holds up." He pointed into the darkness at the edge of the fire. "We're still in Kansas, some east and a little south of Dodge City." A thought suddenly occurred to him. "How are your supplies holding out?"

"We could use some," Dixie told him. The rest of the women nodded, the smell of a town, any town, already in their noses. "The outlaws took most of our bacon and all but a dab of our sugar."

"I'm surprised they didn't find your money," Frank said.

"We can thank Betty's old man for that. He built false bottoms in all the water barrels. They were standing next to their loot all the time, but never knew it was there."

Frank nodded at the folks' ingenuity. "Well, the point is you have money to take on some supplies and still make a good go of it wherever you land. So what do you say? You want to head for Dodge?"

"I'd sure like to have me a real bath and sleep one night in a feather bed." Paula gave the back of her wagon a wistful look. "And I'd like to send a wire to Weldon's mother and let her know he's dead."

Betty Ellington nodded. Carolyn Brandon just stared into the night.

"Dodge it is then," Frank said. "But I have to warn you, it's a wide-open town, ladies. It can get mighty rough when the drovers come through."

"They have more law there than is out here, don't they?" Dixie asked. "Some kind of police force?"

Frank nodded. "They got better than a police force. They got Bat and Ed Masterson. Ed is the town marshal. Bat is the county sheriff."

"You know them?" Paula asked.

"I know them and they know me."

Dixie narrowed her eyes. "What does that mean?"

"We're friends of sorts. They know I won't cause any trouble for them and they know not to prod me."

"Will they have rock candy?" Sara Ellington asked from her spot on the quilt by her mother

Frank winked. "A whole sack of it, darlin'. A whole sack of it."

Paula looked up at Dixie, then over at Frank. Her round face glowed red from the embers. "What about after Dodge?" she said, her jaw set in grim determination. "Our trouble is, we don't know how to get where we're going.

Would you consider guiding us, Mr. Morgan? We could pay you well for your trouble."

Frank slapped his knee. "Take pay for such a pleasure? Are you joshing me? It would be an honor to guide a passel of women as beautiful as all of you."

Dixie shook her head and smiled. "We might get to be too much for you, Mr. Morgan."

"You might at that, but I've always been partial to beautiful surroundings, so I reckon I'll adapt."

"Aren't you the silver-tongue?" Paula gave a coy toss of her head.

"I want to warn you of one thing, though."

Dixie raised an eyebrow. "And what could that be?"

Frank raised his empty cup. "I'm a coffee-drinkin' man, I am, and I prefer my coffee like my women: strong."

Everyone laughed while Dixie took the tin cup and refilled it.

The animals had all been fed. Dog was full of biscuits the girls had given him. Coffee in hand, Frank leaned back against his saddle and groaned. His belly glowed with the warmth of spiced chili and cornbread.

"I'll talk to Bat as soon as we get into town. Explain everything that's happened. He'll make certain no one messes with your wagons or mules. It's a hundred miles or so past Dodge to the Colorado line, but it's early summer, so we've got plenty of time as far as the weather goes." Frank computed the distance in his head. "We can make Dodge by day after tomorrow if we start early."

Betty Ellington tossed what was left of her own coffee on the ground. "I'm ready to go now. I can hardly wait for a bath."

Chapter 9

"Morgan, you no-good son of a bitch." Frank heard the voice behind him as he spoke with the liveryman in Dodge.

He turned to find the dapper-dressed Bat Masterson, derby hat low against the evening sun, standing behind him.

"You're losing your edge, Morgan. Letting me sneak up on you like that."

"Hell, Bat, I smelled your fancy cigar five minutes ago while you were dealing with that drunk cowhand across the street. I saw your reflection in the glass there when you stopped to consort with that loose woman on the sidewalk. Even noticed when you bent over to brush some horse crap off your shiny boots on your way across the street. If I'd wanted to brace you, I'd have done it long before you made it this far." Frank stuck out his hand and grinned. "How you been, you fancy old fart?"

Bat took the hand and gave it a hearty shake. "I'm doing well, thank you for asking. And who you callin' old?"

"Yeah," Frank said. "I get your point."

"I understand you're now the patron saint of lost widows, orphans, and wayward wagon trains."

"You got some spy network. We only been in town fifteen minutes."

"Those women can't stop talking about their hero. Tell me, Morgan. What in thunder have you gotten yourself into?"

"I'll tell you, Bat, I'm not entirely sure. But I do know one thing. It's been an eternity since I've had me a cup of coffee and I'm sportin' a buffalo-sized headache. Let's you and me hunt up a pot and I'll fill you in. It's kind of a long story."

Bat's brother Ed joined them as they walked into the café. A pot of coffee and three pieces of apple pie later, Frank finished telling his tale. Both lawmen shook their heads in disgust. Bat was the first to speak.

"I never heard of anyone named Steve Wilson, but the man you've described is a no-good slave trader and whiskey runner named Ephraim Swan. He hails from somewhere back East himself—Ohio or maybe Illinois. Anyhow, it's got to be him with the white eyebrow and scars."

"Figured his name wasn't Steve Wilson." Frank picked up a toothpick from a little jar on the table. "Ephraim Swan, huh? The name rings a bell."

Bat nodded. "Stealing women is what he does best. He lures them out with all sorts of schemes, then sells them to the highest bidder. Usually down in Mexico. I got a stack of wanted posters for various nefarious activities he's been involved in."

"I'd appreciate it if you'd have your men look out for him while we're in town." Frank began to roll a smoke. "These women are bound and determined to get on to Colorado with their wagons."

"Everything will be safe while you're here in Dodge and as long as you're in the county," Bat said. "Tell the women they can bank on that."

Ed nodded his agreement. "I'll post some men to guard the wagons day and night."

"I appreciate it, boys. Say, I suppose you'll be wantin' my gun while I'm in town."

Ed shook his head. "You wouldn't give us all of them anyway, Morgan. I know you better than that. Too many people gunning for you. Besides, turning in your gun has never worked out here."

"I heard Wild Bill has a little trouble with it."

"He does." Ed darkened. "We have to pick our battles. But his attitude might get him killed one of these days."

"In any case," Bat said, patting his brother on the back to calm him, "you watch your back, Morgan. Every two-bit gun-toter this side of creation is just itchin' to do battle with you on the streets of Dodge City. And that's not counting any hired killers Swan is sure to send to brace you."

"Just watch the women for me, boys." He winked at both men. "Neither of you should have any problem with that. And if one of those folks you talked about shows up and the shootin' starts, hunt your holes and stay out of my way."

Chapter 10

Dixie took her time in the bath. It was an incredible experience after the long miles on the trail. She hadn't realized she'd had so much blood and so many blisters on her. She spent a nickel on a fancy bottle of soap, and hoped the smell of it covered the roughness she still felt when she looked at herself in the mirror. Her once-beautiful auburn hair now looked like broom straw, and her face was chapped and pinked from the sun. She'd done the best she could.

Before the bath, she'd taken the time to buy herself and her girls a new dress each. Nothing fancy, they did have miles and weeks to go before journey's end—but even practical could look nice if it was new—and fit just so around all the right places.

The other women were content to lounge around in the tubs, talking to each other and trying to cheer up Carolyn, who had yet to say a word since the death of her husband and son. Once Dixie felt clean and relatively pretty, she tied a ribbon around her wet hair and went to search out Frank.

Ed Masterson tipped his hat and told her Morgan was in the bathhouse out behind the barbershop and Chinese laundry. Feeling conspicuously unescorted on the dusty street, Dixie paced back and forth under a huge painted sign, that declared: DODGE CITY TONSORIAL EMPORIUM—HAIRS CUT AND TEETH PULLED. J.F. WILLOUGHBY, PROPRIETOR.

"Beg your pardon, ma'am," a low voice said behind her. "Have you seen a beautiful, corn-fed lady hereabouts? She's wearing a ratty old blue dress, not nearly so handsome as the one you have on."

Dixie rolled her eyes and turned to see Frank Morgan, dressed to the nines, standing in the entry to Willoughby's tonsorial. The sight of him took her breath away.

He'd changed out of his tattered trail clothes and into a black suit with a blood-red shirt and black kerchief. His boots were freshly polished, and his hat was brushed and blocked.

"Hope you're going to a wedding and not a funeral," she said, looking him up and down.

"Either one'd be about as sad for a woman who'd try to stand by a fellow like me." Frank grinned. "I'm a tough row to hoe."

"You are a might weedy at that."

"Well, I must say you are . . . I have to choose my words here." Frank took off his hat. "Ravishing. How's that for a two-dollar word?"

"You mean it, Frank? Do I look all right?" Dixie didn't know why, but she needed to hear it from him. She'd been a mother for sixteen years—someone's wife, for pity's sake. She hadn't heard such kind words in a long time, and didn't realize how starved she was for compliments.

"Of course I mean it. You're beautiful."

She tittered and looked at the ground. "You are quite the dashing figure yourself, Mr. Morgan."

"A bit worse for wear, I'm afraid." He took her hand and motioned down the street. "Shall we go for a stroll?"

She nodded. "Where's your dog?" she asked, in order to make idle conversation and take her mind off her heart, which was beating fast at finally being alone with this man. "I thought he never left your side."

"He's in the stable where he can stay out of trouble. I told him to stay there and he'll mind me. You see, Dog likes to gamble too much and he's a bit of a boozer, so I have to keep him tucked away." He chuckled softly, squeezing her hand in his as they walked. "I've arranged for the liveryman to feed him."

"Can I ask you a question, Frank?"

He shrugged. "You bet."

"Are you ever able to take off your gun?" She knew the answer, but wanted to get him talking about it.

"I don't bathe with it if that's what you mean."

"I'll bet you do too." She chuckled and elbowed him softly in the ribs. It was an odd thing that she was allowing herself to be so forward with another man mere days after Virgil's death. But the truth was, without Frank Morgan, the West felt like too big a place for her. Alone, she felt as if she might just blow away on the prairie wind.

"Seriously, Dixie. There are a lot of folks around who'd be mighty happy to see me planted in the ground. There's not a lot of sense in it, but that's the way it is, pure and simple."

She slowed her walk and turned to face him. He was a full head taller than her. "I have to tell you something. Before . . . all this happened . . . all the killing and bloodshed, I didn't understand you. To tell you the truth, I'm not sure I do now."

"It's a hard thing, to kill a man. It changes you, Dixie. You're learning that firsthand, I fear, and I'm sorry it had to come to that. Sorry for you."

She tugged at his arm to start him walking again. Stopping made her feel like she might well up and start crying. Movement felt better, kept the tears sifted down. "I feel so stupid. When you first rode in that day and joined the wagons, I thought if you'd just put down your foolish weapons, everyone else would follow suit." She shook her head. "I thought you could be the one to end all this violence."

She felt his arm stiffen and he drew his hand away. A young man in a mouse-colored slouch hat stood leaning against a hitching post in front of a dilapidated dram house across the street. He was staring at Frank through mean slits.

"I see him," she said, stepping away to give Frank room if he had to move.

"Proud of you." Frank put his left arm around her shoulders and gave her a squeeze. She was amazed at how good it felt. "He's not quite ready for me yet. Still working his tombstone courage to the fore."

"You know him?"

" 'Fraid so. His name's Jack Miller." Frank tipped his hat at a passing couple half their age, out for their own evening stroll. "His brother Dan tried to ambush me some months ago down north of Eagle Pass."

"And you killed him?"

"Had to. Dan Miller wasn't one for talking things over."

"Are there many like this one?"

"More than I'd like, that's for sure."

"And he's going to try and kill you too—to avenge his brother—who also tried to kill you?"

"I didn't make the rules, Dixie. I'm just trying to stay alive."

"Should I get out of the way?"

"Not yet. He's still trying to work up the gumption to pull on me. He might still need another beer or two."

"Will you warn me when he's worked up the courage?"

Frank smiled and gave her shoulders another squeeze. "You're learning quickly," he said. "I think you'll know. Say, where are your daughters?" He suddenly seemed to push the would-be gunman out of his mind.

"I told them to stay at the bathhouse with the Fossman girls and try to cheer them up."

"Think they'll stay there?"

"They'll mind me as good as Dog minds you, I'll bet." She looked behind her. "Miller is following us now."

"I see him. Step in here and I'll buy you a phosphate. They're mighty tasty. Maybe Jack will cool off a bit if I get out of his sight."

A short time later, Frank ushered her back out onto the sidewalk. He stuck his head out first, then took her hand again to lead her back toward her hotel. She'd learned enough to stay on his left side to keep his gun hand free. Miller still loitered on the other side of the street.

"There's no way out of this, is there?"

"Nope," Frank said. "Jack's worked up a full head of steam. I reckon he'll be calling me out anytime now."

Dixie felt as if her head might explode at the stupidity of all this. "Why don't you call the town marshal or your friend the sheriff and get them to put a stop to this?"

"It might get them killed. Jack might be scared of me, but he's no slouch. No, if anyone has to die because of this, it has to be him or me."

Dixie spied one of Ed Masterson's deputies leaning against a post a half a block away, watching. He was a lanky fellow, ten years younger than Frank. He had kind eyes. She shot a glance at Frank. "He's got on a badge. Why won't he do anything to stop this?"

"Because he's a man of the West, Dixie. It isn't the way things are done out here."

"Then what good are they? This is absolutely no different than it was out on the prairie when that gang of killers were after us. We are still all alone."

"I don't know what to tell you. In some ways I suppose we are. Out here a man saddles his own horses and stomps his own snakes."

She shook her head. "You talk about all this killing so matter-of-factly. Aren't you afraid you might die?"

"Never was before." He kept a wary eye on Miller. "Truth be told, until just a few days ago, I didn't have all that much to live for." He gave her a sly wink that made her knees go wobbly. He scooted her out of the way behind a pile of crates. "Now, if you'd be so kind as to stand over here. I believe young Mr. Miller is about to make his play. I can see in his eyes he's made up his mind he can kill me."

* * *

"Morgan!" Miller called from the middle of the rutted street. "Get out here and face me, you back-shootin' son of a bitch."

Frank shook his head. He felt so tired from all this. Jack Miller was an amateur, filled with too much alcohol-induced bravery. It would be a senseless death.

"Dan gave me no choice," Morgan said.

"That ain't the way I heard it, Drifter. Now step out here and let's get to it." Miller's voice was unsteady, hollow.

"All you're gonna do is get yourself killed, Jack." Frank stepped on to the street. The sun was to his back. Stupid kid. "How'll that help your brother?"

"You're getting a little long in the tooth, Drifter. I reckon I can take an old man like you easy."

"Here I am then." Frank's voice went stone cold. "Anytime you're ready, kid."

Chapter 11

It was over in an eye twitch. There was a rocking boom, Frank's Peacemaker belched fire and smoke, and he was left standing alone in the middle of the street.

Miller never fully cleared leather, and his gun slid harmlessly back into the holster, as if it had never even been drawn. The wounded man lay writhing in the street, a red stain on his right shoulder, blood spilling into the street and mingling with a pile of green horse manure.

"Good Lord in heaven," Dixie breathed.

The tall deputy strode over from his hiding place behind the dram house. Frank holstered his revolver and raised his hands.

"I saw it all, Mr. Morgan, sir," the deputy said. He beamed like a young boy talking to his hero. "I saw he prodded you into it. Left you no choice. I need to warn you, though, Miller has cousins."

"Don't they all?" Frank lowered his hands and checked back over his shoulder at Dixie, who still had her hand over her open mouth.

"My kin'll get you, Drifter. I'm sorry I couldn't take care of you for Danny's sake, but someone will."

Frank walked over to the panting man. "You're a mighty bold talker for a man bleeding in a pile of horse shit." He looked the wound over and shook his head. "You're lucky this time. I generally don't have time to aim. If you'll quit thrashing around like this, you might make it. Let this drop and no more of your family has to die."

"You go to hell, Morgan. If I could still use my arm, I'd kill you right now."

Frank drew his gun and ejected the empty brass. He slid another round in the cylinder to take its place, then squatted down next to Miller, looking him square in the eye. In Frank's experience, if he ever had a chance to let a man look into his eyes, see what was behind them, their will to fight him had a way of evaporating.

"Son," he said, tapping the barrel of his Peacemaker on his bent knee. "If you'd still been able to use your arm, you'd be dead right now."

Miller's face went white—maybe from loss of blood, more likely from a sudden rush of understanding.

The deputy whistled two men and a wagon out of the alley by the saloon. He'd done his planning well. The two men loaded a now-quiet Miller into the bed of the wagon. Once they clambered aboard, the wagon rattled off down the dusty street. The deputy followed.

"Is that it?" Dixie asked, still wringing her hands. "Is that all there is to it?"

Frank shrugged. "Oh, there might be some papers to sign over at the marshal's office, but other than that, I think it's over."

"No hearing in front of a magistrate?"

"Reckon not."

"I'm smack in the middle of the Wild West. The dime novels about you are not far off the mark."

Frank lowered his gaze. "I thought you didn't read such nonsense."

"I bought one to take to the bath with me today. It's called *Frank Morgan: Notorious Gunslick and Cold Blooded Killer.*"

Frank sighed. "No wonder so many folks want to brace me."

* * *

The ladies asked if they could stay in Dodge another day. Frank didn't mind. It was still early in the season, and he had nowhere else pressing he had to be. Might as well drift with a bunch of women as by himself.

He saw to the loading of new supplies, while the women worked on sending telegrams back East and seeing to the personal affairs of their husbands. The water barrels hiding the group's entire life savings remained safe in plain sight.

The women were aghast when Frank suggested they all buy some men's britches for the trail.

"Britches." Paula Freeman grimaced. "Why on earth would we do such a thing?"

Frank shrugged. "For one thing, it will make you more comfortable on the trail. When we run into any trouble you'll be able to move a lot faster. Get the older girls some too. I'm not certain what we got in store for us, but if you end up in a saddle, I think you'll get a lot less sore in britches."

"I've never worn britches before," Betty mused.

"There's a lot of things you'll do you've never done before this trip's over," Frank said, winking at Dixie.

Three men loitered near the entrance to the Gilded Lily saloon, and watched the women carry their packages out of the dry-goods store across the street. Frank stood in the shadows and watched the men.

The three looked like brothers, all from the same bad seed. Frank didn't recognize them, but he knew their type: thieves, ne'er-do-wells, trouble hunters. In that respect, they were brothers to hundreds of men across the West.

This particular trio was easy enough to spot because of their redheaded mops that stuck out under worn and dirty hats. Each sported a whole bushel basket of freckles over his face and arms. All wore their guns tied down to their thighs.

Frank's suspicions were confirmed when Bat approached him at his morning coffee on their last day in Dodge.

"The Benson boys have been asking a lot of questions about you and the ladies."

"Three of them, carrottops and spotted as Stormy's rump?" Frank sipped his coffee, leaning back in the wooden chair.

"That's them. I've got informants that tell me they may be connected to Swan and his gang, but I've got no proof." Masterson drew up another chair and the waitress brought him a cup. "They're thieves, though. Take anything that's not nailed down. Bully, the middle one, just got out of prison a month ago."

"That's his name, Bully Benson?"

Masterson chuckled. "I don't know, but that's what everyone calls him. I can't be casting stones, though, with a name like Bat."

Frank leaned forward, more serious now. "You think they'll make a try for us?"

"I'd bet on it. When you get far enough out of Dodge. I've let it be known I'll have men shadowing you until you're well out of the county. I don't think anyone would make a play against you in my territory."

Frank chuckled and put down his cup. "You do have yourself a reputation, Bat."

The sheriff laughed. "Look who's talking."

"We need to keep an eye out for three men who've been watching us," Frank told Dixie while they hitched the mules to her wagon early the next morning.

"Redheads?" Dixie said, sliding wooden hames over the collar of the lead mule.

Frank nodded. "You noticed them then."

"How could we miss three scruffy men like that? They stood around watching us wherever we went, scratching like they were infested with fleas."

"They probably do have fleas, among other things." He didn't tell her about the possible connection with Ephraim Swan. "I am proud of you for noticing them."

"You ought to be really proud of us," Paula said as she road up in her wagon with the Fossman girls. "We each bought two pairs of men's britches for the trip."

"I felt lewd in them when I tried them on." Betty grinned.

"When do you plan to change into them?" Frank climbed aboard Stormy and made ready to take the lead. He waved good-bye to Bat, who stood a few paces away in the dim morning light.

"Not until we're well out of town," Paula said.

Frank raised his eyebrows and winked at Bat. "I can hardly wait."

Chapter 12

Frank led the wagon train out of Dodge as dawn was beginning to color the eastern sky. He looked around for the Benson brothers, but didn't spot them. He hadn't really expected to. They would trail the train until well outside Bat Masterson's jurisdiction.

A few miles out of town, when the sun was well up, Frank reined up next to the lead wagon. Dixie's wagon. Her two girls were riding horseback on the opposite side on animals they'd taken from the dead kidnappers.

They were fine horses too; something most successful outlaws insisted upon, for their very lives depended on mounts with staying power. After hearing what had happened to the women, Bat had arranged with a local magistrate in Dodge to fix up legitimate ownership papers for the animals.

"Keep the girls close to the wagon." Frank nodded at Dixie, then surveyed the uneven plain around them.

"Why? Indians?" Dixie followed his example and began a search of her own.

"Not necessarily. Although there may be a band or two still out here wanting to make a name for themselves. It's those redheaded brothers I'm worried about."

"You think they'll hit us this soon?"

Frank wiped the sweat out of his eyes with his bandanna. "They shouldn't, but who knows? They didn't look to be the brightest in the class. They might not even know where the Ford County line is. In any case, it's best to keep the girls in sight and a sharp eye on the horizon. Pass the word among the women to keep their weapons at the ready."

Dixie nodded and patted the rifle in the seat beside her.

The weather remained warm and cloudless for the next three days, and the wagons slowly ate their way across the endless plain. Nine miles out of Ford County, they pulled up for the night at a tiny settlement made up of no more than a saloon, general store, assay office, and a jumble of surrounding shacks and brush wickiups.

Paula had forgotten to get nutmeg in Dodge, and set off to the store on a mission to find some, against Frank's warning that in this little no-account town, she'd be lucky to find salt, let alone a fancy spice.

Frank walked into the darkened saloon and found he had it to himself. He needed another man to talk to, someone with a low voice to rest his ears.

"Beer," he said, leaning up against the rough bar.

"Comin' right up, mister," the smiling barkeep said through a mouthful of crooked teeth. He looked like each tooth had been removed and put back in sideways. "You the one leadin' all them women west?"

Frank nodded, sipping the froth of his beer. "I am."

"How do you stand it? I could hear you all comin' for the last hour—all that cacklin' would drive me outta my head." He leaned forward on his bar rag. "Ain't they got no other menfolks?"

"Killed. All of them. By a fellow named Ephraim Swan and his gang."

"Heard of him. He's a bad one for a fact, he is. Cold-blooded killer."

"He is at that." Frank took a proper drink of his beer and downed it. "That was tasty. Got one more?"

The bartender drew another beer and put it on the bar in front of Frank. "Best beer in town." He began to laugh, showing all his crooked teeth. "Hell, it's the only beer in town. This one's on the house, friend. Anyone who can put up with a bunch of women on the trail deserves a little reward. Besides, you're a damn sight easier to talk to than those three hotheads that came in here earlier today."

Frank sat up straight at the news and leaned closer to the bartender. "Three men came here ahead of us?"

The man nodded and poured himself a beer. He raised the glass to Frank. "To ownin' your own bar," he toasted. "Yeah, they was real scabby types. Surly too, wouldn't talk to me at all. Kept to themselves altogether."

"Redheads?"

"Yeah. You know 'em?"

"Afraid so." Frank turned to go warn the women, but the Benson brothers poured through the front door before he could take a step.

All three shuffled to the end of the bar and ordered beers.

"We ain't lookin' for no trouble, Morgan." The oldest of the three stood nearest him at the bar.

Frank thought it best to put all his cards out on the table right there and then. Better to face all three together now, than at night on the plains, when he'd have the women to worry about. "You boys are a right smart distance out of Dodge. Did Swan have to draw you a map?"

The brothers started when he mentioned the outlaw's name, as if they'd been caught red-handed stealing cattle.

Frank nodded. "Figures. I thought he'd probably pay someone to do his dirty work."

"We don't know what you're talkin' about, mister," the one called Bully said from between his brothers. The three seemed to go everywhere in order of their ages.

"So you're just out for a little trip?"

"We might be," Bully said. "There ain't no law against it."

"Depends on what you do while you're on that trip." Frank swayed up from the bar and faced the three men. "Now which one of you three is in charge?"

They looked at each other blinking, as if no one had ever put the question to them before.

"I'm the oldest," the one on the end said, bobbing his red head.

"Shut up, Hugh. You may have been whelped before me, but you ain't in charge of nobody." It was easy to see why they called this one Bully.

"Why can't I be in charge once in a while?" the youngest brother whined into his beer.

Frank put his hand on the butt of his gun. "I wish you boys would hurry up and figure it out, 'cause I aim to kill the one in charge first."

All three pushed up and held out their hands. "Hey, Morgan, we said we ain't lookin' for trouble." Bully had a shifty eye. If any of them drew had the gumption to draw, it would be him.

"Yeah, you don't want any trouble, not here in front of witnesses. But you'd sure as hell sneak up and cut all our throats while we're sleeping." He took a step toward the brothers. "Now I want to know which one of you took the money from Swan to come after us. Tell me the truth and I'll only kill the one of you."

"You're crazy, mister," Hugh said, turning to leave.

Frank was in his face now. He grabbed the older brother by the ear. Bully took a step toward him, but Frank jerked his Peacemaker from the holster and slapped him across the side of the head. A couple of Bully's teeth beat him to the ground. Frank stomped down hard on Hugh's boot toe, then gave the screaming redhead a conk on the noggin as well, sending him sprawling and unconscious beside his middle brother.

Frank turned to the youngest Benson, gun in hand. "All right, I just did you a big favor. You're in charge."

The boy swallowed hard, his huge goiter bobbing up and down on a freckled throat. "What do you want from me, mister?"

"First, I want you to put your gun on the bar where my friend here can keep it for you." The boy complied. His knees knocked together.

"Now, you can do me a favor," Frank said. "What are your orders from Swan?"

"N-n, no or-or-orders." He had a hard time talking past the lump in his throat.

Frank thumbed back the hammer. "I'm gettin' tired of askin' you, Baby Benson."

"R-really! We ain't got no orders. I ain't never even met the man. He just put out the word he'd pay ten thousand cash to any man who kills you." Pale to begin with, the boy had gone bone gray, and looked like he might keel over at any moment.

This was bad news. Now every tinhorn gunslick west of the Mississippi would be looking to gain not only a reputation, but ten thousand dollars as well.

"Wh-what do you aim to do with us, Mr. Morgan?" Baby Benson leaned against the bar to steady himself.

"That is a very good question," Frank said, tapping the barrel of his Colt against his thigh. "A very good question in deed. I can't just leave you all here like this. When your fool brothers wake up, you wouldn't be in charge anymore and they're likely to make you come after us. We can't have that, now can we?"

Baby Benson shook his head. "No, sir, I reckon we can't."

Frank stared down at the unconscious men and smiled. His face suddenly brightened. "You can be in charge for a while longer," he told the young redhead. "I got an idea."

Dixie came out of the store with Paula, who was gloating about finding a small vial of nutmeg behind a tin of baking powder, when she heard two shots from inside the bar next door. Both women jumped at the loud sound and started for the door. Dixie had taken to carrying her rifle with her wherever she went, and she grabbed it with both hands, making it ready for use.

Before they could make it inside, Frank met them on the steps, chuckling and shaking his head.

"Are you all right?" Dixie checked him up and down looking for wounds. She didn't see any.

"I'm fine. Just had to shoot the two oldest Benson brothers in the foot."

"What?" Dixie and Paula said at once.

"Shot each of 'em in the foot. They were bound to come after us one way or another. Least this will slow 'em down."

"Weren't there three?" Dixie asked.

"Yeah." Frank chuckled. "But the youngest one's no problem. He'll be busy tending to his wounded brothers for a while anyway. Besides, if a miracle happens and he grows a spine, we'd smell him coming a mile away."

A tall, slender Mexican sat hunched in Ephraim Swan's tent wearing a rumpled white suit and an impatient look. Swan sat across from him drinking from a snifter of brandy.

"How long do you expect my offer to stand?" the skeletal man asked, dabbing at his thin mustache and goatee with a white kerchief he'd taken from his vest pocket. "I, like you, have customers I must keep happy. If I do not bring them a product, then they begin to look elsewhere."

"I'll get them for you, Eduardo. I told you I would and I will." Swan set the brandy on the wooden trunk offered the other man a cigar. "I have run into some, shall we say, unforeseen circumstances. But they are nothing I cannot handle in time."

"Would these unforeseen circumstances be Mr. Frank Morgan, the famous gunman and desperado?"

Swan grunted around his own cigar. "You know of the bastard down in Mexico?"

"Oh, yes," Eduardo said. "He is quite a legend." The Mexican shook his head slowly and took a long draw on his cigar. "I understand your problem, but unfortunately I can only give you one more week. If you somehow get the girls back by then, my offer is still valid. Any time beyond that, and my buyers will begin to look at other markets. They are particularly interested in the redheaded señoritas, so I will give you the agreed price for them whenever you bring them—the *güeras*—the blondes as well. But the price will go down considerably for all the others after this week. Frank Morgan or no, my feet are . . . how do you say it? Held to the fire."

Swan seethed inside, but didn't let is show on his face. "Thank you for the week, Eduardo. I'll make good use of it, I promise you."

Eduardo flicked the ash of the coal off his cigar with a bony finger. "May I ask what you plan to do? I have heard of your reward, and I have also heard this Morgan has killed everyone who has challenged him so far."

Swan tried to keep his face placid. What did this stupid bean-eating scarecrow know about Frank Morgan—or anything, for that matter? If Swan didn't stand to lose so much money, he would have held a lot more than this idiot's feet to the fire. Swan took a deep breath and cleared his throat in an effort to regain his internal composure.

"I have sent the word all over about the reward. Men will begin to come and challenge him in droves. Some will go for him in town; others will try him on the prairie. Sooner or later, he will lose."

"I hope for your sake, Ephraim, it is sooner rather than later."

Swan nodded. "I do as well. I have sent word to a very special man who should be able to speed things up. Once he hears, all our troubles should be over."

"These are not my troubles." Eduardo smirked. "They are yours and yours alone."

Swan smiled broadly. His face hid the inner fury that gnawed at his stomach. If in a week's time he didn't have the

William W. Johnstone

girls, Frank Morgan would still pay dearly—but so would Eduardo. For the next time they met, if the price was lowered one peso, Swan would see the bony Mexican torn limb from limb for all his smart condescending attitude.

Chapter 13

Paula soaked some dried apples, and used a dash of her treasured nutmeg to make an apple pie that smelled good enough to make Frank want to forget the rest of the fine meal. Dog didn't care much for pie, but he did enjoy the steak trimmings and biscuits the girls gave him.

"You ladies are going to fatten me and Dog up so fierce, we won't be able to protect you." Frank chuckled, and used a piece of biscuit to sop up the last of his fried potatoes and pan gravy.

"We like to see a hungry man eat," Dixie said, dabbing a little tear out of her eye with the corner of her apron.

"Well." Frank got to his feet and scraped the last bits of his main course onto a nearby clump of grass. "I don't aim to disappoint you then. Paula, I'd chop you a cord of wood for a piece of that pie." Wood was at a premium on the plains, and they all laughed at how easy it was to promise such a thing.

Dog sprawled out between the Fossman girls, doing his part to cheer up the orphans, and promptly went to sleep. With Frank 's belly full of steak and sweet apple pie, he decided Dog had a pretty good idea.

Dixie squatted by the fire, gathering up the dishes and banking the coals so there'd be some left to cook breakfast. The dying blaze popped and sputtered, casting a warm glow on the woman's face. She smiled at Frank, a wide smile that made the tough gunman's insides turn to jelly

For one night anyway, all was right with the world.

* * *

They made it until noon the next day before the rain came. They were in a low-lying draw and Frank had them push on, fearing they'd be caught in a flash flood. By the time they'd gone two miles, mud began to suck at the wheels. Each wagon left trenches a foot deep in the trail. Stormy moved his feet with great effort, each step making a slurping pop as he withdrew his hoof. The prairie had turned into a maze of muddy streams under the heavy downpour.

Alone as they were on the treeless plain, Frank worried as much about lightning as he did about bandits. There wasn't anything he could do about it, so they pushed ahead.

Frank wiped his eyes with a bandanna and peered ahead of him. Finally, through the wind and rain, he could see what he'd been hoping for.

"Swing left for those rocks," he yelled to Dixie over the driving rain. Tall sandstone monoliths stood a quarter mile away, looking like giant guardians of the prairie. "They'll give us some protection from the wind and maybe keep us from getting struck by lightning."

Dixie clucked to her mules and tugged on the wide leather reins. The stout animals seemed to know rest waited for them at the rocks, and dug in with renewed effort, straining at the harness.

A short time later, wagon canvas was strung and a fire built under it from dry wood Frank had insisted the girls gather for just such an occasion.

Dixie rocked back and forth next to the flames, tugging at the pockets of her soaking-wet britches. She shook her head and looked at Frank. "I don't care what you say. Dresses have an added benefit of not being so uncomfortable when they get wet."

He chuckled, warming his hands by the fire. "I suppose wet britches do take a little gettin' used to."

"It's something I'd rather not try," Paula said. "This is

absolutely unbearable." She had a drawn, pained look on her face.

"I'm going to change back into a dress until these dry." Dixie winked at Frank. "I have an extra skirt if you're uncomfortable, Frank."

Frank scoffed. "That'll be the day."

The rain lasted for two long days. In the cramped quarters under the canvas, tempers simmered and inevitable squabbles broke out between the girls. Berta Fossman accused little Tabby Freeman of stealing a length of green ribbon she wanted to use to tie back her wet hair. There was a flurry of name-calling, and for a moment Morgan thought the girls might come to blows. Berta was stout, and had twenty pounds and at least three years on Tabby. But Frank would have put his money on the Freeman girl in an all-out brawl. She had the look of righteous indignation in her eye, a calm tone in her voice, and though no one else could see it, a cast-iron muffin pan hidden behind her back to defend herself with against the much larger girl.

Luckily, Bea Fossman found her sister's ribbon and after much crying and apologizing, all was forgotten. Frank was amazed at how women could be so all-fired angry with each other one minute, then sit around and gab shoulder-to-shoulder the next, sewing on a quilt together like nothing had ever happened. If it had been boys, someone would have had a bloody nose. He'd seen men go to guns for lesser insults.

On the third day, the sun popped out from behind a gray cloud bank. The camp turned into a huge tangle of lines with dripping clothes and steaming bedding.

Two days later, the wagons pulled into the settlement of Garden City, Kansas, about sixty miles from the Colorado line.

Frank suggested that Paula go on another nutmeg hunt in case she wanted to make another apple pie or two . . . or three. She was glowing at his compliment outside the small mercantile when a well-dressed man in a high-collared shirt and bowler hat sauntered up on the boardwalk.

Frank gave the man a wary stare and turned to face him, letting the women move out of the way and into the store.

"Pardon me for intruding," the gentleman said, touching the brim of his bowler. He had a dark, pencil-thin mustache, which looked like it took a lot of work, under a crooked nose. An assortment of white scars adorned the backs of his large hands. He carried himself with a confident air of strength and grace. A bare-knuckle boxer.

"What can I do for you?" Frank kept his gun hand relaxed, ready.

"My name is George Carlisle." The boxer stuck out a beefy paw. He smiled under his tiny mustache. There seemed to be nothing but admiration in his eyes.

"Frank Morgan." They shook hands.

"I know. You're the reason I'm here."

Frank tensed, waiting for Carlisle to make a move.

"I'm on assignment from a national detective agency," the boxer said.

"Pinkerton?" Frank took a deep breath and shook his head. After what they did to Jesse James's mother, Frank had little use for Allen Pinkerton or his men.

Carlisle smiled, but didn't come out and admit to working for the infamous agency. "I spoke with Sheriff Masterson in Dodge. He told me about the trouble with Swan and his gang."

"And?"

The boxer shook his head. "You've no doubt heard of the ten-thousand-dollar reward Swan has put on your head."

Frank was already watching two trouble-hunting young men strolling across the street toward him like they owned the place. "And what business is this of yours, Mr. Carlisle?" he said while he watched the newcomers approach.

"Swan is a ruthless man."

"I don't reckon I need you to tell me that. Pardon me. It

looks like I have to take care of a little something." Frank stepped off the boardwalk to face the two young men. One of them was big and oafish, with a lumbering gait that left huge tracks in the soft dirt of the street. The other, a head shorter than his compadre, wore a brace of two ivory-handled pistols and a frown.

"Do you think he can use both those guns at the same time?" Carlisle had followed Frank into the street.

"Some are able to. I'm a fair hand with two guns," Frank said without taking his eyes off the men. "Now, Mr. Carlisle, I don't mean to be rude, but there just might be gunplay here. Why don't you scoot back up on the sidewalk where it's safe?"

"I'll be fine." Carlisle didn't move. "This might prove interesting."

The two challengers stopped twenty feet away.

"You Frank Morgan?" Two-Gun demanded.

"I am. What's on your mind?"

The bigger of the two lumbered closer. He had squinty eyes, and probably needed to get closer just to make certain he could see well enough to aim. He stopped five feet away and glared. "I think you're gettin' a little gray around the edges, old man."

"Could be." Frank shrugged. "Happens to us all sooner or later."

"I don't think you're as all-fired good as folks say you are," Two-Gun added. "You look all beat up to me. Maybe traipsin' along with all those women has turned you into a woman your own self."

Frank sighed.

"Who's this dude with you, Morgan? Your nanny?" The big kid sneered. "Looks like he's wearing half a melon on his head."

"I want you to think about this, boys," Frank said. His voice was barely above a whisper.

"We ain't boys," Two-Gun flared. "I beat Matt Sunday not a month ago."

"You killed Matthew Sunday?"

"Damn right I killed him," Two-Gun grumbled. "He's planted in the cemetery on the edge of town."

"You must be fast then. Sunday was supposed to be pretty good."

"He was faster than you," the big oaf drawled, spitting into the dirt and narrowly missing his own boot. He turned to Carlisle. "You know, while my friend shoots Morgan and earns us a quick ten thousand, I think I'll whip your ass just for the fun of it."

Carlisle smiled an easy smile. His left hand shot out in a quick jab, just grazing the big oaf's nose, his right following, pulling the giant's gaze and his guard with it. A brutal left hook smashed into the young man's face. He tottered for a moment, dazed, and then collapsed to the street in a mighty puff of dust.

"You as fast as your friend there?" Frank said, nodding to the unconscious lump.

Two-Gun was silent, but he glared daggers at both men.

"How fast are you?" Frank said, stepping in and snatching both ivory-handled pistols from the young man's holster. "Not fast enough to keep me from doing this." He brought both barrels straight down on, thumping the astonished man on top of his noggin.

Chapter 14

"That was some respectable fisticuffs, Mr. Carlisle," Frank said a half an hour later over a cup of coffee. "Where did you learn to fight like that?"

"I've done a bit of boxing in my time."

"I'll bet your have, sir. I seem to remember reading about a George Carlisle who was bare-knuckle boxing champion on the Eastern Seaboard a few years back."

"Too many years, I'm afraid," the boxer said rubbing his hands.

"So." Frank leaned back in his chair and stared at the man. "What's your national detective agency got an interest in me for?"

"Two things really." Carlisle leaned forward across the small table. "I've been commissioned to offer you a job."

"Not interested," Frank said quickly.

"Don't you even want to hear the particulars?"

"Not really." Frank took a sip of his coffee. "Now, what's the other thing?"

Carlisle put down his cup and smoothed his napkin out on the table in front of him. "It's your son, Frank."

Frank sat up straight. "What's wrong with Conrad?"

"Nothing's wrong. Quite the contrary. He's doing well. He heard about the ten-thousand-dollar bounty Swan put on your head and hired us to protect you."

Frank relaxed. "Damn fool kid," he said, feeling a bit of pride in his chest that his estranged son would worry about him like that. "He should know enough to know I, of all people, don't need a bodyguard."

Carlisle shook his head sadly. "At one time or another, everyone has to rest. That's where we come in. We take up the slack. That's why they call us 'the eye that never sleeps.'"

"So you are from Pinkerton then."

"Afraid so, Morgan. Look at this way. I can be of help to you seeing to it that the women are safe."

Frank rubbed his chin whiskers and thought. This Carlisle was a likeable enough person. He was sure enough handy with his fists.

"What kind of gun do you carry?"

The boxer opened his coat to reveal a shoulder rig and the round butt of a short-barreled revolver. "It's a three-inch Colt with bird's-head grips. I had a little action work done on it by a gunsmith I know in Boston. A real pleasure to shoot."

"Are you any good with it?"

Carlisle laughed out loud and let his coat fall shut. "I'm good. Good enough to know I don't ever want to tangle with you when it comes to gunplay."

Frank finished off his coffee and put a tip on the table. "Well, George, I don't think I'd want to box against you either. Now let's go and introduce you to the girls." He suddenly turned on Carlisle. "But I want you to get one thing straight. You're not my bodyguard. I'm bringing you along to help me look after these women. Are we clear on that?"

The boxer nodded. "Crystal."

George Carlisle rode a tall, flea-bitten gray that had a good deal of white in its eye and a surly disposition. Dog gave the grumpy horse a wide berth.

Frank gathered the women around him and introduced their new traveling companion as an acquaintance of his son's and a trustworthy man. Though Frank considered him somewhat of a dandy, the women seemed to think he was handsome enough. Paula Freeman almost swooned when he dismounted to help her into her wagon.

"Are you certain you can trust him?" Dixie said a short time later as Frank trotted Stormy up next to her. Carlisle had taken a seat on the wagon next to Paula and they were carrying on what appeared to be a lively conversation.

"He seems honest enough," Frank shrugged. "He stood by me in a fight. With my reputation for drawing bullets, a lot of men would have hunted somewhere else to be." He rested his hands on the saddle horn and gazed at the chattering couple in the wagon behind him. "In any case, Paula seems to be quite taken with him."

Dixie nodded. She opened her mouth to say something, then stopped. "How far would you say it is to Colorado?"

Frank pointed to the line of willows and Russian olive trees ahead. "That's Two Buttes Creek. The line runs more or less along there. Should be an easy crossing for us. This marks the beginning of what people are calling the Arkansas Valley. We'll be following the Arkansas River for a good way. . . ."

Carlisle had reclaimed his gray, and rode up next to Dixie's wagon. "Beg your pardon, Mrs. Carpenter. Morgan, did you see that thin line of smoke down by the trees ahead?"

Frank nodded. "I did. This is a well-used crossing, but I suppose I should ride up and take a little reconnoiter before we commit the wagons down the hill. I'd appreciate you keeping an eye on the ladies while I'm gone. Shouldn't take long." Without waiting for an answer, he squeezed Stormy into a gentle, rocking-horse lope toward the creek.

He rode to the lip of the creek bed cautiously, but let himself relax some when he saw another Conestoga wagon alongside four mules grazing on the narrow green flood plain of Two Buttes Creek. A Negro man walked out from under a smoke-colored camp awning with a rifle in hand.

"I'm friendly," Frank called. "Leading a small wagon train west. Mind if I dismount?"

"Step down and have a rest." The man smiled and let the rifle swing down to one hand like a walking cane. "To tell you the truth, I could use some conversation." There was a trace of an accent in the man's voice, but Frank couldn't place it.

He stepped down from the saddle and shook the black man's hand. "Frank Morgan."

The man's eyes widened for an instant. Then he regained his composure. "Pleased to make your acquaintance, Mr. Morgan. I'm Otis Chapman and this is my wife Salina. Those three sets of eyes peaking out from under that canvas tarp are my sons Shadrach, Meshach, and Alphonse."

"No offense, but what happened to Abed-nigo?"

"Alphonse is the oldest. We didn't happen on the Israelite theme until after he was born."

"That's a shame," Frank said. "They're nice names on the ear."

Chapman smiled and winked at his chubby little wife, who shook her head and looked at the ground with a sly grin. "Oh, don't you worry, Mr. Morgan, Salina and I are hard at work to bring forth a little Abed-nigo."

"May I offer you some coffee?" Salina asked, shooing the younger two boys back into the wagon. Frank guessed them to be no more than six or seven years old. Alphonse, who was every bit of seventeen, was allowed to stay out with the adults.

The coffee was tasty, with just a hint of chicory. Salina noticed the expression on Frank's face and smiled.

"My mother was from Louisiana. When she came north to Massachusetts, she brought some fine recipes with her, including the one for this coffee."

Frank held up his cup in a salute and winked. "My compliments to your mother then. So, you're from Massachusetts?"

"Born and educated there," Otis said. "My father was a free man and so was I. I fought with the all-colored 51st."

Frank bowed his head. "You're lucky you made it out alive. Most of the 51st didn't."

"I was wounded about a month before the ill-fated assault on the fort. Were you in the war, Mr. Morgan?"

"Yes, on the other side. Cavalry. From start to finish."

"Does it bother you, seeing a colored man like me out here like this?" Otis looked him straight in the eye as he spoke.

"Mr. Chapman, I didn't own any slaves. Never had a stomach for such a thing, but I wasn't fighting for that. It wasn't about that for me at least."

"States' rights?"

"Exactly. I had to follow the dictates of my conscience." Frank handed the empty cup back to Salina Chapman and stood up with a groan. "How far are you folks heading?"

Otis glanced at his wife. "Pueblo, or thereabouts."

"Well," Frank said, "there's strength in numbers, and if you don't mind traveling with a bunch of women, a New York dandy, an ugly dog, and a man with a price on his head, you're welcome to throw in with us."

"We all seem to be going the same way, and we're bound to bump into each other over and over anyway. I would certainly enjoy the conversations. I don't see why we shouldn't join up. Do you, Salina?"

Mrs. Chapman shook her head. "No, Otis, I don't see any reason at all. As a matter of fact, you boys are beginning to grate on me. I could use a little female companionship."

"It's settled then," Frank said, climbing back on his horse. "Oh, and Mrs. Chapman, one more thing—would you happen to have any nutmeg? One of our women is always on a hunt for good nutmeg."

"Well, of course. I got a whole jar of it."

"Good to hear." Frank said. He trotted off to fetch the others, already tasting hot apple pie.

Chapter 15

Trouble trotted up behind the wagons on the second day after the Chapmans joined the procession—in the form of a longhorn cow and calf. Alphonse pointed it out to Otis, and he in turn rode up to the head of the train to tell Frank.

"Not a brand on either one of them," Frank mused as he and Otis watched the piebald calf suckle. "But they're not wild. A maverick cow wouldn't be caught dead this close to people, particularly with a calf that young."

The wagons had all stopped so the youngsters could come back and look at the new arrivals.

"He's just precious," the little Ellington girl said to her mother. "Can we keep him?"

"Oh, no." Frank shook his head. "They don't belong to us. Livestock will get a man in trouble quicker than wife-stealing around here. We can't keep them from trailing along behind us, but they're on their own."

"Wolves might get them come nightfall," Otis observed.

"Might, but I think the mama will keep a good watch. She probably got separated from a herd to calve and now looks at us as her keepers."

George, who'd been on a scouting trip, reined up his gray beside the Chapmans' wagon and tipped his hat at Salina. "Riders coming in, Morgan. Four of them."

"I see 'em. This is what I was afraid of."

A moment later the four cowboys blew up beside them in

a cloud of dust. Frank took off his hat to fan the air. "You boys sure know how to be a damned nuisance."

"You got a big mouth, mister," the lead cowboy said. He had a loud purple scarf around his neck, and a wide-brimmed hat hung off his back on a leather stampede string. "Maybe somebody ought to close it for you."

Frank raised a hand. "Hold on there. Don't get so riled. I was talking to my friend there as well as you." He pointed at George Carlisle. "He brought in as much dust as you."

"Well," the cowboy said, "I ain't your friend, so shut your pie hole. Them cattle is ours. Down our way, we hang rustlers."

"Well, we're not down your way." Frank smiled. "And the cattle wandered up unbranded. They're not rustled. If they're yours, take them."

"I say they're stolen," another cowboy spit, glaring at the Chapmans. "And I bet I know who stole 'em."

"You'd lose your bet." Frank set his jaw. These men didn't want the cattle back. They wanted a fight. "Now take your livestock and clear out."

"We don't take orders from you, Morgan. Them niggers stole our cattle. Get out of the way. We got ways of dealin' with thieves."

"Stand fast, boys," Frank hissed, but their minds were made up.

Frank's Peacemaker spit fire and smoke. An instant later the lead cowboy lay dead on the ground, his boot still dangling from the stirrup.

The other three cowboys didn't move, but glared at Frank and the others. One of them, an older man, hung back a little from the others and eyed Dixie with such contempt, Frank thought about shooting him on the spot. He had a familiar face, something about his jawline and the way he slouched on his horse . . . Of course. He'd been one of the men with Swan that day on the prairie. One of the men coming to gun him down and take back the women and the wagons.

Frank kept the pistol pointed at the three men. "Your leader there called me by name before he died. Funny, I don't recall introducing myself."

"Everybody knows who you are, Morgan," the youngest of the three cowboys said, his hands raised high above his head. Frank thought it best to let the fact he recognized one of them slide until he could figure out what was going on. He had no doubt he would be able to take all three men, but there were too many innocents behind him and a stray bullets might find an unintended mark. "You boys collect your friend there and git. Take your cow with you."

"Nobody messes with the Circle V," the cowboy on the mouse-brown gelding whispered. "Particularly not some nigger-lovin' two-bit gunfighter with a swelled-up view of his self. My Uncle Vic will have a word to say about this."

"Keep your mouth shut, Sonny," the older cowboy hissed while he tied the dead man across the vacant saddle.

Sonny shook out his lariat and built him a loop. He tossed it easily around the cow's horns. If he was an outlaw, he was a talented cowboy as well. "Let's get back. I'm sure Uncle Vic will want to hear about this." The young man took a dally around his saddle horn and turned to face Frank. A cruel grin crossed his face. "Mark me, Drifter. Your day is comin' and it's comin' soon." With that, he spun his cow pony and took the cow off at a trot toward the southeast and the herd. Keeping their eyes on Frank as long as they could, the other two cowboys turned their horses and followed their hotheaded partner.

"They didn't come from that direction," Dixie said after the cowboys were out of earshot.

"Maybe they were just out hunting strays and ran into us," Carlisle offered.

"Or hunting us," Frank said, sliding his gun back into the holster. "That older fellow was with Swan's men when they came after us on the prairie back before we hit Dodge."

"Swan?" Dixie asked.

"Wilson's real name is Ephraim Swan and he's as bad as they come according to Bat."

"What's one of Wilson's . . . Swan's gang doing herding cattle with the Circle V?" Dixie shook her head.

"I don't know," Frank said, climbing on his horse. "But I don't like it one bit. Everybody stay close. We'll make an early camp. George, you, Otis, and I will rotate a watch tonight. We're a pretty easy target out here like this."

The wagons began to creak forward again and George rode up on his gray, out of earshot of the others.

"Do you think they'll hit us tonight?" He didn't look worried, just interested.

Frank looked back at the empty horizon where the cowboys had disappeared. His jaw was set and he let out a sigh. "I'd say we should count on it."

"Well, you have me and Otis. Alphonse is nigh unto eighteen, so I'm certain he will be able to shoot." George began to tally their forces. "From what Paula's told me, Dixie is pretty handy with a gun."

"Still long odds," Frank said. "Somebody's likely to get hurt if we face them head-on."

The two men rode for a time in silence. Then Frank began to smile. He folded his hands across the saddle horn and looked at George. "It'll be tricky, but I think I just might have an idea."

Chapter 16

Two hours before sundown, Frank pulled the wagons to a halt beside a dense grove of willows and silver olive trees. Wood was in relative abundance, and they enjoyed a roaring fire, hilarious stories from George, and some raucous recitations of Shakespeare from Otis. Dixie made a rich stew out of an antelope Frank had shot earlier in the day. Dutch-oven biscuits and Salina Chapman's shoofly pie rounded out the meal. Alphonse stood guard until an hour after sundown.

Frank wanted the group to sound as loud and as carefree as they could. When Otis brought out a harmonica, each man took a turn around the fire with each of the women. Even Carolyn Brandon danced a bit. A tiny smile parted her lips while Frank took her in a promenade, but she never spoke. Alphonse danced with his mother, and his brothers, Shadrach and Meshach, danced with the younger girls.

The fire crackled and sparks twirled upward toward the stars in the still night air. Otis played every song he knew, and even made some up on the spot. The little group sang and laughed, some of them for the first time in weeks. Even Dog joined in the festivities, barking and nipping at the dancers' heels.

Dixie looked up into Frank's eyes during a waltz. "Do you think this will really work?" Her face was a picture of serenity and trust.

"I don't know, Dix. If it doesn't, we've had a heck of a good frolic for our last night on earth."

Dixie frowned. "That's not funny, Frank."

"Sorry." He gave her a twirl in time to the music. "I think it will, but it's touch and go on a thing like this. I'm counting on what I know about human behavior. Especially outlaw behavior. There's a few of them who'll face you head-on to make a name for themselves, but most don't like to buck the odds. Most outlaws are cowards when you boil 'em down to the bone. Sneak thieves and backstabbers. If those cowboys today were the type to face us, they'd have done it right then when their partner threw down on me."

Otis ended his playing, but Frank kept Dixie's hands. "No, they'll come at us tonight while we're asleep."

By midnight the fire had burned to nothing but a pile of glowing embers and a few flickering flames. The women and girls drifted slowly off to their respective wagons and tents. Otis chased playfully after his wife and children, sending them squealing in all directions.

Frank took the watch. Except for the small remnant of a fire, the camp was dark. Only a thin sliver of a moon hung in the star-filled sky. A rustler's moon. He walked slowly toward a small rise above the little creek that fed the Arkansas River a quarter of a mile away.

A knot formed in his chest. He'd do his part, but it was up to Dixie and the others to make things work right.

He'd walked the route in the light, so he knew where he was going. Still, the way was treacherous in the dark, and Frank took a few steps at a time, watching out of his peripheral vision for any roaming rattlesnakes or Gila monsters. Dog had better night vision than he did, so much of the time, Frank just followed along behind him.

From his vantage point a hundred feet above the wagons, Frank could just make out an outline that looked like Alphonse's coat, hanging on a stick by the dying fire. No one else stirred.

At two in the morning, Dog rose to his feet and stared to

the southeast. A long, rumbling growl escaped his throat. Frank hushed the animal, and slowed his own breathing so he could hear better on the chilly desert air.

It was a quiet sound, almost indistinguishable from the breeze in the willows—the jingle of spurs and bits. Frank watched as six mounted men picked their way along the wagon track. Rifle barrels glinted in the scant moonlight. Hushed voices carried in muffled bits on the wind.

"Careful!"

"Quiet . . . "

"Watch it . . . "

" . . . son of a bitch is a quick one, so get on him fast . . . "

The men moved in around the wagons.

"Fan out," a hoarse voice whispered. "Dammit, Baxter, point that thing at the wagons, not at me."

Frank licked his finger and wet the front sight of his rifle so he could catch a little more of the moon's reflection. His guess had been right on the money. These were cowards— six men standing in the dark ready to execute sleeping women and children.

"Fire!" one of the cowboys yelled. A second later, the area around the wagons was filled with smoke and gunfire. Ten seconds later, six men and two of their horses lay dead and wounded on the ground.

The silence that followed the shooting was eerie and hollow. Below in the darkness, one of the wounded cowboys moaned. George's voice pierced the night from a stand of willows along the creek.

"We're coming out, Morgan. Don't shoot us."

"Careful of the wounded," Frank shouted down. "They may still be able to shoot."

"Help me," a low voice moaned. "I ain't goin' to shoot nobody. Oh, Lord, I'm shot bad."

"Leave him," Frank shouted to the others as shadowed figures began to pour out of the willows and olive trees along the creek bed. "Wait till I get down there."

* * *

"Hell of a plan, Morgan." George gave him a good-natured slap on the back.

Alphonse stoked the fire back up to a full blaze. Dixie stood close to Frank and surveyed the damage the outlaw bullets had done to the wagons. They'd never had the chance to get too many shots off, but the ones they had would have been lethal if anyone had actually been asleep inside the wagons.

"I'd hate to think of what could have happened," she said, tucking her head against Frank's chest. He looked over and saw Paula was pulling George close to her as well.

All but one of the attackers lay dead on they ground. Two horses had been killed by the withering volley of gunfire from Frank, George, Otis, Alphonse, Dixie, and Paula. A third horse was wounded so badly, Frank had to lead the limping animal out of camp a ways and put him out of his misery.

The wounded outlaw was an older fellow. Gray swatches of grizzled whiskers decorated his ratty, twisted face.

"I wish to hell one of you women would get me a cup of water."

Frank nodded at Dixie, who brought a cup. He squatted next to the dying man and helped him take a sip. Most of the water dribbled away out of the corner of the outlaw's lips.

"I need you to tell us what's going on here. Why are some of Swan's men riding for the Circle V?"

"Swan's men riding for the V . . . " the man gasped. His eyes darted back and forth in the firelight as if he didn't know where he was. "Vic. Vic Sutton, you talk to him. He'll hire you on."

"Does Sutton have anything to do with Swan?" Frank gave the man another drink of cool water. The pool of blood on the ground grew by the moment. There were too many holes in him to stop the flow.

"Swan said ten-thousand . . . should do it . . . Lord, I hurt bad. . . .Cindy! Oh, dear sweet Cindy . . . " His voice trailed off.

Frank lowered the dead man's head slowly back to the ground. "Seems like they always call out for their mama or some woman at the very last."

"Wish he could have told us a little more," George said quietly, still clutching a rifle in his hands.

"So do I." Frank got to his feet with a tired groan.

The sun was already a pink glow behind the hog-back ridge to the east. There would be little sleep for any of them for another day.

"We know damn little more than we did before."

George and Otis helped him drag three of the dead outlaws over to the remaining horses and tie them across the saddles. Their guns and ammunition, he stowed in the back of Dixie's wagon. They were beginning to amass quite an arsenal of dead outlaws' weapons.

"You think they'll go back to the herd?" Dixie said as Frank scribbled out a note on a piece of scrap paper.

"I do. Horses generally go to what they know, and these little ponies know where they get fed. Besides that, with these poor buggers drippin' blood all over 'em, the animals will want to get shed of them as quick as they can." He tucked the note in a dead outlaw's shirt pocket, letting it hang out enough so it would be noticed, but not fall out.

"I'm guessing Sutton is trailing his herd to Pueblo. It takes a considerable crew to keep the cattle together and he's bound to be running out of men. I'm hoping he won't try anything for a few days." Frank fired his Colt in the air, and the outlaw horses took off at a trot toward the rising sun. Their loads of dead men flopped like the wings on three ungainly birds.

Frank and the other men spent another hour scratching out graves for the other three before getting ready to move on.

Dixie took his hand. "What did you write?"

"I appealed to Vic Sutton's common sense. Told him to meet me at the trading post fifty miles this side of Rocky Ford and we'd talk like two civilized men."

"That's it?"

"No, I also told him, if I saw any more Circle V boys near the wagons, I'd send 'em back like these poor souls. No questions asked." Frank spit and readjusted his hat. "I expect he'll get my meaning."

Chapter 17

"My lands," Otis said as he rode beside Frank and looked at the distant horizon. This country's so flat, if you look hard enough you can see the back of your head."

Frank chuckled. "It's deceiving, though, my friend. A whole mess of Indians could be waiting up ahead of us over a little swell and we'd not know it until we were smack on top of them."

"That's why you keep riding ahead to scout like you do." Otis nodded. "I thought you just didn't like the smell of the mules."

"Little of both, I guess." Frank grinned. "Listen, there's a little fart of a trading post about two miles up that way." Frank pointed off to his right with an open hand. "I'd like to borrow Alphonse to go with me and check things out. I told Sutton to meet me there. I've seen him ride, and I need someone who can scoot back here if something happens to me."

Otis beamed at the compliment of his eldest son. Then his face grew tense. "Death follows you, Morgan. I'm honored that you want my boy to go with you, but his mama would have my hide if anything happened to him. I'm a fair rider. Why don't I come along with you?"

"I appreciate your concerns," Frank said, slowing his horse so he could look Otis in the eye. "Mr. Chapman, it's a hard country out here and your boy is young and inexperienced. I'd feel safer if he was with me than here, if the Circle

V boys come ridin' in here again. I was hoping you'd stay with the wagons and help George look after the women and your little ones."

Chapman rubbed his jaw in thought. "I agree then. You take care of my boy, though. You're right about it bein' a hard country. Trouble is, Mr. Morgan, I don't think you have any idea how hard it can be for a black man."

"I see your point. We'll be careful. Anybody crosses young Al and they'll answer to me. I'm a father myself." The two men shook hands.

Alphonse Chapman was a natural horseman, and easily kept stride with Frank as they let their horses eat up the ground between the wagons and the scabby adobe trading post. He was too polite a boy to speak unless he was spoken to, which was fine with Frank and one of the chief reasons he'd brought him along.

"You follow my lead," Frank said as the two dismounted outside the earth structure and tied their animals to a cedar hitching rail. Dead coyotes hung by their back legs from the exposed timber cross-beams of the roof along the outside of the building. Flies buzzed around the freshest ones nearest the door.

"Stockmen pay a bounty for each critter killed. They don't do anything with the carcasses, though, so old Ramiro uses them for decoration for his combination tradin' post and bar." Frank could see Alphonse was turning up his nose at the rank smell. "They don't smell too good when they're alive either. Anyhow, Ram thinks the bodies frighten off the evil hobgoblins or some such thing."

"I'm surprised they don't scare off the clientele," young Chapman said in a rare outburst of words.

Morgan chuckled. "Probably would." He waved his hand around to show the wide-open space around them. "But old Ram sort of has a corner on the market way out here."

One other horse stood tied outside the trading post. It bore a Wine Cup brand—a ranch miles away from the Circle V.

"Ram Solis is a friend of mine," Frank said as they walked through the door into the dim interior of the trading post. "Anything happens to me, you do what he says and you'll be all right."

Alphonse nodded.

Ramiro Solis was a bear of a man, with a pockmarked face and a smile that belied his lonely, smelly existence.

"Morgan, my dear old compadre," the big-bellied man said in the smooth tenor voice of an opera singer. "Why you not come to see an old man more often?" He pulled Frank to him in a huge backslapping hug and whispered in his ear. "The man in the corner has been asking about you. I think he is a hired gun."

"Good to see you too, Ram, you old cuspidor." Frank kept an eye on the solitary man in the back of the room while he spoke. "You gonna hug me to death or offer me and my young friend a beer?"

"Of course, of course." Ram plodded back to the makeshift bar. "A beer and then some coffee. No?"

"You got that right." Frank smiled and pointed to a small table, motioning for Alphonse to sit down.

"I'll have a cup of that coffee too when you get a chance," the man at the rear of the room said as tipped his chair back and took the makings for a cigarette out of his vest pocket. He stared at Frank and began to roll his smoke.

"Been waiting for you quite a while, Morgan," he said as he licked the edge of his paper and twisted the ends a bit to keep in the tobacco. "What's kept you?"

"Well, if I'd known you were waitin', I'd have got here faster." Frank turned to face him, shooing Alphonse out of the way, against the side wall.

"Don't worry about the nigger boy," the man said, lighting a match on the sole of his boot. "My contract's on you. There's no money in killin' him."

"So that's it, Mr . . . "

"Gamble, Nick Gamble out of Uvalde, Texas."

"Gamble?" Frank shrugged. "Sorry, never heard of you."

Gamble's face twitched at the thinly veiled insult. To a hired gun, reputation was second only to speed at the draw.

"Mind tellin' me who hired you, Gamble?" Nick sipped at the beer Ram gave him. "I'm kind of at a loss here."

Gamble motioned to the empty chair at the table next to him. "Why don't you join me, Morgan? We can chat for a while before we get to the dirty work. I got no particular malice toward you. This is just business."

"I'll stand," Frank said, finishing off his beer. "Who's paying you to brace me?"

The hired gun shrugged. "Not exactly sure. A representative gave me the money. Half before . . . half after the job is done."

"Hope you spent the first installment wisely," Morgan said. " 'Cause it's awful unlikely you'll ever get to see the rest of it."

The gunman laughed at that. "Sit down and relax for your last few minutes on earth, Morgan. You're too tense. You have a great sense of humor. We could have been friends under different circumstances, you and I."

Frank's voice grew cold. "I doubt that. I don't hire my gun."

"Ahh." The gunman wagged his finger. "You don't hire it for money, but you do hire it in a manner of speaking. You hire it for a cause. Let me hear you deny that, Morgan."

"There's a difference, Gamble. If you can't see it, then I feel sorry for you."

"Suit yourself." The hired gun dropped his cigarette on the floor and stood, crushing it out with his boot. "I'll go ahead and kill you now then, while my coffee cools."

"I'll give you this, Gamble. You got a certain style. But unless you plan on talking me to death, I'd just as soon you made your play. I'm tired of listening to your cock-a-doodle bullshit."

Gamble's face twitched again and his nostrils flared.

The hired gun was fast. He matched Frank's draw for speed, but to do so, he had to rush. Morgan didn't.

Gamble's aim went wild, missing by a good two feet and knocking the horn off a stuffed antelope head on the wall behind the bar. Frank's bullet tore into the gunman's chest, sending him staggering back against his table, then onto the ground. His heavy pistol clattered harmlessly to the ground.

He stared straight ahead, gasping for air, the hole in his chest sucking air. Even lung-shot and in the throes of death, Gamble struggled to fulfill his end of the contract and bent to jerk a derringer out of his boot. He blinked, trying to find Frank.

"Stop it, Gamble," Frank yelled. "It's over."

"I took the man's money," the gunman croaked.

Not one to argue with the gaping maw of a .45-caliber derringer, Frank put a round between Nick Gamble's eyes. The bullet tore out the back of the man's skull, spattering gray matter over the table and chair behind him.

Alphonse Chapman leaned out of his seat and vomited on the floor.

Frank kicked the tiny double-barrel away and calmly reloaded. The gunman twitched once, then lay still.

"Mr. Gamble, he should have stayed back in Uvalde, Texas," Ram said, staring at the mess on his none-too-clean floor. "I'll get a mop and a bucket." He turned to Frank. "You want another beer?"

Frank shook his head. "No, thanks. You got an undertaker around here?"

"Only me. I did have a Goshute wife, but she ran off or got stolen." Ram brightened as though he had an idea. "I know. I can hang the body outside with the coyotes."

"I think we better bury him. I'll pay you for your trouble. If a man named Sutton comes by, tell him I'm sorry I missed him, but my word still stands."

There was a shuffle in the doorway behind him, and Frank turned to see a dark silhouette.

"What word is that, Morgan?"

"Come to mop up after your hired gun, Sutton?" Frank let his hand fall to the butt of his Peacemaker.

The trail boss walked into the room and looked at the mess that had been Nick Gamble. "He's not one of my men." Sutton wore a pistol on his left side. The leather whang still covered the hammer spur. His right hand was a tight mass of white scar where his thumb and forefinger used to be. A common accident for a cattleman used to dally-roping strays—must have gotten his hand caught between the saddle horn and the rope. He was a cowboy and a mean one at that, but Vic Sutton was no gunfighter.

He ordered a beer and looked into it while he spoke, barely containing his contempt. "I got your message. You're damned fast on the trigger, Morgan." He took a long slug of his beer and then stood back from the bar. "I'm losin' a lot of men I can't afford to lose."

"Tell that to the women and children they were about to murder."

Sutton waved him off. "Don't blow smoke up my ass. Those men were after you, not the women."

"Hard to tell it from where they were aimin.'"

"Listen, Morgan. As far as I'm concerned you're no better than those men you sent back to me. You're all two-bit gunslingers with a short life and no savvy for God's honest work. But this has to stop. Some of Swan's men hired on with me, but they're all gone now. I can personally vouch for all the men I got left on the crew."

"What about your hotheaded nephew?"

Sutton turned to finish his beer. "Aw, hell, he thought you were stealin' cattle and did what any cowboy who rides for the brand would do."

"With a little too much rush to judgment maybe?"

"I'll give you that, Morgan. Is it over?"

"As far as I'm concerned." Frank took a step closer so the trail boss would be sure to understand him. "Me and you, we're hard-put types, Mr. Sutton. You just want to get your herd to market, and I aim to see these wagons safe and sound to their destination. Neither of us has got much slack when it comes to our goals. I don't want to kill any more of your men. You know that. So keep 'em clear of me. You're a tough old cob, and I trust your word—so you trust mine. The terms of my note still stand. If I said any different, well, then I'd be blowing smoke up your ass."

Chapter 18

Three scorching days after Frank killed Nick Gamble, the wheel on the Freeman wagon shattered and fell off the axle. The tired wood and metal gave way with such a loud pop, George Carlisle drew his bird's-head Colt and scanned horizon for attackers.

"You're mighty fast, Georgie," Frank ribbed the boxer. "If a broken wagon wheel ever tries to brace you, it doesn't stand a chance."

Carlisle took the jab with good humor, and dismounted to help with the repairs.

Though the families had sold most of their possessions before leaving Indiana, the wagons were still carrying extremely heavy loads. Each woman still had a fair amount of her own possessions. The Fossman and Brandon wagons had been so badly damaged during the rescue as to make them unusable, and their things were divided among the other three vehicles to even out the loads.

In order to fix the broken wheel, the mules had to be unhitched, and the entire wagon's contents unloaded under the blazing sun. Rather than ride to find wood, Frank unbolted the wagon's own tongue, unhooked the double trees, and used the stout piece of oak as a lever to lift the still-heavy wagon up high enough to put on the only spare wheel.

It was a tedious, back-breaking affair without the proper tools, but after much labor, copious amounts of sweat, and an equal measure of cursing that drove the women and children scurrying into the cactus, the wheel was finally in place.

No sooner had the sweating men reloaded the numerous heavy trunks and bags, some of which they swore contained anvils and railroad ties, than Betty Ellington pointed out that one of her mules had thrown a shoe.

Frank groaned and cast his eyes back and forth around the other exhausted men. "Any one of you besides me know anything about shoeing stock?"

"Not that I'm willing to admit," George groaned, mopping his glistening forehead with a towel Paula brought him.

"I'm a pretty poor hand at it," Otis said. "I quick just about every horse or mule I try to put a shoe on."

Frank sighed and trudged toward Betty and her mule. "That's what I figured. Alphonse, grab the shoeing box out of the back of Mrs. Carpenter's wagon and come learn an honest trade."

The families had had the good sense to have extra shoes made for each of the mules before leaving Indiana. It should have been a simple matter of cleaning up the hoof with a quick application of the rasp and then nailing on the new shoe, which had already been fitted to the mule's foot. But this particular animal was a leaner, and Frank spent as much time jabbing it in the ribs with his shoeing hammer to get it to stand up as he did pounding nails.

Twenty minutes of struggling, half bent under twelve hundred pounds of a cantankerous bag of bones, took its toll. Once the nails were all turned, wrung off, and clinched tight, Frank handed the mule's lead off to Betty and sat back on the ground.

"I'm getting too old for this," he sighed, rubbing the small of his back. Dixie handed him a cup of water. He took a sip and poured the rest of it over his head. Dixie laughed, showing all her beautiful teeth, and filled his cup again. He took another swallow, then threw the rest at her, wetting the front of her britches and causing her to gasp in surprise.

"River's not more than a half a mile away," Frank said. "We could all use a bath. Don't you think?"

"A bath." Paula perked up from the back of her wagon at the mention of the word, and Betty turned from hitching her mule to look at Frank.

"A bath, a swim, call it whatever you want. I'm tired, I'm hot, and my old back hurts. I imagine most of us share the same feelings. A little cold water would be good for what ails us."

A half a mile and twenty minutes later, Frank brought Dixie's wagon to a halt above the bank of a gentle bend in the Arkansas River and set the side-brake. The other wagons creaked to a stop behind him.

The girls and younger Chapman boys wasted no time jumping out of their respective wagons. They scampered down the steep incline like so many squirrels, excited at the prospect of a swim.

Betty Ellington stood by her wagon, her arms folded staunchly in front of a heaving chest. "Wearing men's britches is one thing," she said. "Swimming with men is an entirely different matter."

"You wouldn't be wearin' the britches while you swim," George joked, giving Paula an obvious wink.

Betty set her teeth and stomped one foot on the ground like an angry buffalo. "I do not intend to . . . "

Frank raised a hand. "Now simmer down, Betty. The river makes a pretty little bend here and pools out nicely on that far side. You women go on upstream there through the willows and have your swim. Me and the boys'll stay down here and splash around in the shallows and get cooled off."

Betty's decency preserved, the women began to coble together some towels and fresh drawers and trooped off through the willows.

"You think there might be snakes in there?" Dixie said. She and Paula were the last to leave the men.

"Don't think so," Frank said. "As you're about to find out, that water is a little more than on the cold side. There could be some on the bank, though, so keep your wits about you."

"If you see one just give us a yell." George winked. "We'll come running over to check on you."

"I'll bet you would at that." Paula giggled like a girl half her age.

Frank raised his hand as if to pledge. "We promise not to peek more than once or twice."

"Well." Dixie nodded slowly. "Gentlemen, you will get no such promise from us."

The two women turned in unison and walked slowly toward the stand of willows and cottonwoods that would separate them from view. They didn't look back, but the wiggle in their walks made it plain they knew the men were watching them.

"You ever been married?" Frank asked a few moments later as he began to strip down by the bank and hang his clothes on the willow brush. Otis and his boys already splashed and played in the knee-deep water.

"Yes, as a matter of fact I was," George said, paying careful attention to how he laid out his pistol next to the bank—out of the water but within easy reach—an action that impressed Frank as much as the man's speed with a gun or his fists. "I was married to a beautiful young woman from Pennsylvania. Her father is a large landholder there and the family had a great deal of money."

"Ah." Frank nodded. "The family didn't take to you then?" He winced as he stepped into the cold current.

"Actually, her father and I got on quite well. We had two children and a very nice home in upstate New York. I got along with the family fine. It was my wife I had a hard time getting along with. Through the years, I came to learn one of life's valuable lessons—beauty doesn't guarantee tranquility.

You know what the Good Book says?" George kicked at the water with his toe, as if in deep thought.

Frank shrugged. "I reckon I've got as much cause to read the Bible as anyone, but I'm not certain what it says on that particular subject."

"It says, and I quote, 'It is better to dwell in the corner of a housetop, than with a brawling woman in a wide house'—Proverbs 21:9."

"Truer words were never spoken," Frank said, easing deeper into the water. It was cold enough to take his breath away, but it didn't seem to be affecting George. "So, if you don't mind me sayin' so, you don't seem to think Paula is going to be a brawling woman."

George chuckled. "Fortuna—that was my first wife—she was young, barely twenty when we married. I had to watch her grow from a spoiled girl into a brawling woman. Took a while to get there, but once she did, it was a sorry sight to behold. Paula already is what she's going to be. She's been through a lot and held up remarkably well, don't you think?"

"I do. I'm glad you two seem so taken with each other. In my opinion, Mr. Carlisle, she could do a lot worse."

"I was going to say the same thing about you and . . . "

A shrill scream carried through the cottonwoods above the rush of the river. Both men scrambled immediately for the bank—and their weapons. Frank yanked up his britches and grabbed the rifle, not even taking time to hitch on his gun belt and pistol. George was right behind him, bird's-head Colt in one hand and his hat in the other. Not wanting to be left behind, he hadn't bothered with his drawers or his trousers.

They hadn't gone ten steps when a single gunshot rang out, echoing across the water's surface. Otis shooed his boys to the safety of the bank while Frank and George redoubled their speed. More shrieks and cries of panic came from the women's side of the river bend. Before the men made the tree line, they were met by two red-faced cowboys, neither of them over seventeen, spurring their horses away from the women as fast as their mounts would carry them.

Frank aimed the rifle at the approaching cowboys. He was certain George followed suit behind him. Caught between the swimming women and two armed, half-naked men, the frightened cowboys reined up and raised their hands.

Both tried to talk at once, a slurry of apologizing stutters and stop-and-start tongue-tangled yammering that got Frank laughing so hard, he couldn't have hit them if he'd tried.

"Oh, dear Lord, we . . . didn't know there was naked women down there," the pudgy boy on a buckskin gelding whimpered.

"Honest. Honest to God, sir," his baby-faced partner finally got out, his hands shaking enough to scare flies away. "Chance is tellin' the gospel truth. Mr. Perkins sent me and him to find a place to cross the herd, that's all."

"We swear it." Poor Chance grimaced and squirmed like he needed to go the bathroom.

Frank lowered the rifle and glanced behind him to see George do the same. He seemed unabashed to stand naked in front of the world with only his hat and pistol.

"Go ahead and put your hands down, boys," Frank said, rubbing his eyes and trying not to laugh anymore and embarrass the frightened youngsters. "You said Mr. Perkins sent you on this scout?"

"Yes, sir," Chance moaned. "He never said nothin' about lookin' out for no naked women. Good Lord."

Frank stifled a chuckle in a cough behind his fist. "Would that be Mr. Luke Perkins of the Double Diamond?"

The boys brightened at Morgan's tone. "Why, yes, sir," Chance said. "He's our boss. Do you know him?"

Frank nodded. "I do." Completely relaxed now, he cradled the rifle in arms across his bare chest. "Luke's a good friend of mine."

There was a flurry of activity in the trees. The boys' horses began to prance again from their riders' nervousness.

Chance gave a pleading look to the men. "Mister, will you vouch for our innocence? That naked skinny woman with the dark hair tried to blow our heads off just for stumblin' on 'em like we did."

"That'd be Mrs. Ellington." Frank smiled. "She's right particular about her decency."

Jasper shot a forlorn look over his shoulder, then hung his head and cringed lower in his saddle. "I'd hate for it to get back to my mama that I was kilt by a naked crazy woman. I don't think she'd ever get over it."

Dixie, Paula, and Betty trooped over the small rise at the tree line, armed to the teeth and wearing nothing but their lacy underthings.

Frank quickly explained the misunderstanding, and George removed his hat for the ladies and put it where it would do the most good.

"Well," Dixie said, raising an eyebrow at Frank and a now-squirming Carlisle. "I suppose since we women don't have to save the day, some of us should go back and make ourselves more presentable." The women stood elbow-to-elbow, looking at George, giggling at the fact that sooner or later he would have to turn around and walk back to his clothes or risk stumbling backward over the stony path.

"Would you ladies be so kind as to avert your eyes?" The boxer cleared his throat and tried to keep some modicum of dignity. Despite his age, he was still well muscled, and the women, enjoying their game, seemed in no hurry to let him slip away scot-free. Paula giggled, but none of the women budged.

"I see," he said. "Well, then. In that case I will bid you ladies good day then."

George gave a little bow, and to the dismay of Frank, the frightened cowboys, and the startled women, returned the hat to his head, did a slow about-face, and marched back to get his clothes.

All three women gasped in embarrassment and covered their eyes with their hands.

Nobody but Frank saw it, but Paula Freeman peeked.

Chapter 19

"How far back is the herd?" Frank asked the cowboys over coffee a short time later once most of the group had regained some composure. The incident had even lightened Betty Ellington up a little.

"An hour at most," Jasper said. When he wasn't under the gun of a crazy naked woman, the boy turned out to be a pretty intelligent cowhand. "The herd's pretty dry, though, so they're likely to speed up some when they smell the water. Mr. Perkins had us keeping them well away from the river until he decided to cross."

"Good thing we had our little bath when we did then," Frank said. "This river'll be a mud pit for hours."

"You been on drives before?" Chance had already drunk four cups of coffee, and was beginning to get a little jumpy.

"A couple. I worked on a ranch as a boy, right alongside your Mr. Perkins a good deal of the time. I'm sure he's mentioned me."

"He may have, sir," Jasper said. "But you ain't told us your name yet."

"You're right, boys. All this excitement has caused a slip in my manners." The gunfighter extended his hand. "Frank Morgan."

Both cowboys' jaws dropped. Chance spilled his coffee.

Dixie's mothering instincts kicked in automatically. "Close your mouths, boys, before something crawls in and builds a web."

The cowboys obeyed. "Yes, ma'am," they both whispered in unison.

"You're Frank Morgan?" Jasper gasped. "The boss talks about you all the time. I read a book about you once."

"Well, don't believe everything you read," Frank said. "Some yahoo could easily write that you were shot at by a naked crazy woman with raven hair. On the face of it, it would be true, but people could read whatever they wanted to into the circumstances."

Jasper nodded, his mouth open again. "But you're Frank Morgan. No foolin'?"

"No foolin'," Frank said, patting the young man on the back. "You boys better get back to the herd or if I know Luke, he'll have your hides and mine too for keepin' you."

"Yes, sir," the boys said at once, clambering to their feet.

"Mr. Perkins still scared of snakes?" Frank said as he walked the boys to their horses.

Chance nodded with a grin. "You know the boss all right. He kills every snake he sees and has us do the same."

Frank began to laugh to himself. "When we were about thirteen, we were out gathering some maverick cows down in southwest Texas. A young German boy—can't recall his name—he killed him a fat, five-foot diamondback rattler. That snake was big around as my leg and had a head as wide as a shovel. Well, sir, this kid snuck up where Luke was snoozin' and coiled that bugger up on his chest. Poor Luke woke up with that huge spade-headed serpent starin' back at him." Frank and the boys were laughing so hard, it was hard for him to finish the story.

"Well, he tore the blankets off him and shot the snake in half. Once he realized it was already dead and we were all laughing our fool heads off, he grabbed up a branding iron and lit out after the poor German kid. I believe he would have beat him to death if he could have caught him." Frank shook his head and dried the tears of laughter out of his eyes with his bandanna.

Dixie looked on dumbfounded. "That's the worst story I ever heard. It's just awful."

"Awful funny, ma'am," Jasper said, tipping his hat. "It was a pure pleasure to meet you, Mr. Morgan. We'll tell the boss you're here and he'll be along directly."

"You do that." Frank patted the boy's horse on the rump. "I'd love to see that old fart."

The boys turned their horses and galloped off toward a growing cloud of dust that approached from the south.

The herd was getting close.

"You ladies are in for a real treat." Frank put his arm around Dixie's shoulders and gave her a squeeze.

"Is George going to go swimming again?" There was a twinkle in her green eyes.

"You're a scamp. Your know that? No, he's not. But a huge cattle herd is certainly something to see. We need to put the wagons next to the trees. Then we can watch the crossing from that little knoll up there. We're upwind, so the dust shouldn't be too bad." He squeezed her shoulder again. "It'll be a sight to behold."

She pulled away and looked up into his eyes. "You, sir, are the sight to behold, Frank Morgan." She nodded once as if to put emphasis on her point. "I just thought you should know I feel that way." She turned back and repositioned his arm around her again. "Now, let's go watch those cattle."

Dixie sat between Frank and her girls as the huge herd rumbled across the river. The two bumbling cowboys had chosen well, picking a wide spot past the swimming hole where the channel spread out and the water slowed and shallowed.

Her insides felt in as much upheaval as the roiling herd. From the day she'd met Frank Morgan, she'd been at odds within herself about her feelings for the man. First because Virgil was still alive, then because he was so recently dead.

As time wore on and she watched the gunfighter move and interact with the others in the train, she felt herself falling in love with him. Then she'd watched him shoot the man on the street—watched him deal so much death. There had to be an end to all the killing.

After she'd heard about the fight with Nick Gamble, she'd decided that there was no way she could be happy with a man surrounded by so much pain. Content with her decision, she'd watched him work so hard to fix the wagon, shoe the mule, and then cheer everyone up with the suggestion of a swim. She watched the way he joked with George, the way the young cowboys revered him. This was such a different side of him—a side she had not seen—a playful side that loved life and the good and simple things that went along with it. He was so excited about running into his friend Luke, he looked as if he might burst.

As the last of the bawling cows splashed and heaved their way up on the far bank, Dixie changed her mind again. She could make him happy. Frank Morgan needed saving. No matter how good he was, how quick he was, the life he lived made it certain he would meet an untimely death.

Dixie nodded to herself and smiled at him without speaking. She would help him settle down, build something permanent with his life. He had saved them. It was only right and proper that she should save him.

Less than two full days' ride to the south, Ephraim Swan leaned against a scrubby piñon pine and cleaned the dirt out of his fingernails with a tiny silver-handled knife.

The news of the Circle V cowboys' debacle had been enough to make him slap Carmen so badly he knocked out two of her teeth. It really didn't matter. He was getting tired of the sleepy-eyed tramp anyway. He'd already decided to kill her and dump her with that slimy bastard Eduardo the next time they met.

That time had come.

"Why don't you get down off your horse and have some brandy, my old friend," Swan said, folding up his small knife and wiping his hands on the front of his trousers.

The tall Mexican beamed at the thought of good brandy and shrugged.

"Do you have the redheads and the others?"

"You know I don't, Eduardo, so why do you ask?" It was difficult for Swan to hide his contempt for the other man. "Come, let us drink and we can discuss the new terms."

The Mexican shrugged. "*Bueno.* I am happy to see you understand. I was afraid you might take this . . . how would you say it . . . a little more to your heart." He climbed down from his saddle and rubbed his bony hands together in front of him. "I would truly enjoy some of your fine brandy."

Swan gave a tiny nod of his head, and two outlaws sprang on the startled Mexican and pinned both his arms to the sides of his white suit.

"*Que es eso?* What is the meaning of this?" he cried, but he didn't attempt to struggle.

Swan stepped up and took the man's nickel-plated pistol from the holster under his coat.

"You greasers always do go for the flashy stuff, don't you?" The outlaw twirled the shiny pistol around, watching the way the sun glinted off the gleaming barrel.

"Why do you do this, Ephraim? I can make you a very rich man."

"You already have, Eddy."

The tall man glowered back at him, incensed at such rough treatment. "You should not forget, *mi companiero,* I know many very powerful men."

Swan spit in the man's face. "And you should not forget, I am one of those powerful men." He swung the nickel revolver sideways, catching the surprised Mexican in the temple with a loud whack.

Eduardo's eyes rolled back in his head and his knees

buckled. The outlaws on either side of him struggled to keep the swaying man on his feet. He shook his head to clear it, and spit out a mouth full of blood.

"I still have clients who will pay a high price for the blondes and redheads." His voice was a whine now. "I told you that."

Swan nodded. "I know you did, Eddy. You told me that." He leaned in so he was nose-to-nose with the Mexican. "But you know what? I don't care anymore. I don't give a rat's ass about your clients or their prices. You think you're the only damned slaver in the world who wants to buy young freckled kids and fresh women? You can't be that stupid."

"Come now, Ephraim." Eduardo rolled his jaw back and forth, still smarting from the blow from his own pistol. "We can still talk about this. I can assure you it will be mutually beneficial for each of us."

Swan stood and stared at the captive man. His breathing quickened and his nostrils flared. He shook his head back and forth and screamed. Eduardo flinched, but the outlaws holding him stood rock solid.

"All my work, Eddy!" Spittle flew from Swan's mouth as he railed. "All my hard work and you can't wait another day? What the hell's wrong with you and your people? This is gone far beyond selling any women and redheaded orphans. This is personal now. You know what I'm gonna do to those women when I see 'em? I'm gonna skin every one of 'em alive and hack the rest into pieces so none of your stinkin' clients will ever get to enjoy 'em."

Swan stood panting, glaring at the victim of his tirade. "In another week you and I could have been richer than we are already, but you just couldn't wait. Now in another week Morgan and all the women will be dead."

His voice grew suddenly quiet and he raised the sliver pistol. "And you don't even have a week."

The shot cut short Eduardo's scream for mercy, and the two outlaws let his body slump to the ground.

Swan pitched the gleaming pistol on top of the dead man, and wiped a bit of blood from under his own eye. That always seemed to happen when he shot people at such close range.

Carmen had stuck her lolling head out the tent flap during all the screaming and commotion. Her dirty-blond hair stuck out in every which direction, and her eyelids hung half-closed against the bright sun.

Swan motioned her out with a flick of his wrist.

She tried to blink her eyes open wider. "But, darling, all I got is this sheet wrapped around me. I ain't decent."

"Carmen," he barked, "you haven't been decent since you turned thirteen. Now get out here like I tell you."

The dazed blond woman stuck a timid foot out the tent flap, and then made her way over to where Swan stood beside the dead Mexican slave trader.

She clutched his arm until he shrugged her off. Then she swayed, blinking up at him with her foggy eyes. "What's wrong, sugar? What do you want me out here for?" A pale shoulder peeked out from the sheet.

The other men began to gather around. Some grinned, others chuckled openly. Some tied their horses to the scrubby pine trees, to free up their hands. They all knew what was about to happen.

"What I really want is to be shed of you," Swan spit. "Now get out of my sight."

The girl blinked and looked at the brush and open ground around her. "But Ephraim, honey, there's nothing out here but cactus and snakes—and I ain't got no shoes." Her chest heaved and she began to cry. "You can't just leave me out here. I'd die for sure or get killed—or worse. There's Indians out here." She was sobbing full-tilt now, her dirty arms wrapped tight around her chest. "All I got's this damned sheet."

"I almost forgot about that," Swan said. He grabbed the sheet and yanked it off the crying woman.

She screamed and tried to cover herself with her hands. "Ephraim, what the hell are you doin'?"

"You don't have any dignity, Carmen, so stop pretending." Swan turned his back and carried the sheet back toward his tent. He yelled over his shoulder to the men as he went inside. "I'll be ready to go in an hour. I'm finished with the girl, boys. Do whatever you want to with her, then dump her with the greaser."

Carmen began to scream and spit as the men closed in around her. Swan poked his head back out the tent. "But keep her quiet, will ya? I'm gonna have a little nap."

Chapter 20

Luke Perkins cut a fat steer out of the herd and with the help of Frank and George, butchered it for a reunion barbeque. The women busied themselves making yeast bread and pies, while the men and cowboys not riding herd gathered as much deadfall wood as they could drag up. The soft cottonwood and willow burned fast, so they would need a lot.

By sunset, the beef sizzled and smoked over a huge bed of coals. The rest of the herd was strung out for nearly a mile, mooing and milling, content to graze on the narrow strip of green that lined the bank. There was hardly a breath of wind and with the sun down, it cooled off just enough to make fire and close companionship feel warm and welcome.

"I miss a good old mesquite fire for barbeque, don't you, Frankie?" Perkins leaned back against his upturned saddle, the fleece under-lining forming a backrest, his blanket a padded seat over the rocks—a cowboy easy chair. "Ain't nothing like a hardwood for barbeque."

"I don't miss the thorns," Frank said. He licked grease off his fingers. "I've had enough mesquite thorns to last a lifetime. The meat is good, though, and that's a fact."

"Yeah, it's all right. I've grown a little particular about my beef," Luke said, getting up to check the rest of a huge haunch that dangled over the coals. "It'll do, I reckon." He was a tall man, completely bald, with a huge mustache that hung over his upper lip, like the cowcatcher on a steam engine.

The rich aroma of bread, roasting meat, and baking sweets filled the air in the little riverside glade. At the edge of the clearing, three Mexican cowboys, adopted by Luke in their early teens, huddled around a shovel blade over a bed of coals away from the main fire.

"What are they cooking over there?" Dixie asked. "It smells wonderful."

"*Tripas,*" Frank said, grinning at Perkins.

"What's *tripas*?"

"Tripe, Mrs. Carpenter," said Luke. "They're cooking the guts. Mexicans love the stuff." Luke looked over at the boys, who crowded around their sizzling delicacy and stirred it with a stick as it fried on the hot shovel blade. "It really ain't so bad once you work it around in your mouth some and get it chewed up and swallowed."

Dixie shuddered. "Personally," she said, "I'd rather eat the shovel. Eating a gut sounds disgusting."

"I know people who eat snakes. Now that's what I call disgusting." Luke cast his eyes back and forth on the ground around his saddle to check for the slithering reptiles—just to be on the safe side. "When was the last time you went home to Texas, Frankie?"

"I drifted through Amarillo a few months ago, but I haven't been home in a coon's age. It would just bring trouble to my friends if I went back."

"You're getting old, Frank. Most of the men back home who wanted to kill you are either already dead or gummin' their food by now."

"What about Jim Taggart? He and I don't exactly see eye-to-eye since I killed his brother back before the war."

Luke waved that off. "That big bucktoothed Irishman who was sweet on Julie Sweeny killed him last winter."

Frank nodded, staring into the fire. Home. It would be something to ride out to the old home place again. Better not to dwell on it, though. No matter what Luke said, his appearance would only rekindle smoldering hatreds and stir up old feuds.

Frank decided it was best to change the subject. "Looks like you're doin' pretty well for yourself, Luke."

The rancher shrugged. "The Double Diamond turns a profit if that's what you mean, but since Lisa passed on, my heart's not in it anymore. I'm happier out here on the trail than I am back at the ranch. We all got our ghosts that haunt us."

"Amen to that." Frank raised his coffee cup. "Amen to that." He took a sip and gestured toward the Mexican boys. "It must be a heavy burden bein' trail boss, guide, father confessor, and nursemaid to all these adopted children of yours."

"Yeah, well, there are benefits to startin' them young." Luke dipped his head toward Chance and Jasper. The two boys seemed to do everything as a pair. Together, they now laughed and whispered in hushed tones with the Fossman twins.

"If I raise 'em, I know I can count 'em in a pinch. I wouldn't give you a dab of horse crap for the best hand Vic Sutton has. Those boys ride for the money. My boys are family. They ride for the brand. You wouldn't catch any of my men workin' for Swan or the likes of him, ten thousand dollars or no. Wouldn't matter if it was a hundred thousand dollars." Luke spit over his shoulder, covering his face with the palm of his hand in deference to the ladies. "I'll not have a man I can't trust. I find someone like that in the ranks, and he can draw his wages and scoot."

"You need to be a daddy," Frank said as Dixie brought him a refill for his coffee and a hot piece of Salina Chapman's pie. "You'd make a good one, for a fact."

Paula tended to George's every need, and brought him his pie and coffee. Salina served Otis.

To everyone's amazement, Carolyn Brandon, her

normally disheveled hair tied back in a green satin bow, brought a huge piece of pie, a linen napkin, and a fresh mug of coffee to Luke.

He smiled up at her and took the dessert. He patted the saddle pad on the ground next to him. "Take a load off those pretty little feet, darlin'. There's enough of this here for the both of us."

Carolyn knelt down beside him. "I'd like that very much, Mr. Perkins," she said—the first words she'd spoken in weeks.

"Well, now, aren't you just the prettiest thing this side of Texas or heaven. Call me Luke."

Frank watched as his friend chatted with the heartsick woman, complimenting her hair and her dress. Luke Perkins had a way with people, particularly the fairer sex.

Everyone ate their fill, and then at Salina's insistence ate some more. Surrounded by a virtual army of Luke's cowboys, Frank felt like he could relax a notch for the first time in recent memory.

The fire died down to embers, blown to life now and again by each breath of passing breeze along the river bottom. Cowboys began to drift back to the herd to relieve their compadres riding night owl.

Frank was intensely aware of the warmth of Dixie's body. She sat right next to him, her hip pressing against his leg, her hand in his, resting on the bend of her knee.

A whippoorwill cried in the cottonwoods down by the river.

"That's odd," Frank whispered. The night seemed too reverent to warrant loud talking. "You don't hear those birds too often this far out."

Dixie shivered and leaned her head against his shoulder. "It sounds so lonesome. Makes me feel like crying."

Frank sighed. Words were unnecessary. He was content to sit next to this strong, beautiful woman and say nothing.

"The girls are already in bed," Dixie said at length. Her voice was soft, almost liquid. She kept her head where it was.

Frank gazed into the remnants of fire. He was beginning to feel a little light-headed. He thought it funny how he could stare down the meanest hombre on earth without so much as breaking a sweat, and yet this little woman was making it hard for him to think. He nodded. "I reckon it is time to turn in."

Dixie didn't budge.

"Frank?"

"I'm still here, darlin'. You'd fall on your head if I moved."

She giggled and sat up to look him full in the eyes. "Frank Morgan, I'm a full-grown woman in case you haven't noticed. So I'm going to be bold and say this straight out before I change my mind." She was close enough that he could feel her breathy words on his face. "I don't want to sleep alone tonight." Her chest heaved and she bit her bottom lip. The speech given, a look of panic began to cross her face and she opened her mouth to speak again.

Frank smiled and put a finger to her lips.

"I don't either," he whispered. "What do you say we go down by the river and find that whippoorwill?"

Dixie sighed. All the tension seemed to leave her body. She disappeared to the wagon, and returned a short time later with some blankets and a pillow. She held it up in front of her.

"I could only find the one," she whispered so as not to wake the children or other women.

Frank gave her a wink. "I don't reckon I'll be needin' any pillow. I'll have you."

He took her hand and they slipped quietly into the night.

* * *

Two hours later, Dixie Carpenter, recent widow and thirty-six-year-old mother of two girls, lay next to a sleeping Frank Morgan and smiled up into the white curtain of stars that draped across the night sky.

Two months ago she would have been perfectly content to stay cooped up in her cozy little home near Terra Haute, Indiana, with her grumpy husband, growing children, and basically dull existence. Before she left on this trip, Dixie had never even slept outdoors. The lumpy tow-filled tick in the wagon had been almost unbearable at first compared to her feather bed at home. As time went on, though, she'd grown somewhat used to the hard conditions of the trail, and except for the sleeping arrangements, even flourished.

Now, lying on top of a maze of tree roots that crisscrossed under her blanket and bit into her bare back like a rope bed without the mattress, she found she was as comfortable as she had ever been in her life.

Frank slept quietly beside her, his strong chest rising and falling with each breath. Her head was cradled on his shoulder, his sure arm wrapped around her, holding her as if he was afraid she might escape if he let her go. He didn't need to worry about that.

Even surrounded by the warm comfort of his body, Dixie felt her heart flutter inside her. She'd really done it now. She hoped Frank Morgan was half the man she judged him to be. If he left her now, she didn't know what she'd do.

The roots finally began to get to her spine, and she rolled a little to change positions. Frank clutched at her in his sleep and then relaxed. He whispered her name, then didn't stir again.

On her side now, her face against his neck, his mouth breathing softly in her ear, she whispered back to him.

"I love you, Frank Morgan."

She held her breath to see if he would answer. He'd said

it, before but she'd supposed lots of men said it during such amorous circumstances.

He coughed a little and hugged her to him.

"Me too," he whispered in her ear.

Dixie froze, waiting to see if he would say more. When he began to snore softly, his lips brushing against her ear, she relaxed. She didn't want to sleep anymore. She just wanted to lay in the arms of this wonderful man and plan—plan for everything the future might hold. For the first time in weeks, Dixie Carpenter, recent widow and thirty-six-year-old mother of two, knew she could handle it.

Chapter 21

Two hours before dawn, Frank squatted by the chuck wagon at the Double Diamond camp. Up and down the river, the cattle were beginning to stir. A few mama cows that had snuck into the herd of steers at the start of the trip lowed for their babies, telling them it was time to eat.

The remuda of horses stood on a long picket line, stomping and snorting as they waited for the wrangler to give them their morning ration of oats.

A column of bleary-eyed cowboys, Chance and Jasper in the lead, queued up for bacon, biscuits, and coffee. Tired as they were, a whisper rumbled up and down the breakfast line when the boys rubbed enough sleep out of their eyes to see Frank Morgan had come to their camp for a visit.

"I've tasted worse." Frank sipped the tepid coffee and tried to keep from spitting it out.

"Where? From the back end of a buffalo?" Luke looked down at his breakfast plate and grumbled. "I'd love to have a plate of ham and eggs right now, with some fluffy buttermilk biscuits as big as a cat's head all smothered in real redeye gravy."

"I seem to recall you said you were happier out here on the trail." Frank held the cup of coffee for warmth on his hands, but decided against drinking any more.

"I was. Then you had to go and introduce me to that Carolyn Brandon. She's got me thinkin' about soft beds and good meals." Perkins tossed the plate on the ground with the food uneaten—an act that could get any other cowboy on the crew a severe tongue-lashing from the cook.

"Truth is, Frank, I reckon I'm getting' as old as you. That Carolyn, she's real sweet and I been awful lonely since Lisa passed."

"I think you'd be good for each other."

"Good, because she's decided to come back to Texas with me after I get this herd to the railhead."

Frank beamed at his friend. "Good for you and good for Carolyn."

"There's even more to it than that. Berta and Bea have decided to come with us too. They are right smitten with Jasper and Chance, and the feeling appears to be mutual. In a few years . . . well, who knows how it will work out?"

"You'd adopt the whole lot of them if you could," Frank said.

"How about that Dixie Carpenter? A body would have to be blind as a mole not to see you two got a little thing goin'."

Morgan shrugged. There was no use denying it to Luke or himself. "Yeah, I reckon we got something goin'."

"Well, then, when you two get hitched, ya'll can come home and settle down—stop all this driftin'."

Frank held up his hand. "No one said anything about marriage yet, partner. It hasn't even come up."

Luke slapped his leg and laughed, deep in his belly. "Oh, oh, boy, you don't think so? Sure it's come up. A woman Dixie's age don't look at your eyes like that because she wants you to take her to the church social. And she sure as shootin' don't walk off with you into the dark." Luke grinned at his friend. "Yeah, we seen the two of you, and so did George and Paula while we were all slippin' off to find our own little slices of the night. Take it from me, a single woman brings you a piece of pie and sits by you around a campfire and she's dreamin' of tying the eternal knot."

"So you and Carolyn already talked about getting married?"

"Yup, late last night. We'll get hitched first chance we get. To be such a quick hand with a gun, you're a little slow on the uptake, boyo." Luke suddenly got quiet and he leaned in close to Frank. "Let's get serious for a minute, okay?"

Frank shrugged. "Sure."

"You got a considerable number of men after you."

"I do. It's been that way for some time. This is not a new situation."

"Well, you got a woman to think about now. I ain't sayin' you should run scared or any such thing. I'm just suggestin' that you think about comin' home. Quit wandering around and getting yourself shot at."

"You think that if I came home, no one would try and prod me?"

Luke shrugged. "I don't know, Frankie, but for the most part at least, if you came back to Texas, you'd be among friends. Dixie could have a home. You know enough about women to know they got a need to put down roots."

Frank sighed. "Home to Texas; it's something to consider."

Luke groaned to his feet and reached out for Frank's cup. "Don't worry about drinkin' the coffee. It'll probably kill the grass, but go ahead and pour it out."

The trail boss stuck out his big hand. "Well, I got a herd to move."

He whistled up the rest of the crew and shouted, "If we ever want to get to Pueblo, we best get movin'!"

By the time Frank made it back to the wagons, Dixie was up and tending to a large Dutch oven full of biscuits. A tall, blue-speckled coffeepot sat at the edge of the fire. He wondered how she could look so beautiful on so little sleep.

"I hope this is some of your famous brew," Frank said pouring himself a cup. "I can't begin to tell you how bad that cow-camp coffee was. I've heard of folks throwing in some eggshell to settle the grounds. I believe they threw in the whole egg." He took a sip, closed his eyes, and savored it.

"Did you eat?" Dixie asked.

"I had a piece of biscuit to be polite. At least I think it was biscuit. It was dark, I mighta been eatin' a hunk of firewood or a cow patty."

Dixie fed him a full-course breakfast, and gave him a peck on the cheek for dessert. Luke sure did know women.

After he ate, Frank hitched the mules. As brave a man as he was, with what he intended to do, he needed to hitch up his courage as well. Once the teams were well in harness, he called Dixie and the girls over to where he stood. He folded his arms in front of him and stared at them. For all his planning, he didn't know how to begin. Just looking at Dixie's bright and expecting face took all the starch out of him.

Faith, the oldest at almost seventeen, cocked her head to one side. "What's wrong, Frank? You look like you just swallowed a bug." She had her mother's forthright attitude and spunk.

Frank raised his hand. "Be still a minute. I have something I need to tell you and it's eatin' a hole in me to keep it inside. It's important."

Dixie started to speak, but Frank shushed her. "All right, here's the way things are going to be. I want you girls to listen and listen good. First, you are both going to get a good education. There are some top-notch universities back East, and I expect your mother would be happy for you to attend any one of them once you're old enough. I'll pay for it, so that shouldn't be a problem. I'll not have any stepdaughters of mine going through life as uneducated women with schooling becomin' so important in this day and age."

Dixie and both her daughters gasped, but Frank plowed ahead.

"Your mother wants to go to Denver, so we are going to go on up there and be married. After we're married, if she's willing, we'll travel down to Texas for a while. If we like it

we'll stay. If not, I have a nice spread in New Mexico. It's re-
mote, but it will do." Frank took a deep breath and unfolded
his arms."Now, I've said my piece."

Both girls stood slack-jawed. Faith spoke first. "Are we
supposed to call you Daddy or Mr. Morgan?"

"Frank will do just fine."

"Will you really pay for our schooling and board and
everything back East? I always wanted to be a doctor." The
wheels were already turning in Laura's head.

"I said I would and I meant it." He looked at Dixie. "All
of it. Now, you girls run on. Me and your mama have a thing
or two to sort out among ourselves."

After the girls were gone, Dixie stood staring at Frank, a
silly grin decorating the corners of her mouth.

"That," she said, "was the strangest way to propose I've
ever heard of."

"I believe in getting straight to the point. Does my plan
meet with your approval?"

She touched his face. "What do you think?"

He raised his eyebrows. "I think we need to hurry and get
married so you can make an honest man out of me."

Ephraim Swan sat in his folding wooden chair and
watched the sparks from the huge cedar fire spiral upward
and disappear into the blackness above him. The drovers
they'd robbed the night before, near the little speck on the
map where Colorado, Kansas, and Nebraska all came together, had left him richer by thousands, but he still felt
hollow knowing Frank Morgan was alive and free to roam
the country after the way he'd mucked everything up.

Times like this made him feel like he'd been too hasty to
get rid of Carmen. She'd been dull-eyed and stupid, but at
least she had provided some distraction from time to time.
Now he had nothing but the buzzing talk of the other men as

they divided up the loot to take his mind off the man he'd grown to hate more than anything in the world.

It wasn't so much the loss of money, though he had stood to gain a considerable amount from the transaction with the Mexicans. There was always more money to steal from this puny settler or that hapless miner who struck it rich just long enough to brag about all his gold to the wrong people. No, there was money aplenty to be had in any number of ways.

Swan hated to be beaten. He despised the fact that Morgan had been able to kill so many of his men, that he'd been able to keep the women safe all by himself, when Swan, with his virtual army, hadn't been able to get them back.

Gamble, who had been touted as the best hired gun around, hadn't even come close to besting the stupid drifter.

In a few days, the wagons would be well into civilization and it would be all the more difficult to get at them. He knew the families had put their entire life savings somewhere in those wagons. He'd talked the ignorant men into doing just that. But the closer they got to towns and banks, the more likely each of the women was to make a deposit and put the money where he couldn't get to it.

Swan looked deep into the glowing coals of the fire. He realized it wasn't the money he was after at all. More than that, he just wanted Frank Morgan dead. If the gunfighter was too fast—or just too damned lucky to be killed—then so be it.

Swan lifted his head and howled at the stars like a crazy wolf. The men closest to him around the fire jumped at the horrific sound. One outlaw gave a little yelp.

"I've worked it all out, boys." Swan stood and clapped both hands together, rubbing them in front of him like a fly. "We been goin' about this all the wrong way. I shoulda kept after that train from the very beginning. Gather around and let me tell you what we're goin' to do."

He bent to pitch more wood on the fire, and it rose up in a tall pyre in front of him, bathing him in orange light and warming his face as he spoke. He knew his huge shadow danced in the juniper and piñons behind him, and he saw the awe in the eyes of his men.

"The wagon train with the soon-to-be-dead Frank Morgan and all his women will be pullin' into Pueblo soon. I say we head that direction and when opportunity rears its head we whack it off." He stared hard at all the men around him. These men knew him. They'd all seen what he was capable of doing when he was upset.

"I've been offering ten thousand dollars to the man who kills Frank Morgan. I'll say this once so listen to me good. I'm uppin' my offer to double. That's twenty thousand to the man who kills the worthless puke. If you can get to him before I do. But any man who wants the money better light a shuck and hurry, because tomorrow, I'm headin' for Pueblo and when I get there, I aim to kill Frank Morgan myself or die tryin'."

Chapter 22

As slow as the wagons were, they still moved faster than the ambling Double Diamond herd. Perkins wanted the cattle to be as fat as possible when they got to the market, so he let them laze along and didn't rush them.

Frank had a three-day lead by the time the wagons rolled into the outskirts of Pueblo. They pulled to a stop next to a line of scrubby cedars by the dilapidated remnants of on old log-and-stone structure.

The closer they got to the town, the more animated Otis Chapmen became. He asked Frank a number of questions about the surrounding country, particularly the area to the north, toward the big gorge.

"You ever hear of a place called Cripple Creek?" he asked, out of earshot of all the others.

"Sure, Canyon City's about forty miles that way." Frank pointed to the northwest with an open hand. "The place you're lookin' for is a bit north of Canyon City." The gunfighter grinned. "Your secret's safe with me. I never had the lust for gold."

"I didn't fool you much, did I?"

"I've seen people with gold fever before, Otis. It's what brought all these women out here with their husbands in the first place. Some folks strike it rich, others don't. No matter how you look at it, from what I've seen it's mighty hard work for what you get back."

Chapman nodded. "I suppose I'm after the adventure more than the gold."

"Good to hear. The search for gold generally amounts to a fool's errand, but if you got your heart set on it, and that kind of attitude, I say Godspeed. When are you pulling out?"

Otis pranced like a horse left too long in the starting gate. "As soon as we can provision up. Salina and I are anxious to get up there and stake a small claim."

"Make certain you get enough to last the winter." He shook the man's hand. "It's been a pleasure knowing you and your family, Mr. Chapman."

"The pleasure was all ours. I'd say we'll meet again one day."

Not one for prolonged good-byes, Frank tipped his hat to Salina and the boys. "Hope so," he said, and went to find Dixie.

"Chapmans are leaving us," he said when he found Dixie at her wagon. He leaned against the wagon wheel and rolled himself a smoke while he watched her. She puttered around the camp, tying off the cook tarp, unpacking utensils, and taking stock of what they might need to buy in town.

"Where are the girls?" Frank asked.

"Gone on in with everyone else. They promised to stay with Betty and keep out of trouble."

Frank nodded. "How long ago did they leave?"

"Ten—fifteen minutes. George and Paula said they'd come back about three and stay with the stock while we go in. Look at these peppers, Frank." Dixie held up two-foot-long string of bright red chilies. "A sweet old Mexican woman in a red scarf came out and sold them to me—along with some fresh tortillas. I thought we could have chili tonight. What would you think of that?" She leaned up against the wagon next to him.

"Sounds good. That señora, did she have her head?"

"What's that supposed to mean?" Dixie gave him a quizzical look. "Of course she had her head."

"You don't know the story of old Pueblo and the Christmas massacre?"

She shook her head. Her auburn hair shimmered under a mid day sun.

"Well, on Christmas Day back in '54, a bunch of Ute Indians came up to the old fort that used to stand pretty near where we are right now and asked if they could come inside and work out a peace treaty. The way I heard it, the poor Mexican folks inside were well into a good drunk from all their festivities, so they let the thievin' buggers in. The Utes killed all but a woman and a couple of kids right here in the fort."

"That's awful. Right here where we are." She snuggled closer to his shoulder.

Frank shrugged. "Or thereabouts. Legend has it that the Utes cut the heads off all the women. For years trappers and traders coming through this area have told stories of seeing headless women walking around Pueblo and wailing in the dark."

"Headless?" She shuddered and put her arm around his waist to pull in even closer to him.

"That's what the legend says."

"Do you think it's true?"

"The massacre happened. That's a fact."

"What about the ghost part?" Dixie cast her eyes through the sparse trees, then ducked her head against Frank so her voice was muffled. "Do you think the ghosts of those poor headless women still haunt this place?"

"No." He grinned. "But it makes for a good story to make your woman bunch up tight and close-like."

Dixie jerked away and narrowed her eyes. "You're awful, Frank Morgan." She tried to look mad, but couldn't keep from grinning.

"I reckon I do have a bit of a mean streak." Frank chuckled.

"Just the same, I think it would be better if you stayed right next to me."

She collapsed back into his arms. "I wouldn't have it any other way. Let's get married here, Frank. Let's not wait any longer. It doesn't have to be anything big, but we could do it before Otis and Salina leave. How about it, Frank? Are you still in the mood to marry this old woman?"

It was Frank's turn to shudder. "I don't know which should scare you more, Dixie darlin', headless Mexican ghosts or marryin' a rough old cob like me."

She looked off toward the sleepy little town. "I'm sure they got a justice of the peace or a minister or somebody who could do it proper."

"All right," Frank said, pounding his fist on the top of the wagon wheel. "We deserve some happiness too, don't we?"

"Yes, we do." Dixie covered the gunfighter's calloused hand with her smaller one.

"I'll go on into town, get the license, and pay the fees. You tell the girls to drag out their Sunday best, because you're gonna have a wedding tomorrow."

"Tonight, Frank. Who knows what the world will be like tomorrow? Let's just do it tonight." Her green eyes seemed to burn a hole right through him. She gave him a coy nod. "Then later, we won't have to go sneaking off into the bushes."

Frank kissed this stubborn, beautiful woman and grabbed her by both shoulders, staring at her face. "Tonight it is then, soon-to-be Mrs. Frank Morgan."

"Promise? No matter what?"

Frank took off his hat and put it over his heart. "You have my word on it, darlin'."

Dixie stayed with the wagons while Frank saddled Stormy and loped into town. There was a warm breeze in his face, and he felt a little dizzy as he slowed his horse to an easy trot adjacent to the little pink adobe cobbler shop at the edge of town. He looked down at Dog, who trotted beside them, his tongue lolling out, black lips pulled back as though he was smiling.

"Am I doin' the right thing, boy?"

Dog whined, keeping pace with the jigging Appaloosa. His ears perked up at the direct attention.

Frank looked down and grinned. "You're no help at all."

Frank had the marriage license in hand an hour later. He still needed Dixie's signature, but the justice of the peace assured him that could be taken care of just before the ceremony—especially for the famous Frank Morgan.

He stepped out onto the baked-clay road, returned the hat to his head, and drew in a deep lungful of high desert air— one of his last breaths of air as a free and single man. There was something to be said for drifting. He thought of Dixie, her green eyes and soft face. There was something to be said for settling down as well.

George Carlisle reined up in front of the justice of peace's office and dismounted in a hurry. He looked up the street behind him, then at Frank. Two Mexican women were walking into the office behind him, and George held his peace until they were out of earshot.

"What's the matter, George? You look a little green around the gills. You decide to get married today too?"

"You need to watch yourself, Morgan. I've been in town two hours and already run into someone who wants to kill you."

"One of Swan's men?"

"Likely. A towheaded giant they call Dakota Bob." George nodded back down the street toward a false-fronted saloon called La Paloma Blanca: The White Dove.

"From what people tell me, he's been sitting in there playing cards and spewing on all day about what he intends to do to you and your wagon train of women."

"I see." Frank pulled his Peacemaker and checked the rounds. "Don't know why I thought this town would be any different. Until I address this problem with Swan, there'll be no rest from these two-bit gunmen out to make their fortune." He slid the revolver back into its holster.

"What do you want to do, Frank?" George reached under the edge of his jacket and touched the bird's-head grip of his pistol. "You know I'll back your play."

"I know it, and I appreciate it. But there's no sense in you taking the chance of gettin' yourself hurt. Paula would never forgive me."

George waved that off. "And Dixie would never forgive me. Forget it, Frank. This is not about my job now. You're my friend."

"You could help me the most by going back to the wagons and checking on my wife-to-be. I'll keep my head in the fight better if I know she's being taken care of."

"All right," George said. "But I don't like it. Why don't we go get Dixie settled with Otis and Salina? Then we can both go take care of this."

The gunfighter swung into his saddle. He patted the folded papers in his vest pocket. "No, I reckon I better go on and see to this Dakota Bob now before he finishes his card game and comes to bleed all over Dixie's weddin'." Frank touched the brim of his hat, nodded, and spun his horse on its haunches to lope up the street toward the Paloma saloon.

Frank knew two things. If something needed to be done, it was better to get to it right away—and it was generally better if he tended to it by himself.

Chapter 23

Flies darted and buzzed around the entrance to La Paloma Blanca as if even they knew better than to go inside. Frank looped Stormy's reins over a rough cedar rail in front, next to a gaunt bay with a sagging lower lip. He told Dog to stay outside and guard the horse.

Inside, the bar was busy for an early afternoon. It was two o' clock—siesta time—and those that couldn't sleep chose to come and spend their afternoon rest in the smoke-filled air of the greasy establishment.

The buzz of several card games hummed under a pall of smoke in back of the dim room.

Two Mexican hostesses slouched at the bar, sipping clay cups of mescal. Both looked well past their prime. One was at least as old as Frank. The other, though younger, filled her threadbare peasant dress to the point of bursting. Chubby, round cheeks almost hid her tired eyes. Both smiled dutifully at Frank, but neither seemed to have the energy to get up and speak to him.

The bartender was a short, dark man with a stained apron and yellowed shirt. He had a curled black mustache and wore his hair slicked straight back.

"Can I help you, Señor?" he asked, putting both hands flat on the surprisingly tidy bar.

"Beer?" Frank said, nodding to the older of the two women, who stared at him as if he were a juicy steak.

"I am sorry but we have no beer," the bartender said. "The

supplies have yet to be delivered from Denver. I can offer you some of the best tequila this side of the Mexican border."

"No, thanks. Gives me a whompin' headache. You got any coffee?" Morgan scanned the room.

"Of course, Señor. I have sugar as well if you wish. Except for beer, we have anything you might desire after a long day's journey under this sun." The bartender dipped his head toward the two women at the end of the bar.

Frank suppressed a shudder, and thought of sweet Dixie back at the wagons. "Black coffee will suit me just fine, thank you."

It was easy enough to tell which of the cardplayers was Dakota Bob. The hulking man sat at a table of dust-covered drovers, chewing on a green cigar as big around as a small shrub. He was winning, and the drovers were too afraid of him to get up and leave.

Bob took a match out of his vest pocket and lit it on the end of a yellowed thumbnail. He touched the flame to the gray ash of his cigar and puffed it back to life. He was clean enough, but his clothes looked homespun and poor. His long blond hair was pulled back into a tight braid, tied off at the end with a leather string and a brown eagle feather. Frank guessed him to be in his late thirties.

"Hurry up and bet, boys," the big man bellowed. "I got me a date with Mr. Frank Morgan as soon as I win all your hard-earned cash."

Frank leaned against the bar and drank his coffee, watching the blowhard.

"Yes, sir, boys, after I put a bullet in Morgan's gizzard, then I'll show them women what a real man is like." He thumped his chest. "It'll take most of 'em just to satisfy a man like me."

Frank had heard enough.

"And what kind of a man is that?" he asked, still leaning against the bar, coffee cup in hand.

Dakota Bob froze. Slowly, he put his cards on the table

and turned his head toward Frank. "Did I hear a little ground hog chirpin' over there?"

"Nope. Just me." Frank toasted him with the coffee cup. "I was just wonderin' what kind of man it was who would have to go around blabbin' about killing somebody they never met and molesting a bunch of defenseless women."

Bob's already pink face flushed red. "What are you tryin' to say, mister?" He pushed back from the table and stood.

Frank shrugged and set down his cup. "Oh, nothing really. Name's Frank Morgan. I was just wondering why you don't just come and find me instead of sittin' around in here all day talkin' about it. Then it hit me. I figure you just need the time to work up the courage to look me in the eye."

"You cocksure, uppity son of a bitch. It's gonna be a pleasure to skin your sorry hide."

The drovers scattered to the edges of the room, leaving what money they had on the table. They didn't want to be in the line of fire, but they didn't want to miss the show either.

"Well, I'm here, Bob. You go ahead and do what you think you need to, because I got things to do."

Dakota Bob's hand dropped to his gun.

Morgan stood, his Peacemaker smoking in his hand.

The other gunman swayed, staring into space. He'd drawn his pistol and cocked it, but hadn't had time to fire. He grabbed at the edge of the table, flipping it as he fell and scattering money and cards across the dusty floor.

The outlaw slumped, both legs splayed out in front of him. He raised his gun. A look of surprise crossed his face. "You . . ."

Frank's Colt spit fire again, knocking Bob backward. The cocked revolver slipped from his grasp and hit the floor beside him. The impact caused it to fire, and Frank ducked instinctively.

He heard a yelp behind him, and saw the heavyset barmaid clutch her round behind and slide to the floor. Frank couldn't speak Spanish, but he understood enough to know she'd been shot in the rear end. The poor woman squealed like a stuck pig while the bartender and other woman knelt to check on her.

Frank walked up to Bob and found he was still alive.

"You bastard," the outlaw said. "I can't feel my legs."

Frank kicked the gun away and squatted next to the dying man. A growing pool of blood soaked into the dirt floor under him. "Afraid I shot your spine out, Bob. Wish I could have killed you cleaner."

The man gasped. He was losing color quickly in his face and his big hands began to flutter.

"Tell me who sent you," said Frank.

"Mean son of a bitch named Ephraim Swan. Meaner than me by a long shot."

Frank nodded and got to his feet.

Dakota Bob clutched at his pants leg. "Don't just leave me here. I can't move. Show some mercy, for pity's sake."

"Like you would've showed those women?" Frank shook his foot loose and left the hired gun to face his death alone on the dirty floor.

At the bar, the older hostess had the wounded girl's dress pulled up to her waist so she could check on the wound. The chubby prostitute bit at her knuckle and wailed as if the world were about to end.

"How is she?" he asked the bartender.

"Oh, Señor," the little man cried, clutching at his chest as if he was the one who'd been shot. "The bullet, it passed through her buttock."

Frank nodded. "That's not so bad then. It could have been much worse."

"You don't understand, *patron*. Margarita, she is lazy.

She didn't work too much before. Now she will milk a little wound like this and be good for nothing for weeks." The bartender ran a hand through his slick hair and swore. "Oh, *Dios mio.* I was a poor man to begin with. Now I will be ruined for sure."

Frank gave the man ten dollars for the damage, and told him he could have what had spilled off the table and whatever was in Dakota Bob's poke.

Frank reloaded and walked out of the dim bar, leaving the bartender wallowing in his sea of troubles.

He slipped the Colt back into his holster and took a deep breath. As long as Ephraim Swan was still alive, he would have trouble of his own.

Chapter 24

Dixie didn't have anything white, but decided it didn't matter. Once the other women found out she and Frank had decided to go ahead and tie the knot, they all joined in to make everything ready.

Carolyn Brandon worked on a pie crust and kept looking toward the southern horizon. "I wish Luke were here. I hate to think about him sleeping all alone out there with the snakes while we're having a wedding and a party." Carolyn had become animated after she'd met Luke Perkins, as if she'd been reborn. Her girls had noticed it, and begun to come out of their own stupor and giggle and play like the others.

"He'll be here soon." Dixie patted her on the shoulder. She'd heard about the shooting, and couldn't help but wonder if things would always be this way. She wanted to marry him—wanted it worse than she'd wanted anything in a long time—but as much as she trusted Frank and respected his ability with a gun, she hated the idea of worrying about him every time he left her sight. One thing Dixie was sure of: Frank Morgan was worth fighting for, there was no doubt about that.

A few moments later, Frank came riding up to camp. He dismounted and started over to Dixie until Betty chased after him with a wooden spoon.

"You get out of here, mister. It's bad luck to see the bride before the festivities."

Surprised by the sudden outburst from the women, the gunfighter jumped back aboard his horse and trotted off.

Safely out of range of Betty and her spoon, he wheeled his horse and waved at Dixie.

"If you need me to come rescue you from these wild women, give me a shout. I'll be with George and Otis trying to figure out the secret to you females." He turned and rode away.

Just seeing him—looking at his smile—put all her fears to rest.

The Pueblo justice of the peace was a bushy-haired old gent who seemed disappointed Dixie was marrying Frank instead of him.

"You sure you want to go through with this, little lady?" the man said, giving a thoughtful rub to his three-day growth of gray chin whiskers. "Someone as pretty as you is bound to do a whole bunch better if you'd just wait a dab."

Dixie blushed at the compliment and looked at Frank, who stood beside her. She wore her best green linen dress and a white ribbon in her hair. The girls had picked her a shock of wildflowers, and she held the bouquet in her hand.

"No," she said. "I've made my choice. I believe I'll stick to it."

"Take a good look at him, now before we do this—that mean look in his eye, the cruel grin," the J.P. said out of the corner of his mouth as if Frank couldn't hear every word he said. "You still got time to change your mind. Remember, this is Frank Morgan, the notorious gunman and killer."

Frank cleared his throat and glared at the old man. "Judge, you might do well to follow your own advice and remember who I am."

Dixie giggled behind her flowers, and Frank continued.

"It's not too late for me to go get a priest. After he's done with your last rites, he can finish up with the weddin'."

The old judge set his jaw and hurried through the ceremony. When he finished, he shook his head in sorrow as he looked at Dixie.

"I do believe you broke that man's heart," Frank said after they were outside. "He fell in love with you as soon as we walked in the door."

Betty and Paula began to herd everyone back toward the wagons, where they'd laid a sumptuous meal of lamb, tortillas, and roast vegetables. It was getting dark, and the cook fires cast shadows among the canvas wagon tops. A cool breeze blew.

Frank had hired a young guitarist, and everyone danced late into the night.

"The girls are going to stay with Betty tonight," Dixie whispered as they swayed to a slow Spanish waltz.

Frank shrugged. "I don't care if they stay in the wagon."

"Frank! It's our wedding night." She tried to pull away, but he held her tight and kept dancing.

"I don't care if they stay in the wagon because I got us a room at the hotel in town." He felt her relax again. "A woman like you shouldn't have to spend her honeymoon on the trail."

"You spoil me."

"That lecherous old judge was right about one thing. It's a hard enough life you've chosen, just livin' with the likes of me. I reckon you deserve to be spoiled a little."

"What about that poor woman who got shot in the behind?" Dixie asked later as they walked slowly toward the hotel.

"It was only a flesh wound." Frank chuckled. "And she certainly had plenty of behind to spare."

"Frank, that's not funny. My rear's not as small as it used

to be either. You wouldn't like it if I got shot there, would you?"

"Well, no, darlin', I would not." He gave her a swat on the rump. "Your beautiful little rump is one piece of real estate I plan to guard with my life."

Chapter 25

The Chapmans pulled out for Cripple Creek before noon the next day. Frank could tell Otis was antsy to get moving, and had only stayed around for the wedding because Salina had made him.

Luke Perkins arrived late that evening, two hours ahead of his herd, and walked straight into the arms of Carolyn Brandon. Now that he was back, she stuck to him like glue, even going with him to sell the cattle. She even refused to ride a separate horse, but rode behind him, clutching the cowboy around the waist as if he might fly away if she let go of him.

If Luke minded the attention, it didn't show on his face. His great, bushy mustache was turned up in a constant grin from the moment he rode into town.

"What are you going to do now?" Luke asked Frank over a cup of coffee that evening.

"We're not certain yet." Frank looked at his new wife.

"We're heading right back for Texas," Carolyn declared. "Betty says she's coming too. Says there's nothing for her here so she might as well. Luke says he knows a widower in Lampasas who she might get along with real good."

Luke gave a sheepish look at being caught in his matchmaking. "You remember Dobb Barker, don't you, Frankie? His wife died a year ago and I think he and Betty could both use someone to talk to. Don't you?"

Frank squeezed Dixie's shoulders and smiled. "I'll tell you what I think, Lucas Perkins. I think you're stealin' all my women. One minute I'm surrounded by them, the next minute they've all headed off to Texas with you."

Dixie and Carolyn both laughed.

"Why don't you just come with us then?" Luke leaned forward, his bald head shining in the firelight. "There's safety in numbers. You'd be better off with us."

"What about it, Dixie? We got nothing but ourselves pullin' us north. If you still want to see Denver, well, I'm game. If you'd care to try our hand in Texas, well, I'm up for that too."

George and Paula came up from their evening stroll and announced that they had decided to leave the next morning for New York.

The little group talked and planned late into the evening, plotting out their futures.

Frank and Dixie decided they would let the girls go with the rest of the group while they got what they could for the wagons and belongings. They would honeymoon in Pueblo and follow by train about a week later.

The decision made, Frank felt lighter. They got a room in Pueblo for a week, and the two began to set about selling the wagons. Everything went smoothly until the third day.

Vic Sutton rode into town just after noon. He found Frank at the livery working out a deal to sell all the mules.

"I don't like you much, Morgan," the rancher said, driving the stable owner away with a withering stare. "But I don't like what's about to happen even more."

Frank perked up at Sutton's tone. "What are you talking about?"

"Swan and a band of his gang are on their way. He says

if he can't get anyone good enough to kill you and your woman, he'll just have to come and do it himself."

"His funeral," Frank whispered.

"No," Sutton said, shaking his said. "It don't matter how fast you are if he shoots you in the back. He don't intend to face you in the street. There ain't a fair bone in that sorry bastard's body."

"When?"

Sutton shrugged. "I talked to him two days ago and started straightaway to warn you. I reckon I got a day on him. Listen, I don't give a hoot in hell if he guns you down in a fair fight. But I won't have him kill you like a dog in the street. If I was you, I'd get on the next train out of town."

Frank stuck out his hand. "I'm much obliged to you, considerin' how you feel."

Sutton shook hands with his crippled hand. "Just take your woman and get while the gettin's good." With that, the rancher mounted his horse and loped away.

The next train came through at eight the next morning. Frank had never been the type to run from a fight, but he had Dixie to think about now. He sold what he could, deposited the money in the bank, and drew most of it back out in the form of a cashier's check.

Dixie packed her best dresses in a leather valise, while Frank arranged with a man at the depot to have Stormy berthed in a boxcar with Dog.

At eight-thirty, the train hissed away from the Pueblo station with Mr. and Mrs. Frank Morgan safely on board. Dixie breathed a sigh of relief as they picked up speed moving north to the line that would eventually take them east.

"I have to admit, I was beginning to get scared there for a

while," she said, leaning her head against Frank's shoulder. The train picked up speed.

"I'm glad to be out of there." Frank looked out the window and watched the hazy Blue Mountains toward Rye fade into the distance behind them. "We're going the wrong direction, but we'll work our way back south when we get the chance."

He patted her on the thigh and sighed. "My darlin', I don't know what you had planned a few months ago. To tell you the truth, I'm not sure what my own plans were, but no matter what happens from this day on, it's been a great adventure. We have sure enough seen the elephant."

"What does 'seen the elephant' mean?" Dixie put her hand on his. "I don't think I've ever seen an elephant in my life."

Frank chuckled softly. "I reckon it means seein' it all through to your goal even though you lose a good part of your kit. Makin' it through the storm, so to speak. I heard this story about a farmer back years ago who wanted to go to town and see one of those circus elephants. Seems he wanted to see that damned elephant more than anything in the world. Well, he loaded up his cart with all his produce to sell in town so he'd have enough money to go to the circus. On the way there he heard the elephant had escaped. He was awful upset about the news until he ran smack-dab into the doggone thing in the road. It scared his horse so much the cart overturned and spilled all his vegetables on to the ground. The huge beast ended up trampling all the goods and killin' the horse before the circus tenders could get it under control."

"That poor farmer," Dixie said. "What did he do then?"

"Well, darlin', that's the point of the story. See, his friends offered their condolences and asked him how he felt about losing of all his stuff. You know what he said?"

Dixie shook her head.

"He said, losing everything didn't matter, for he had seen

the elephant and that was what he'd set out to do in the first place."

Frank leaned away a bit so he could look Dixie in the face. "I reckon I'm not much of a speech giver and my words generally get me in trouble, but now that I've had the pleasure of meeting and marrying you . . . "

Dixie giggled. "Don't tell me, now you've had a chance to marry me and have a proper honeymoon, so you feel like you've seen an elephant."

"No, darlin', I was going to say that now that I've got you, it really doesn't matter what happens. With you, I've had the main course. Everything else is just gravy."

"You've got a funny way of saying things, but you make sure make me feel good about myself. I've never been compared to an elephant or food before that I can remember and been so happy about it."

Weary from constant worry, the two fell asleep to the motion of the gently swaying train.

Two hours later, Frank was startled awake by the squeal of screeching brakes on metal wheels. He and Dixie were both thrown forward in their seats.

"The steamer on this old bucket leaks like a sieve," an elderly miner said from behind his newspaper across the aisle. "Sometimes they have to stop here to take on more water."

Frank nodded. The sun shone fiercely through the window and his nap had made him thirsty.

"You want something to drink?" he asked Dixie.

She rubbed her eyes and yawned. "That would be nice. I could use a stretch. I'll go with you."

The conductor assured them they would be stopped for twenty minutes, so Frank and Dixie both got off to walk around. There was no more than a windmill and tower set up by the tracks in the red sandstone, and a small spigot at the base of the windmill drizzled water and created a small oasis in the red dirt.

A green bush had sprung up from the abundant water, its branches covered in delicate yellow blossoms. Dixie cupped her hand to drink from the spigot, and stopped to admire the flowers while she dried her hands.

"How's that ring fitting you?" Frank touched the gold band on Dixie's finger. It shone brilliantly in the sunlight. "Looked like it might be a little small."

"Oh, the ring fits fine. A cow kicked me in the knuckle when Faith was a baby, and it's been a little on the big side ever since."

"I could have the ring stretched a little."

"It's fine," she said, admiring the ring. "Believe me, Frank, I never want to take it off."

A shiver suddenly ran up Frank's spine—the familiar feeling he got when something was wrong. Two boxcars back, Dog confirmed his fears and broke into a barking, growling frenzy within his confinement. Frank drew his Colt and stepped in closer to Dixie, putting her between him and the windmill.

"What's wrong, Frank?"

A bullet slammed into Frank's back before he had time to answer. He staggered, then slumped into Dixie's arms. She screamed and wrapped her arms around him in an attempt to hold him up.

He struggled to get to his feet. The Peacemaker felt heavy in his hand. "Get down, Dixie," he tried to say, but it only came out as a whisper and he wasn't sure she heard him. Another shot tore into his shoulder, exiting through his right arm.

More shots rang out, and the conductor shouted for everyone to get back on the train. Frank heard the hiss of steam as the engine began to pull away, leaving them behind. Horses squealed and rough men barked out orders.

Frank was aware of Dixie's screams. Blackness began to

envelope him. Another bullet hit him in the leg. He felt it strike like a powerful fist, felt it rip at his muscle and break bone, but he no longer felt any pain.

He dropped the pistol and gazed up at his wife. Her beautiful green eyes were filled with terror—and there was nothing he could do.

Chapter 26

"Can you hear me, mister?" A husky voice penetrated the fog of Frank's sleep. He tried to answer, pushed everything he had into forming the words, but they simply would not come.

"Saw his eye twitch. That's a good sign," the husky voice said. Frank felt as if he were floating, drifting. He'd often floated with his eyes shut on the river near his home as a boy. . . .

"Needs a doctor." This voice belonged to a woman. Frank wondered if it might be his mother. She'd often warned him about the cottonmouth moccasins that lurked along the brushy shores of the Brazos River. She hated it when he drifted like this. It would be just like her to think he was snakebit.

"There ain't no doctor for forty mile." It was the husky voice again. "If this one is supposed to live, it's up to us and that Lord Almighty you talk to so much."

"I'll pray over it while we drag him home," the woman said. "He looks like a fighter, this one does."

"Bad as he's hit, he'd better be," the husky voice said.

Frank tried to speak again, but it was no use. Warm currents tugged at his arms, and he felt like a stick slipping out of a swirling eddy to drift again, enveloped in the comfortable brown waters of the lazy Brazos River.

* * *

Sam and Abby Bergin sat in their respective rockers and watched Frank sleep. During the day, Sam worked the mine, and except for when she took her husband soup or a piece of mutton, Abby kept a vigil on her patient.

She was by nature an extremely pious woman, extolling the virtues of the Good Book to everyone she met and, under normal circumstances, reading to Sam by candlelight while he pecked away with his hammer and chisel in their little mine.

She kept cool towels on the injured man's forehead. He'd taken a nasty fever two days into his ordeal, and she worried about that more than the loss of blood—which had itself been substantial. She'd used sage and wild chamomile to make a poultice to draw out any poison left in the man's system, and checked the wounds daily for any red or abnormal puffiness. He didn't appear to have any lead still in him, so that was a blessing. Once she felt the herbs had done their job of drawing out anything unholy, she dabbed each wound with a bit of honey to stave off future infection.

The mine had been showing some color lately, but the couple had little to offer except a straw mattress over a slung-rope bed, clean bandages, mutton soup, and constant nourishment to the soul from Abby's reading of the Bible.

She'd started off that morning reading from Habakkuk, a short book that in her estimation was too often overlooked or skimmed too quickly by the preachers back in civilization.

"O Lord, how long shall I cry, and thou wilt not hear! Even cry out of violence, and thou wilt not save!"

Her patient stirred, struggling to speak. His eyes clenched in effort, his strong face distorted in pain.

Abby leaned forward in her rocker and put a little check mark by her verse with a pencil stub so she would remember where she'd stopped, then slipped the thin leather bookmark between the pages of her Bible before she closed it.

The cloth on the man's forehead was near steaming from his fever, and she dipped it in the basin beside his bed. After wringing the excess back in the bowl, she placed it back on his brow and touched him gently on top of his head.

"There now, son," she chided him gently. "Don't try and talk just yet. You save yourself and fight this quietly. Me and Sam, we've done all we can. It's up to you and God now. You're gonna have to fight if you want to live."

Abby sat back down in her homemade rocking chair and found her mark in the Bible. "Let's see here, where were we? Here we are. *'Behold ye among the heathen, and regard, and wonder marvelously: for I will work a work in your days, which ye will not believe, though it be told you. . . .'"* She looked across her spectacles at the sleeping man. "Now, listen up. This is when it starts to get bad. Poor old Habakkuk," she said.

Frank was no stranger to pain. He'd been shot before, even broken a few bones—but the hurt he felt as he slowly became aware of his surroundings made what little breath he had come in short gasps. His head throbbed as if he'd been kicked between the eyes, and his shoulder pounded enough to make his teeth ache.

He willed his eyes open. The dim adobe room slowly fell into focus, and he became aware of two people standing with him. One of them, a woman, brought him a cup of water and helped him drink it. She spoke in soothing tones, and he recognized her voice, but he didn't know how.

The cool water chased away some of the pain, and he found enough energy to smile at the woman holding the cup.

"I'm obliged," he whispered. His voice was weak as thread.

"I won't ask how you feel, boy," the old man said. "You look like hammered shit."

"Sam!" the woman scolded. "You mind your language. Can't you see the hand of the Lord at work here?"

Frank smiled. It was good to be back among the living, even if the living were prone to an argument now and then. He felt a knot, low in his belly, and realized he probably hadn't eaten in some time.

"I'm . . . could have a little something to eat?"

"Hallelujah! Glory be to the Lord Almighty." The woman raised her hands above her head. "I prayed last night, and God told me if you'd just wake up and eat, you'd be all right. Thank you, thank you." She hustled into the other room, and came back a moment later with a wooden bowl of soup.

"I made you some beef broth," she said. "It's been cookin' for the last two days so it's pretty rich. Stick-to-your-ribs good for you." She spooned a little into Frank's mouth. He hated being fed, but his own arms felt like lead anchors and he needed to eat.

"You're damn lucky we found that stray steer. I have to eat mutton stew mornin' noon and night." Sam smiled even though his wife gave him a chastising stare for his language.

"God provides for his own," she said, giving Frank another spoonful of broth. "Just like Abraham's ram in the thicket so's he wouldn't have to kill his own son, Isaac."

"Don't mind her," Sam said. "She can't talk less'n she relates it to the Good Book."

"I'm Abby and this is my husband Sam, the gentile infidel," the woman said. "We're the Bergins."

"How long have I been out?" Frank found he was full after only a few bites of soup, and he had to fight to keep that down.

"Over a week," Sam Bergin said. "You sure soaked up a lot of lead. I was sure you was done for. Them outlaws really wanted to see you dead. They would have finished you off for sure if me and some of my infidel friends hadn't ridden up." He gloated at his wife.

Abby nodded. "The Lord works in mysterious ways."

The food helped to clear Frank's mind, and he jerked as he remembered his own wife.

"Dixie?" he gasped, wincing from the pain of his movement.

Sam and Abby looked at each other. Neither spoke.

"She's dead, isn't she?" Frank saved them the trouble.

"God called her home, son." Abby said, a tear in her eye. "I'm sorry. We buried her out by Wolf Mesa. It's a pretty spot."

"You might like to know we shot two of the buggers that killed her." Sam stared down at the dirt floor. "Wounded another, but he was well enough to hang last Saturday."

Frank groaned. Dixie was dead. He'd not been able to save her.

Abby put a cool towel on his head. "You should get a lot more rest. We can talk some more in the morning."

"What's your name, boy?" Sam asked before Frank drifted off.

"Morgan," he groaned. "Frank Morgan." He waited for the couple to gasp or show some other sign of astonishment that they had a famous gunfighter in their home.

"Good to meet you, Mr. Morgan," Sam said. If he recognized the name, he didn't act like it.

Frank awoke with a tall blond man standing over him holding a hat in his hands. He assumed it was the next morning because he was hungry again.

"I bet money that you wouldn't make it, Morgan."

"Glad you lost your bet," Frank groaned.

The man smiled, showing a row of perfect teeth. "Me too. I'm John Stout, the sheriff of El Paso County. You feel like talking a little, mister?"

Stout had a baby face, but Frank slowly came to realize he was even younger than he looked.

"I could talk. What do you want to know?"

Stout pulled up a rocking chair. "You remember much about the attack?"

"Not much. All happened pretty fast." Frank turned his head on the pillow so he could look Stout in the eye. "Was . . . was my wife abused, Sheriff?"

The man shook his head. "No. Bergin and his drinkin' buddies happened on you right after the ambush. But there is something you should know. By the time they got to her, the ring finger on her left hand was gone."

"Gone?"

"They cut it off. Made a trophy of it, I suppose."

"Was it Swan?"

"Looks like it. Before we hung the old boy Sam wounded, he told us as much. All right, Morgan." The sheriff scooted the rocker up closer to the bed. "You had a horse and a dog on that train. I got them both boarded at the livery at the Springs. That Appaloosa is a mighty handsome animal. I could get you a good price for him if you want."

"No, I'll keep him, thank you." Frank set his jaw.

"Listen to me, Morgan. I hate to be the one to break this to you, but you got shot up pretty bad. You aren't going to be doin' much ridin' again. Hell, I don't know if you're even gonna walk without a cane."

Frank closed his eyes. "I surprised you once, remember? Now, I'd be obliged if you'd send my horse and my dog back here. I'll pay you for your trouble."

Stout flashed his wide grin again. "That's just what I wanted to hear, my friend. You're a fighter." He nodded. "And by the time this is all over, you'll need to be."

Chapter 27

"You got anything in there about vengeance and such?" Frank sat propped on his pillow against the wall. He had graduated to feeding himself.

"Well, we got the whole Book of Judges," Abby said. "There's a heap of the Lord's hand of fury in there. I'll read to you about God's left-handed servant Ehud stabbin' the wicked king in the guts. Sam likes it when I read that part."

"That'll do," Frank said, finishing off his stew.

It was nothing short of a miracle he was alive at all. He'd been shot in the shoulder, back, and both legs. One of the bullets had gone through the bicep of his right arm.

It had been almost a month since the ambush, and Frank had yet to walk without Abby or Sam's help. They showed him every courtesy and treated him like a son.

Sam disappeared to work in his mine every morning. In the evening, he sometimes went to share a drink with friends in nearby Manitou Springs. When Abby wasn't cooking mutton stew, she sat at Frank's side and read to him from the Bible, picking where to start each day by closing her eyes and letting the pages fall open to "whatever place the Good Lord directs."

Day by day, Frank could feel himself getting stronger. The need for a reckoning against Swan kept him going, pushed him through his pain.

One Sunday, Sam walked in and interrupted Abby's Scriptures. She must have been expecting him, because instead of her normal rebuke, his intrusion only drew a soft smile.

"I made this for you," Sam said as he came through the door. He held out a wooden crutch, carved out of peeled cedar and cushioned with a piece of wool. "Me and Abby been talkin' and we figured it was time you got up and around." The old man twisted his hat in his hands and beamed as he offered Frank the present. "You're welcome to stay with us as long as you need to. We just thought you might want to go on a walk or two without us taggin' along all the time."

Frank took the crutch and scooted to the edge of the bed. "I don't know what to say, Sam. You two have been nicer than a hard man like me deserves." He pushed up on the wood while the Bergins watched his progress.

It took him a few wobbly minutes, but he finally got to his feet. He felt light-headed as soon as he stood up, but that passed and he took a tentative step.

The crutch fit perfectly, and Sam beamed like a father who'd just given his son a new horse.

Frank hobbled around the room. Sweat popped out on his forehead from the exertion. After one round, he collapsed back on the bed and leaned his new gift against the wall next to him.

"Thank you, Sam. Thank you both, for everything." His body was unaccustomed to any exercise, and he found himself short of breath. This healing was hard business for one who'd always been so self-sufficient. "I'll try a longer gallop tomorrow," he panted.

Frank ate mutton stew, listened to Abby read her Scripture, and walked a little further every day.

Three weeks after Sheriff Stout's first visit, the lawman made good on his promise and delivered Stormy and Dog out to the Bergin place. When he saw Frank come out to

meet him, hobbling on the cedar crutch, the sheriff cocked
back his hat and folded his hands across his saddle horn.

"Well, I'll be." He whistled under his breath. "I leave for
a day or two, and come back to find you running around like
a jackrabbit."

"Told you I'd surprise you." Frank grinned. He knelt down
slowly to rub a delighted Dog behind his ears. "I figure I'll
be off the crutch in another week—movin' slow, but on my
own."

Stout dismounted and ground-tied his gelding. He held
onto Stormy's lead rope. "We'll go put your horse in Sam's
corral if you feel like a short stroll. I'd like to talk to you for
a minute."

"Sure thing." Frank had walked the short, sandy path to
the pole corral a dozen times that day. One more would do
him some good. He found he only needed the crutch about
half the time, and he used it more to rest than to walk.

"Morgan," Stout said after he turned Stormy out and
pitched him a flake of hay. "You're getting better. That's
plain to see. What are your plans after you mend?"

"I suspect you know, Sheriff, or you wouldn't have bothered to ask just yet."

"Frank, listen to me. I been hearin' stories about you since
I was a sprout. You're the fastest gun I ever even heard of,
but you're hurt and weak." The baby-faced sheriff leaned
back against the fence. "You know as well as I do that the
law will catch up with Swan sooner or later. There's no use
for you to get killed in the meantime."

"There's no law in No Man's Land," Frank whispered. The
thoughts of Ephraim Swan brought a new sense of strength
to his legs. "It's a code I live by, Stout. The same code that
would make you hunt a man to the ends of the earth if he
killed one of your deputies."

The sheriff shook his head. "But that's the law. It's different."

"No, it ain't." Frank scratched Dog on the head. "I appreciate you bringing out my animals."

"That's a fearsome dog. He almost bit my hand off till I mentioned your name." Stout seemed to realize it was time to change the subject. "I suppose I'd best be goin'."

"Sheriff." Frank turned to head back toward the house. "I wonder if you could do me one more favor."

"You bet," Stout said.

Frank leaned on his crutch and took a sheet of paper and pencil out of his shirt pocket. He licked the tip of the pencil, scribbled out a note, then handed it to the sheriff.

The other man read it and gave a nodding smile. "Not a problem. I'll take care of this as soon as I get into town." He swung onto his horse. "You're a good man, Morgan—no matter what those boys from the East write about you."

"Not too good," Frank whispered under his breath.

Frank's strength came back slower than he wished, but it did return. He began to extend his walks further out into the hills and canyons surrounding Sam and Abby's place. When he wasn't walking, he spent a good deal of his time at Dixie's grave, talking to her.

He told her of his plan to go after Swan. He knew she'd be against it, but it didn't matter. He thought she should be in on the planning.

Once he was able to dispense with the crutch, Frank began to build a stone fence around the grave. He started by gathering up all the loose sandstone blocks he could find within easy walking distance. The weather was warm, and it felt good to work and sweat with his shirt off.

When all the stones of appropriate size were gathered, Frank borrowed a hammer and chisel from Sam and quarried more from the large sandstone cliffs near the grave. The white scars on his arm and side were drawn and tight, but it felt good to stretch them. It felt good to build something for Dixie.

Frank spent three weeks working on the wall. Sometimes he worked for hours on a single stone to get it to fit just right and lock in with all the others. He'd always been good with his hands, but he wanted this to be perfect. He had never been the type of man to cry, but after all the weeks of building and healing, when he finally laid the last stone on top of the three-foot-high wall and erected the slab marker he'd carved himself, he sat down on the ground beside his wife's grave, put his face in his hands, and wept.

Chapter 28

Walking without a crutch was all well and good, but shooting was another thing altogether. Frank strapped on his Colt again for the first time six weeks after the ambush. Sam was kind enough to provide a half-dozen wiskey bottles, and Frank set them up against a sandy hill a quarter mile away from the house.

His arm had tightened from the scar tissue, and he felt awkward at first just drawing the heavy gun from the holster. Frank's hand didn't react like he needed it to. An action that had once been pure instinct now had to be relearned—step by slow, plodding step.

Frank knew how to shoot. His history was enough to prove that. But knowing how to shoot and making your body do it were two different things.

The first six shots kicked up sand around the bottles. Frank emptied the pistol and tried again. This time he hit two of the bottles, but he had to be painfully slow and he knew if bottles could shoot back, he would have been in trouble.

After twelve depressing rounds, Frank decided to work on form and speed to keep from wasting bullets.

Draw, thumb, squeeze, click . . . re-holster and repeat the process. Frank practiced hundreds of times, until his arm and shoulder ached and his thumb was raw from cocking the hammer. By the times coyotes began to howl at a crescent moon, he was weak as a newborn babe and had to limp back to the house.

Sam and Abby never asked him how things were going, but there was a constant supply of rich stew and plentiful readings from the Word.

After a week of practice, Frank finally began to feel like his old self. Fall had come to the Colorado foothills, and the crisp air put him in the mind for a hunt. He broke all six bottles on his first try, and slid the Colt easily back into his holster. There was definitely a new chill in the air. After almost three months, he was finally ready. Ephraim Swan might not know it yet, but his time had come.

"You done what?" Sam scratched the top of his gray head as if Frank was speaking another language, and Abby broke into tears.

"Sheriff Stout took care of all the paperwork at the bank in town. There's ten thousand dollars there in an account under your name. A fellow I know put that amount as a bounty on my head. I figure you folks saved my life, so you earned at least that much."

Sam opened his mouth to speak, but nothing came out.

Frank put up his hand. "You've treated me like I was kin. I can never repay you for that. Sam, you're getting too old to be scratchin' around in that dark old mine. Come out and see the world while you and Abby are still spry enough to enjoy it."

"I feel like you are my kin," Abby said through her tears. "You don't owe us nothing, Frank. A good turn is its own reward."

Frank knew the good-byes would be hard, and he'd had Stormy and a packhorse saddled and ready before the Bergins knew he was about to leave.

"Please take this money with my thanks. As long as you're able, I'd appreciate it if you'd look after Dixie's grave."

The couple stood arm-in-arm and waved as Frank climbed aboard Stormy and turned to leave. When he looked back, he saw that even old Sam had started to cry.

"I'll come back and look in on you when I can," he said over his shoulder. There was frost on the ground and Dog whined to get on the trail. All the emotion in the air was getting to the poor animal.

"You do that, son," Abby said. "God go with you."

Frank rode away slowly. Before he was out of earshot, he heard Abby say to Sam, "You know what I want to buy first? A new Bible . . . "

Frank provisioned in Manitou Springs. He bought .45's for his Colt and several boxes of .44-40's for his rifle. He still had a sackful of buckshot.

Sheriff Stout walked up just as Frank finished throwing his diamond hitch and tucking the edges of tarp around his top load on the packhorse.

"I guess you healed up enough to go on and get yourself killed. On the revenge trail now, eh, Morgan?"

He gave the lawman an icy stare and tied off the dead end of the hitch rope. "Call it what you like. Swan's not about to answer to the law anytime soon. He may as well answer to me."

"From what I hear, he's got upwards of fifty men working for him. That's an army where I come from."

"You know how to eat an elephant, Sheriff?" Frank caught the stirrup in his hand and brought it to his boot toe. His muscles were still a little tight in his legs and back, and it took some effort to get in the saddle.

"No, Frank, I don't reckon I do. How do you eat an elephant?"

On his horse, Frank leaned down and stuck out his hand to shake with the sheriff. "One bite at a time, John. One bite at a time."

He headed east, intending to work his way south as he went. He made up all kinds of reasons why he should take this more out-of-the-way route; he needed a little more time to heal, more time in the saddle to harden him for what was ahead—but the truth was, he wanted to steer clear of anything and anyplace that brought to mind his time with Dixie.

It didn't work.

Two days out, Frank realized he was just south of Sand Creek, the site of the infamous Chivington Massacre, where scores of Black Kettle's Cheyenne women and children were surprised and butchered while huddled under an American flag. The attack had been fierce and one-sided.

The Dog Soldiers were no shrinking violets. There had been atrocities committed on both sides—but Sand Creek . . . Morgan shook his head when he thought about the killings and mutilations he'd heard about. He was glad he'd never had to explain something like that to Dixie.

The morning sun burned away the frost in no time, and the day began to heat up. Thirty miles out of Manitou Springs, he stopped at a small spring to take off his coat and get a drink. When he bent to refill his canteen, Frank managed to surprise a large rattlesnake who'd curled up on a stone to sun itself.

Instinctively, Frank whipped the Colt from his holster and snapped a quick shot at the snake. He was far enough away that he was in no danger from the reptile's venom, but he was close enough that his blood ran cold.

Not from fear of the viper—but because he'd missed.

Chapter 29

If he'd access to a mirror—which he didn't—even Frank wouldn't have been able to recognize himself. Abby Bergin's mutton stew was rich enough, but the nagging pain from his wounds and the anger he felt over Dixie's murder churned constantly in his stomach and had worked to keep his appetite small. Though he was a powerful man, he'd never been on the heavy side, and now his face was drawn and hollow. The muscles in his arms were strong from building the stone wall around Dixie's grave, but they were long and sinewy. He reckoned if anything happened and the coyotes got his body, they'd be awfully disappointed. He'd likely be as stringy as a spent gaming rooster.

His salt-and-pepper hair had decidedly more salt than it had only sixth months before. Where he'd always kept it short, it now hung long and wild, like a windblown mop when he took off his hat. He'd let his beard grow as shaggy as a buffalo bull. The darkness of it accented the deep circles under his eyes and the hollows in his gaunt cheeks.

He went four days on the trail without anyone recognizing him, and reveled in his anonymity.

The cool fall weather and short daylight had prompted Stormy and Dog to break out their winter coats, and they looked almost as unkempt as he. The closer he got to No Man's Land and Ephraim Swan, the more he realized he would need to make arrangements for another horse if he wanted to slip in unnoticed. It wasn't exactly a big secret that

Frank Morgan rode a stout Appaloosa gelding and was always accompanied by a devoted cur dog.

Twenty miles south of Black Mesa, the unofficial landmark that designated the beginning of No Man's Land, was a run-down log trading post run by an old, snaggle-toothed outlaw named Bob Fitzsimmons. Everyone called him Three-Toed Bob.

There were several stories floating across the plains as to how and why Bob had lost the all but three of his toes. Some said it had to do with frostbite in a big blizzard back it the fifties. Others said he got himself captured by a band of Comanche down by the Red River and they'd done the hacking before he managed to escape. From his experience with Comanche, Frank figured they would have cut off a lot of things more important than a man's toes.

Some folks believed the toes had just rotted off because the old outlaw was so mean-spirited. Frank couldn't really argue with that theory because he'd seen Bob in action. They'd always gotten along well enough, though, and from what Frank had seen, Bob's mean streak only flared up when he was provoked—and never toward innocent women and children. The gunfighter shared that particular tendency himself.

Bob had spent the last five years in the Nebraska state prison and according to all recent accounts, had decided to go more or less on the up-and-up, minding his own business at the trading post, since his release.

Low, gunmetal clouds boiled in a broad sky as Frank neared the log-and-canvas trading post. The smell of rain hung heavily in the air, and a cold wind kicked at the tufts of brown, wilted grass. The sky looked like it might open up at any moment, and Frank was glad to get somewhere out of the weather.

He tied Stormy up to a low pine rail out front of the long, narrow building. Dog hunted him a place under a stack of old crates that looked like it was made just for him.

Three-Toed's place smelled like cheap whiskey and mildew. Old Bob himself stood behind the rough plank bar. Behind him was a small array of bottles, sacks of salt and flour, two double-barrel shotguns, and boxes of cartridges. The whole caboodle was stacked precariously on a set of flimsy wooden shelves held together with horseshoe nails, and looked like one good sneeze from the retired outlaw might bring it down around his shoulders.

"What'll you have?" Three-Toed said as Frank walked up to the bar. He had long gray hair pulled back in a ponytail and tied with a leather whang.

"Whiskey," the gunfighter said. He made no attempt to disguise his voice, but didn't identify himself either. Bob would be a good test to see if Frank was as unrecognizable as he thought he was.

"Lucky you made it when you did," Three-Toed said, getting a half-full bottle and shot glass. "I believe this rain could turn too snow without too much trouble."

Frank threw back the whiskey, and shivered despite the relative warmth put off by the potbellied stove at the end of the bar. "Got anything to eat?"

"Boiled meat and potatoes."

"What kind of meat?"

Three-Toed shrugged. "Like I said, boiled."

Frank gave a somber nod. "I reckon I'll just have another whiskey then." There wasn't much danger of getting drunk on the watered-down mixture.

Three-Toed chuckled. "I'm just joshing you, friend. It's mule-deer doe. Good too. I got a damned Digger Indian works for me. He has to take a wagon far and wide just to keep me in firewood this time of year. He shot the doe just yesterday."

"In that case, I'll take some. How you been gettin' along, Bob?"

Three-Toed leaned over the bar to peer at Frank's face. He shook his head and combed a hand over his gray hair. "Am I supposed to know you from somewheres?"

"Well, I sure hope so. We spent a whole winter holed up together in the Absaroka—back when you had all your toes."

"Morgan? Is that you?" Three-toed poured himself a glass of the hard stuff he kept hidden behind the bar.

Frank winked and gave a little nod. "In the flesh."

"I heard you'd done crossed over." Bob rubbed his eyes and blinked to clear them. "I swear, Morgan. You're all but wasted away. You look near dead now."

"I nearly was. Don't have much fat to spare, so if you could hurry with that meat and potatoes I'd be much obliged."

"Comin' right up." Three-Toed disappeared behind a quilt partition, and came out with a steaming bowl.

"Swan's been tellin' everyone how he killed Frank Morgan and his wi . . ."

Frank took a spoonful of the broth and meat. It was not Abby's mutton stew, but it was hot and savory enough to chase the chill away from his bones. He shook his head and waved off the mention of Dixie. "She's dead, Bob. Not talkin' about her don't make me any less comfortable with the fact. What's he saying?"

Three-Toed took up a glass and began to polish it. "He says he jumped you out north of Pueblo somewhere. He don't make no bones about the fact it was an ambush, but you know how folks are. They was beginning to believe all those books about you—beginning to think you might be bullet-proof."

Frank put down the spoon and looked the old outlaw in the eye. "What does he say about my wife?"

"You don't want to hear this, Morgan." Bob began to polish the glass faster. It looked clean, but his hands needed something to do.

Frank nodded. "You're right. I don't want to, but I need to know for certain what happened. Tell it. Tell it all."

Old Bob slumped like a chicken-killing dog that knew it was about to get a beating. "He cut her finger off. Tells everyone she was alive when he cut it off. Keeps it in a little corked bottle full of alcohol. He wears her weddin' ring on little leather string around his neck." Bob trailed off, but cast his eyes down at the ground. Frank could tell there was more.

"I need it all."

"He said he liked to listen to her scream." Three-Toed looked up suddenly. "If I'd a known you were still alive, I'd killed him for you last time he was in here."

Frank pushed the bowl away. His appetite had vanished with the news of Dixie's suffering. "No, I'm glad you left it to me, Bob. This is something I need to take care of personally."

Though there was no one else in the room, Three-Toed Bob leaned over the bar and spoke in a hushed tone. "Swan and his men have taken over a little burg out east of here about seventy-five miles away. They done run off or killed all the decent folks. I ain't never been there, but I hear it's mighty flat, just like here. Be awful hard to sneak up and take potshots."

"I don't intend to. This is something I need to do face-to-face."

Bob rubbed the top of his head again. "I can give you rough directions from what I've heard people say, but I'm not exactly sure where it is."

"I'll find it." Frank pushed away from the bar. "In the meantime, I need to get my horse out of the rain. I'll pester you for a cup of coffee, then if you got a place I can bed down for the night, I'd be much obliged."

"I got a barn and a shed. Take your pick."

"Barn sounds fine."

"You know, Morgan." Three-Toed leaned over the bar and was talking in his conspiratorial voice again. "Gettin' in—I don't reckon that will be much of a problem. I just can't say you'll be able to get yourself out of there."

Frank let his fist bounce up and down on top of the bar. He sighed. "Well, Bob, I don't much give a damn whether I do or not."

Chapter 30

Frank settled Stormy and his packhorse in the barn and threw two flakes of hay in a feed bunk. The stout Appy pinned his ears and chased the short-coupled bay packhorse to the other side of the rough wooden bin. Once the eating hierarchy was established, both horses calmed down and began to munch their hay. It was still chilly in the drafty barn, and steam rose from the backs of the wet horses.

It was raining in earnest now. Frank wove his way through a maze of drips from the leaking roof, and found a surprisingly dry spot by the stack of grass hay. He threw his saddle and kit there and rolled out his bedroll.

Once he was certain nothing would get wet, he left Dog to guard everything and went back inside for a cup of coffee.

He stomped his feet to get the mud and grass off as he came in from the storm.

"Shut the damn door," a potbellied rowdy said from the bar. A taller, redheaded man about Frank's age stood beside him. They were drenched to the skin and drinking coffee as fast as Bob would bring it. "You're lettin' all the wind in."

"My apologies." Frank closed the door. He was surprised by the presence of the two men. They must have tied their horses around the building.

"You got a room to let?" Red asked.

"Got a shed that don't leak much," Three-Toed said, pouring a cup of coffee for Frank. "It's a damn sight better than a tent on the plains."

"I don't aim to sleep in no tent on the plains," the fat cowboy whined. "And I don't fancy sleepin' in no leaky shed either. What's the matter with your barn?"

"Occupied," Three-Toed said.

"By who?" Red shot a glance at Frank. "The scarecrow? Why, he's so skinny I doubt he'd get wet if he stood out in the rain. Ain't that right, scarecrow?"

"Like the man told you"—Frank took his cup of coffee and calmly drank a sip—"the barn's occupied."

"The whole damn barn?" Chubby whined again.

"Yep," Frank grunted over the lip of his cup.

"We're sleepin' in the barn." Red waved Frank off and turned back toward the bar.

"Listen, boys." Frank put his coffee on the table next to him. "I don't want any trouble, but I do want to be left alone."

"I don't know who you think you are." Red spun around. "I ought to wring your scrawny neck, but it'd be too easy. I seen bed bugs bigger'n you down in Fort Worth."

Chubby took up the cause, and interrupted his whining to pick on Frank. "You got a gun there on your hip, scarecrow. You know how to use it, or you carry it around to keep yourself from blowin' away?"

Frank looked at Three-Toed, who stifled a laugh. "I do all right. I think it would be best if we let this drop." Frank was not a man to back down, but he didn't want to waste any bullets on this pair of would-be desperados. Neither had the hardened look of a gunfighter.

"How about if I just drop you?" Red leaned back against the bar. He seemed convinced his bravado would be enough to make Frank flinch.

"Here now!" Bob growled from behind the bar. "I believe I've heard about enough of this."

"You shut up." Red turned and glared at him. "Mind your own damned business."

Bob set his jaw. "This is my place. What goes on in here is all my business. You can calm down or clear out."

Frank shook his head. "Just let them be, Bob. It's their funeral."

"What's that supposed to mean?" Chubby stared over pink cheeks.

"Should I tell 'em who's gettin' ready to kill 'em?" Three-Toed hobbled to the potbellied stove to get a fresh pot of coffee.

"I guess it won't hurt. They seem bound and determined to get killed. They wouldn't be able to tell anyone my little secret."

"Well, I don't give a damn who you are, mister." Red stood away from the bar. "I'm fixin' to put a hole in you."

"Boy, that'll be a feat if you pull it off," Three-Toed said. "A passel of truly fast guns have tried to kill Frank Morgan before."

"Frank Morgan?" The whine had crept back into Chubby's voice. His face went pale and he looked ready to sleep anywhere but the barn.

Red scoffed. "So? So what if you are? You look like you got one foot in the grave already. All you need is a little nudge." He turned to his partner. "Don't worry about him. He's a has-been. Probably all broke up and boo-hooin' over his dead wife."

"I think we ought to let this alone." Chubby had a tiny lick of sense after all.

"I ain't backin' down from nobody." Red stood his ground. An evil sneer crossed his face. "You know what, Morgan? I wish I woulda been there when Swan went after you." He shook his red head back and forth. "I hear tell that wife of yours was a hell of a fighter."

"You're steppin' over the line, Jake," Chubby whispered.

Red put out his hand to silence his partner. He kept his eyes on Frank. "She screamed and whimpered like a baby, they say. If I'd have been there, I woulda showed her what a real man was like. I coulda made her yowl like a—

The bullet from Frank's Colt slammed into Red's belly

before he knew Frank had even drawn. Chubby frowned and fumbled for his own pistol until a bullet pierced his chest. Both men slumped, then slid to the floor.

Three-Toed gimped around the bar and pulled both men's guns out of their holsters so they didn't get any ideas before they died.

Red tried to get up, but his boots slid out from under him. Chubby moaned and clutched his chest with a bloody hand.

Three-Toed gazed out the greasy window. "Well, hell. I ain't diggin' no damn holes in this rain."

"I ain't dead," Chubby whined.

Three-Toed poured himself a cup of coffee and offered to top off Frank's. "You will be shortly. And so will your foul-mouthed friend." Bob limped over to stand above the redheaded gunman. "You'll likely be the one to go first, though. Bullet done tore up your gizzard. Your innards is leakin' out all inside you. Seen it before. You won't last long."

"You can go to hell, you crippled old fool," Red spit through gritted teeth.

Bob nodded and looked out the window again. "Just for that, I think I'm gonna dump you in with the hogs out back. I got a boar out there as big as a damn buffalo. He'll finish you off in no time, bones and all. That way, I won't have to dig no holes at all—rain or shine."

"I need a doctor," Chubby groaned.

"What you need is a miracle, boy." Bob shook his head. "You're hit as hard as your fool partner."

The heavyset man began to weep. "Don't throw me to no hogs. Please."

"Why not?" Bob sipped his coffee. "Hogs gotta eat too."

Chubby's cries grew softer, then stopped altogether. "He's done expired," Bob said, looking at Frank. "Damn, I sure thought the other one would go first."

"It's tricky guessing at that sort of thing." Frank shook his head as he looked at the bleeding man. After what the outlaw had said about Dixie, Frank felt no pity for him.

"I'm hurt bad." Red blinked his eyes. He seemed to have forgotten what kind of behavior had gotten him where he was. "I'm awful thirsty. Could one of you boys get me some water?" He was suddenly wracked with pain and doubled over. "Oh, Lord, I hurt."

Frank sat down and poured himself a glass of the good whiskey Bob had forgotten to hide again. He hated to listen to this, and thought he might have to put the man out of his misery.

"I see angels." Red's voice had gone soft now, the hard edge leaking away with the blood that pooled on the ground around him. "They're comin' for me now, singin' a beautiful song."

"Them ain't angels," Bob said. "Them's Hell's buggers comin' to drag you off to your eternal reward."

Red's eyes were still open—looking for angels—but he was past hearing.

Frank stood up. "Come on," he said quietly. "I'll help you drag the bodies outside. I guess they'll be sleepin' in the shed after all."

Three-Toed raised a bushy eyebrow. He'd always been a quick one when it came to figuring out ways around work.

"I killed 'em," Frank said. "But I don't fancy feedin' anyone to the hogs."

Bob shook his head. "I got a better idea. There's an old dry well out behind the shed. We can dump the carcasses down there. It's deep enough they won't smell."

"All right," Frank said. "Let's get the mean one first. I'm tired of looking at him." He grabbed a boot and Three-Toed did the same. The dead outlaw's arms trailed behind him as the two men dragged him toward the door.

"You got a Bible around here, Bob?"

"I did." Three-Toed looked around the room. "Oh, yeah, the leg broke off the stove and I been usin' it to prop the blasted thing up. I can't read a lick. At least now it's doin' me some good." The dead man's head thumped when they dragged it across the timber threshold. "Why, you plan on sayin' some words over these scoundrels?"

Frank nodded, hunching his shoulders against the rain as they sloshed with their load through the mud. "I might. Thought I could read them a little bit out of the Book of Judges. I don't know what good it'll do Red here, but it'd make me feel some better."

Chapter 31

"You do a good business here," Frank said later over coffee and cake Bob got out of a tin. He said he'd been saving it for a special occasion. It tasted like wood pulp, brandy, and raisins, but Frank choked it down anyway.

Three-Toed seemed to like it well enough, and dabbed at his saucer to get at every last crumb. "I reckon. It's awful lonely out here, but it beats ridin' the hoot-owl trail. That's a miserable life. Prison was bad, but it was a damn sight better than that."

Frank put up his hand when the other man offered him more of the sawdust cake. "No, thanks, I've had enough. Didn't you have a woman with you up at that post you had up on the Platte?"

Bob hung his head. "Yup. Crow half-breed named Willow. Now that woman could cook a deer haunch. She weren't too much to look at, but she kept me warm in the winter, that's for certain."

Frank didn't pry, but Bob pushed ahead like he needed to talk about it. "I reckon I know how you feel, Frank." The ex-outlaw gazed out the window again. "I came home one day and found my place burnt to the ground with my wife inside it." He wiped a tear from his eye. "Damn. Poor little Willow, she was ugly as a stump, but I ain't that much to look at either. I did love that gal."

"You find out who did it?" Frank said, understanding the other man's pain.

Bob nodded. His eyes blazed with the memory of his own fury. "I found out all right. Three whiskey peddlers wanted to put me out of business. They just killed Willow for meanness. I caught up to 'em about Medicine Bow. Took 'em in the middle of the night. Kilt every mother's son of 'em." Bob brightened. "Cut the leader's cajones off. Made me a little medicine bag out of it. Wanta see it?" He started to get up, but Frank shook his head.

"I'll take your word for it," he said.

"This revenge stuff is ticklish business, Morgan. It can eat you up—take my word for it."

Frank sighed. "Maybe it already has, Bob. When you killed those whiskey peddlers—did it make you feel better?"

Three-Toed shrugged. "Some. Least ways I knew they wouldn't be able to slaughter any more innocents. Justice was served, I reckon."

"That's all I'm looking for," Frank said. "Justice."

The other man gave him a crooked smile. "If anyone can mete that out to Ephraim Swan, it's you, Morgan. I just hope you live long enough to take some pleasure in it."

The next morning Frank chose a rangy black from the two outlaw horses. It bore no brand but where he was going, there wasn't anyone likely to check such things. Bills of sale belonged to the man with the fastest gun.

Bob promised to take good care of Dog and the horses.

"Anybody can pull this off, you can, Drifter," Three-Toed said from the small canvas awning over his front door. Rain still drizzled and the plain was a muddy mess. "Shoot straight and give no quarter, 'cause you'll get none from the likes of Swan and his gang."

The black had a smooth, five-beated gait and ate up ground with a vengeance. Two days ride from Three-Toed's trading post took Frank to the edge of a set of scrubby flint hills that sheltered Swan's town. He figured he was roughly twenty miles from the Texas line.

"Luke," he whispered to himself and the wind. "If this works out, I may just come check up on your sorry hide."

The town was just how Frank had envisioned it: ramshackle, tumbledown buildings all badly in need of repair. What had once been a thriving little community was now home to some of the most vicious killers on earth. Sullen eyes lined the muddy streets under leaky wooden awnings, watching Frank's approach—sizing him up as a dog might size up a bone.

"Watch all you want to, boys," Frank mumbled to himself. "You're apt to see a lot more of me in the next few days." As long as no one recognized him, he felt relatively safe.

He reined up the black in front of the largest building in town. It was a two-story affair of sun-bleached wood and peeling white paint. A crude, hand-painted sign hung above the awning: THE OXBLOOD.

"Saloon or hotel?" Frank asked a grinning man who lounged under the awning whittling on a short stick. A pile of shavings littered the cracked boardwalk at his feet. He'd been there a while.

"Both," the man replied, glancing up under the brim of a broad, high-crowned hat. "If you don't mind bad whiskey and buggy beds."

Frank looped the black's reins over the hitch rail. "You stayin' here?"

"Hell, no. If you're smart, you'll stay at one of the abandoned shacks around town. Some of 'em have beds, some of 'em don't. If they ain't occupied, they're up for grabs." He pointed with his open jackknife up the long narrow street. "I'm floppin' at that old green one up from the old church. Just stay 'way from that."

"What, your shack?"

"I meant the church. Swan turned it into his private

headquarters. He don't take kindly to uninvited guests." The man went back to his carving. It didn't look like he was making anything in particular, just working away at the stick. "I expect that shack on the other side of mine is empty. Fellow that was in it got himself shot this morning."

"Much obliged," Frank said, pulling the collar of his mackinaw up around his neck to ward of the rising wind. He climbed back aboard the black and nodded to the man with the stick. "I'll go stow my gear and come back and get something to eat. If you're still here I'll buy you a cup of coffee."

"I'll be here," the man said. "I got nowhere to go."

The dead outlaw's shack proved to be comfortable enough. Anything of value had already been taken, presumably by whoever had done the killing. All that was left was an old saddle blanket and a half a Sears Roebuck catalog someone had been using for paper in the outhouse. A rope bed sagging in the corner was the room's only furniture, but the dead man did leave behind a couple of beeswax candles to ward off the darkness.

Frank took the worn old Bible Three-Toed had given him out of his saddlebags. The black-leather front cover, all of Genesis, and most of Exodus bore the deep imprint of the stove foot, but he could still read most of it. He tossed it and his blankets on the bed. The candles would come in handy later if he wanted to read a little about vengeance, righteous indignation, and such.

Frank didn't have much. He'd left anything of value except his Peacemaker and Winchester back at the trading post. The old outlaw had promised to sell everything and send the money to Dixie's girls. He'd also scratched out a rough will; leaving the information about his sizeable bank account so the girls would never want for anything should anything happen to him.

After he stowed what little gear he had, he rode to the livery stable down the block from the Oxblood. A bent old man, smoking some noxious herb in a corncob pipe, took his horse and promised to grain and water it well. He told Frank he'd see the animal got a good home if he didn't happen to come back. Frank assured the man he'd be back. The old fellow drew deeply on the pipe and chuckled. "You'd be surprised," he said.

The man with the jackknife still whittled away at his stick on the front porch of the Oxblood when Frank slogged back through the mud from the livery.

"You survived your first half hour in town," the man said, glancing up from under his huge hat. "That's a good sign."

"Some kind of record?" Frank stepped up on the boardwalk and scraped the mud off his boots. He pulled out his makings and rolled himself a smoke. When he was finished, he held out the papers and pouch to the other man.

"Don't mind if I do." The man folded his jackknife and stuck his whittling stick in the pocket of his gray wool vest. Once they'd both lit up, he held out his hand.

"Johnny Nugget."

Frank shook Nugget's hand. "Joshua Bean," he said. He knew the other man's name was likely an alias as well. "This looks like a good place to lay low for a while."

Nugget shrugged. "As long as you keep spendin' money and don't get crossways with some of the hot-tempered sorts around here, Swan will let you hang around. If your money dries up, you're out on your ear—or worse."

Frank rubbed his chin and thought. "You got some short-fused ones around here, do you?"

"Hell, yeah. We got Amos Crocket. He's the one shot the man who was floppin' in that shack you're in now. He musta looked at him wrong. Jim Nettles—he's the fastest gun in Wyoming. Bob Worth rode in a few days ago. He's . . . "

"I've heard of him. He's supposed to be as fast as Frank Morgan," Frank said with a straight face.

"Ain't nobody as good as Frank Morgan was. Shame he's dead. Swan brags about it all the damn time."

"You know Morgan?" Frank asked.

Nugget shook his head. "Wish I had. He knew my . . . never mind. What say I take you up on that cup of coffee?"

"You're on," Frank said, wondering what the young man was about to say. "I'm in the mood for a beefsteak."

"Hope you got plenty of money. Food's higher than a cat's back around here. If your can afford it, they serve up pretty decent vittles. Cook appears to know what he's doin'. Almost makes you forget he was sentenced to hang for poisoning a feller with an apple pie."

Nugget unfolded himself from the wooden chair and stood up. He was a young man, not yet thirty, with broad muscular shoulders and powerful arms as big as some men's legs. For all his muscles, though, he didn't quite make it to Frank's shoulder in height.

"Go ahead and make a comment about it. It don't bother me." Nugget watched Frank's face for a reaction.

Frank looked him right in the eye. "What do you mean, Johnny?"

"In case you haven't noticed. I'm awful short."

Frank grinned and slapped the other man on the back. "Well, in case you haven't noticed, I'm awful old. I think we'll get along just fine."

Chapter 32

Dixie's finger floated in a corked bottle on a shelf behind the bartender. Frank stumbled when he walked up to the bar and saw it. His stomach roiled. He clenched his jaw and fought to keep from vomiting. There was a familiar pounding in his ears, and he was carried instantly back to the day of the ambush. The smoky room seemed to close in around him.

"You all right?" Nugget asked, staring at his face. "You've gone white as a sheet."

Frank snapped out of his daze and forced himself to stare at the grizzly decoration. "That's Morgan's wife's finger."

"Yeah," Nugget grunted. "Tells you somethin' about Swan, don't it?"

"Let's get us a table," Frank said, turning his back to the bar. His stomach was rebelling again. Looking at the finger, he couldn't help but think of Dixie. If Swan would have been in the room, he'd have shot him right there and let the chips fall where they might.

Once seated along the back wall, he was able to calm down some. He rolled another smoke and surveyed the crowd. He figured there were around twenty-five outlaws seated at various tables around the room. Four bar girls worked double duty tending to the rowdy crowd, enduring leers and comments, but amazingly enough, no groping. Swan must have certain rules about his working women, Frank thought. They likely didn't give out anything for free.

"The boys at the bar are sure enough giving you the once-over." Nugget inclined his head toward a motley group of four outlaws. "One of 'em is bound to try you. They check the sauce of every newcomer."

"Oh, yeah? I'd hate to see the fella who tried you."

Nugget chuckled. "See that feller with the bandaged flat nose spread all over his face, talkin' like he can't quite open his mouth—that's Tom Shively. He's the smart-mouthed bugger that decided he wanted a little lesson from me in fisticuffs."

"And you gave him one." Frank smiled.

"Yes I did. I . . . Oh, no. You done grabbed Big Un's attention and that ain't good. He's like a dog with a bone once his tiny brain grabs ahold of something." Nugget smacked his lips and shook his head slowly. "No, this ain't good at all."

"Big Un?"

"That's all I ever heard anyone call him. Dammit," Nugget hissed. "He's comin' over here. Don't say nothin' to rile him, Joshua. I seen him kill two men with his bare fists and I only been here a week."

Frank turned to see nearly seven feet of stinking, red-faced outlaw lumbering his direction. If he ever wanted to get to Swan, he had to deal with these idiots who wanted to test him.

Frank had been in his share of fistfights and if he'd learned anything, he'd learned that if there was sure enough going to be a fight with a larger opponent, he'd better try and get in the first blow. He chuckled to himself in spite of the situation as the giant made his way over to the table. He wondered if George Carlisle would ever forgive him for what he was about to do, but in a fight with someone as huge as this, the Marquis of Queensbury rules went straight out the window.

"I'd hate to be your horse, you fat-assed son of a bitch," Frank said, shifting to the balls of his feet to get ready to move.

Big Un was half drunk, but he was surprisingly fast, and he picked up speed like a locomotive at the insult. "I'm gonna rip off your arm and beat you to death with the stump," the giant growled in a voice higher than Frank had expected.

The gunfighter feinted left, then ducked right behind the ogre, springing up behind him and hopping up on a chair. He grabbed the brim of the big man's hat with both hands and jerked down with all his might, yanking it down over the giant's ears and effectively blinding him.

While Big Un struggled to pull up the tight hat so he could see again, Frank hit him twice as hard as he could in the unprotected kidneys. The man yowled in pain and swayed on his feet. Taking advantage of his unsteadiness, Frank grabbed up a wooden chair and swung it across the back of the man's legs like an ax to a tree trunk.

The huge outlaw fell with a resounding thud, knocking over two tables and spilling whiskey as he went down. The hat was still pulled tight over his forehead and eyes, and his ears stuck absurdly out to each side of a broad face.

Without waiting for his opponent to recover, Frank reared back and kicked the downed man square in the side of his head. He put all the power he could muster behind the blow, and his boot connected with a sickening crack. Spittle and blood flew through the air. Bits of teeth clattered against the far wall. The big man twitched, and Frank kicked again.

Big Un moaned once, then lay still. Bloody drool oozed from his half-open mouth.

His Goliath down, Frank bent over and rested his hands on his knees, panting. Even though he'd never even been hit, he could tell the fight had taken a lot out of him.

"Well, I'll be damned." Nugget came up and toed the unconscious outlaw. "I never thought I see that big bastard bested in a fight."

"I wouldn't want to be you when he wakes up," another man said, whistling in wonderment by the bar. "He'll kill you first chance he gets."

"I doubt he'll be able to see straight for a couple of weeks," Frank managed. He was still panting. He readjusted his own hat and sat back down at the table across from Johnny Nugget.

A wilted little blonde with a gold front tooth brought two beers and set them on the table in front of Frank and Nugget. She was skinny as a picket rail and looked no older than seventeen or eighteen.

"On the house, boys." She smiled and batted her painted eyelashes. "We all enjoyed the show. Besides, I was the unlucky girl who drew the short straw tonight, and I had me an appointment with that big galoot later." She looked Frank in the eye. "Mister, you saved me a hell of a lot of trouble and grief."

Frank counted out a handful of coins and gave them to the girl as a tip. When she left, Johnny sipped his free beer.

"I ain't believin' this. You did good, Bean, but Big Un's gonna kill you when he wakes up."

"I don't think so."

"Why, what do you plan to do, shoot him?"

Frank ran a finger down the condensation on the side of his beer mug. "If I have to."

Nugget shook his head. "Big Un don't even carry a gun. You'd be able to claim self-defense anywhere else, but the folks in this town have their own special set of rules. They'd hang you for sure if you shot an unarmed man. Even one as big as Big Un."

Frank sipped at the froth on top of his mug and shook his head. "You know what that hat did beside make it so the big son of a bitch couldn't see me?"

"What?"

"It kept his eyes from poppin' out of his thick skull. I kicked a man like that once before and sent one of his eyeballs flying across the room just like Big Un's teeth." Frank took a long draw on his beer. "Believe me, Johnny. When he wakes up, I don't think he'll be seein' much of anything including me."

Johnny Nugget set his beer down on the table and stared across the table. "Bean, are you as bad as you think you are?"

"Badder." Frank winked. "By a damned sight."

Big Un finally sputtered back to consciousness twenty minutes and six pitchers of cold water later. He struggled to his feet with the help of three friends, and promptly vomited all over them. It took two more to keep him from falling over and help drag him out the door.

Frank tried not to smile. No, Big Un wasn't going to be much of a problem—he wouldn't have time. Just getting over a kick to the head was a full-time job.

Frank and Nugget both ordered steaks, and sat for a time enjoying being left alone. There was a different sort of notoriety that came with beating the giant, and though the rest of the bar had stayed away from him, if he wasn't the talk of the place when he was a newcomer, he was now.

Every eye in the bar turned to him every few minutes, studying, probing, sizing him up, and trying to figure out how they would beat him. A rumble of angry voices began to grow among a group of outlaws at the bar. Frank cut his steak and savored the bite of meat. It was a little tough, but it was a change of pace from mutton stew. The group became more animated. It was only a matter of time before someone tested him with something more deadly than Big Un's fists.

The test came before he finished his supper.

"You ain't Joshua Bean," a man shouted from the bar.

Frank set his knife and fork down on top of his unfinished steak and wiped his mouth with a checkered napkin. The room had gone dead quiet, and the grating sound of his chair sliding back on the wooden floor made the men at the table next to him jump.

"I know who you are," the man screamed from the bar. He was red-faced, and the veins on the side of his neck throbbed as he spoke.

Frank stood, expecting to be gunned down by everyone in the room as soon as the word of his true identity escaped the challenger's lips. He nodded at Johnny Nugget, and prepared to take out as many of the outlaws as he could.

"You're Jim Crawford," the man screamed. Spit hung from the corners of his lips. "I figured it out. You're the lousy bastard who killed my cousin up in Ogallala."

Frank slowly let out a tense breath and held up his hands. "Now hold on a second, mister, I'm not Jim Crawford. You don't want to be shot by somebody you don't even know."

The man's beet-colored head shook as he spoke and looked as if it might explode at any moment. "You're a liar. You was hired by the Circle T to kill homesteaders. One of the men you kilt was my cousin." The man's bloodshot eyes raged at Frank.

Frank's hands dropped closer to the butt of his gun. He shook his head slowly, trying not to incite the frenzied man any more than he already was. "I'm gonna tell you this one last time. I'm not Jim Crawford and I don't hire out my gun." He stood quietly waiting for the other man to make his play.

It wasn't long in coming.

Chapter 33

The screaming challenger had good intentions when it came to avenging the death of his cousin, but he proved to be no fast hand with a gun. He clawed at his holster, missing the pistol altogether as Morgan's bullet tore into his belly and knocked him against the bar. When he finally managed to jerk the gun to clear leather, it slipped from his fingers and clattered to the floor. The man sputtered and gasped as if all the air were being let out of him.

"You shot me, damn you." He put a hand over his bleeding belly and grabbed at the edge of the bar with the other. The color drained from his face and he stared with big doe-eyes, blinking in disbelief. "I can't believe I let a skinny-ass old man like you shoot me."

Frank cast a glance around the room before he re-holstered. Too often there was some hotheaded friend who acted on the spur of the moment and ended up getting himself killed as well.

"You were the one that wanted a fight." Frank slid his Peacemaker back into the holster once he was reasonably certain things were calming down. "I told you you were making a mistake."

The outlaw's boots slid out from under him and he sat down hard on the floor. His free hand jammed into the top of a cuspidor brimming with tobacco spit. He cussed and jerked his hand away, spilling the slimy contents across the

William W. Johnstone

floor and sending the men around him scrambling to get out of the way.

"That ol' boy's about as fast as I've ever seen," a man said from the table next to Frank.

"I seen Smoke Jensen work one time. This feller's faster than him."

"He's fast, but Frank Morgan coulda taken him," another ventured.

"Ain't nobody as fast as Frank Morgan," the bartender said, getting a mop for the spilled spit but ignoring the gut-shot man altogether. "I seen him once down in Del Rio. He killed nine armed men in a single gunfight. Damnedest thing you ever did see."

A collective murmur went up from the crowd.

Frank grinned to himself. Nine men, eh? That would be a damned fine thing to see, since he'd never set foot in Del Rio. This being dead was doing more to build his reputation than the dime novels.

"Somebody help me!" the wounded man cried from a mixture of sticky brown juice and his own blood.

"You're done for, Hal," a man next to him at the bar said. "Just do the right thing and go ahead and ex-pire."

"I ain't done in yet," Hal groaned. "I ain't gonna do any such thing as expire."

"Wanna bet on that?" The bartender leaned over the bar to look at the wounded man.

"Can I have your saddle?" the first man asked, kneeling down so Hal could hear him. "I always been partial to that saddle. You know that."

"You go to hell," Hal spit, and tried in vain to sit up a little straighter.

"Well you don't have to get all in a huffin' fit about it." The cowboy stood and walked back to his beer. "I'll just wait until you're dead and take it then. Gosh, try to be decent for once and what does it get me?"

"I need me a doctor!" Hal moaned.

"You need a box," the cowboy who wanted his saddle said into his drink.

The bartender took out a gleaming bowie knife. He had a wild look in his eye, and Frank could only guess what he was hiding out for.

"You want us to operate?" The bartender held the knife in front of Hal's face.

"Just go on and let the man die in peace," Frank whispered.

The bartender looked over his shoulder and returned the long knife to his belt. "Take him outside and let him do his dyin' out there."

The excitement over for the time being, Frank looked at Nugget. "I'm ready to finish my steak. How about you?"

"I could eat," Nugget said, shaking his head. "Joshua, you're an interesting sort to hang around."

An attractive little brunette with a sunburned face and an easy smile brought two cups of coffee.

"Thank you, Velda." Nugget smiled up at the woman. She returned his look with a playful, catlike growl. It was obvious these two had a little thing going.

"Your friend here's pretty good with a gun." She gave Frank the once-over with a fearsome pair of brown eyes that probed him so hard, it made him want to duck behind something. "My friend Suzette says she would surely like to get her hands on you." Velda threw a glance over her shoulder. "You saved her from a night with Big Un and she's eternally grateful. Big Un's done paid, so she'd let it be his treat."

"I . . . I'm flattered," Frank said. "But I've had a mighty rough go of it lately when it comes to womenfolk." He was telling the truth.

"Suzette's just what the doctor ordered then. She's got sweet shoulders to cry on if that's what you need." Velda raised her dark eyebrows up and down. "And the other parts of her ain't too shabby either."

Pretty, wilted little Suzette stood with her back to the bar, leaning against her hands and smiling hungrily in

Frank's direction. She looked so young—like one of Dixie's daughters—that it turned his stomach.

"Tell her thanks but I'm gonna have to pass this time," Frank mumbled.

Velda looked back over her shoulder and shook her head. Suzette slumped for a minute, then turned her attention to another cowboy at the bar. A group of poker players at another table hollered for more beer, and Velda sauntered off to tend them, giving Johnny one last playful wink.

"That woman could stare the hide off a grizzly," Frank said after she was gone.

Nugget chuckled and slapped the table. "And that ain't the half of it," he said.

"I need some air." Frank stood and stretched his aching muscles. He was bone-sore and stiff from the fights.

"You're bleedin', Joshua." Nugget nodded downward.

Frank looked at his side. A small spot of blood dotted his shirt halfway between his armpit and his belt on the right side—his gun side. He shrugged, more aware of the pain than he had been.

"Likely I got some of Big Un or Hal's blood on me," he said.

Nugget raised an eyebrow. "Let's go for some of that air."

Once outside, the men rolled smokes and Nugget dragged up another chair so they could both sit down.

"You want to tell me about it, Bean?" Nugget spit a fleck of tobacco off is lip. "You're hurt. They might not be able to see it in there, but I can."

"I'm all right enough." Frank smoked his cigarette and stared into the darkness.

Nugget leaned forward. He kept his voice low so passersby couldn't hear him. "Listen to me. I don't care how fast you are. In case you didn't notice it, those hombres in there are animals. If they smell blood or catch a whiff of weakness, they'll turn into a pack of wolves and rip you to pieces, believe me."

"I hear you," Frank said.

Something about Johnny Nugget didn't quite add up.

"All right," said Frank, "I got scraped up a little a while back and I'm not completely healed."

Nugget leaned back and took out his jackknife and whittling stick. "I figured it was something like that. Scrape with the law?"

Frank shook his head. "No, had to do with the woman trouble I was talkin' about."

Nugget began to whittle. "I see."

"Mind if I ask you something?" It was Frank's turn to lean forward.

Nugget shrugged.

"What did you do to end up in this place?" Frank chose his words carefully in case his suspicions were wrong. "You just don't seem to fit in with the rest of these outlaws."

The short man kept whittling as he spoke, taking long slivers off the soft wood and letting them fall into his lap.

"Killed a man back down in Dimmit. It was him or me, but he was friends with the sheriff, so I had to light out for somewhere to hide."

"Just happened?"

"Not too long ago. Does it matter?"

Frank threw down the stub of his cigarette. "Guess not. Just seems odd a man with one killin' under his belt would come to a place this bad to hide out."

Nugget kept to his whittling. "I don't know. A man does what he thinks is best. You came here."

Something about the tough little man gnawed at Frank. He'd been having a hard time putting his finger on it . . . until Nugget had asked about Frank's scrape. That was it.

"What if I told you my scrape was with the law?" Frank said, keeping his voice low and steady.

Nugget shrugged. "Your business."

"What if I told you I killed three young deputies who tried to arrest me? Men with families just out doin' their jobs?"

Frank watched as the young man bore down harder with his jackknife. Nugget stopped and looked up, eyes blazing under the wide brim of his hat. He pointed with the open blade. He started to speak, but Frank raised his hand, interrupting him with a sharp whisper.

"Your secret's safe with me, Nugget."

"And just what secret is that, Mr. Bean?"

"No outlaw worth his salt would give a prairie dog's scruffy behind if I killed a half-dozen lawmen. I can see it in your eyes. It's eatin' you up inside that you made friends with me."

Nugget stared hard at him for a long moment, then waved him off, leaning back into his chair. "Hell, Bean. More'n half the fools here have murdered lawmen. I can't get too particular about who I partner up with."

"You said 'murdered,' not 'killed.' Sounds like it really bothers you."

The young man slumped in his chair. "I've seen you shoot. I know I can't beat you, Bean. Where do we go from here?"

Frank shook his head. "Nowhere, Johnny. I reckon I'm here for the same reason you are. All I want you to do is stay out of my way."

"So you didn't kill three deputies?"

Frank shook his head and lit another cigarette. "Not even one."

Nugget looked relieved. "How'd you know I was a badge-toter?"

"I didn't live this long by being wrong very often about my hunches. I can generally tell who to trust."

"Well, sir, you called it right this time." The younger man swapped the jackknife into his left hand and held out his right. "Tyler Beaumont, Texas Rangers Company F."

"The Frontier Company," Frank mused. "I used to know a Ranger who was fair hand with a gun. He was assigned to Company F—and not too damned tall now that I think of it. Had fists like twelve-pound sledgehammers. You mighta known him. Went by the name of Sherman Beaumont."

Tyler grinned. "My father."

"Thought there was a resemblance."

"You knew my father?" Interested now, the Ranger folded his pocket knife and put it away. "Can I ask your real name?"

"Sure. It's Morgan."

Nugget clucked his tongue. "Frank Morgan," he said under his breath. "Makes all the sense in the world now. My father used to talk about you all the time. Said you were the fastest, steadiest man he ever laid eyes on. I heard him say once that the Rangers were lucky you landed on the right side of the law, because it would have taken a whole company to bring you in if you'd decided to go outlaw."

"How is old Sherman?"

The young Ranger looked down. "He passed over two years ago. Tangled with a sick coyote one night in camp. Hydrophobia took him." Beaumont shook his head. "Awful thing. Just watching him drove my mother mad herself. She just quit eatin' after he died and wasted away. To tell you the truth, that's why I volunteered for this mission."

"Sorry to hear about that," Frank said. "Sherman Beaumont was one of the finest men I ever met. A credit to your creed." The gunfighter gave a slight chuckle. "He wasn't quite the fastest, but he was the most accurate shot I've ever seen, with pistol or long gun."

"He was good." Tyler smiled.

"I watched him part the hair of an old Mexican who was trying to steal one of our mules. The poor old fellow just wanted it to feed his family and didn't mean us any harm. We could ill afford to lose any stock, though, so your papa, he fired off what we thought was a warning shot. He was too kindhearted to try and kill the starvin' Mexican, you see.

"Well, the poor fella was stopped about two hundred yards from us makin' water. When your pa shot, the old man just fell over like he'd been poleaxed and the mule came trottin' back to us." Frank chuckled, remembering. "When we went to check on the body, we saw your daddy had creased him good right down the center of his hair—grazed him good and made him think twice about stealing Ranger stock. Sherman ended up giving him a whole poke full of food—most of what we had really."

"That was my pa. Thanks for the story, Morgan. I heard about what Swan did to you and your wife. I'm sorry."

"We all got our crosses to bear." Frank leaned forward again. "You said you volunteered for some kind of mission?"

"In a few days, more than three dozen Texas Rangers are going to ride down on this town and drive all these vermin back to hell where they belong."

"What ever happened to 'One riot, one Ranger'?"

"In case you haven't noticed, partner," the young lawman said, "there's generally a riot on every corner in this no-account little burg. Hell, you caused two and you only been here—what, half a day?"

Frank's face hardened. "Listen to me good. I don't care if you kill every soul in this town. But remember one thing—Swan is mine."

"Why not let the law handle this, Frank? Better yet, why don't you let me deputize you and you can ride with us."

Frank shook his head. "Can't do that, Tyler. What I have in mind for Mr. Swan has nothin' to do with the law."

Chapter 34

That night, Frank lit one of the beeswax candles and lay on his rope cot flipping through the pages of Three-Toed Bob's battered Bible. His back and right side ached with a throbbing pain that took a while to dull. It never did go completely away.

Before he went to sleep, Frank read for a time about Jonathan, the son of Saul, killing a whole garrison of Philistines. He pictured the mighty army falling and fleeing before what they saw as an inferior force, and thought about the cocksure outlaws hiding out in this town. They were about to learn a hard lesson in justice.

He set the leather-bound book on the floor beside his bed, and checked his pistol one last time before he blew out the flickering candle. The night was a frosty one, but he dispensed with building a fire and pulled the blankets up tight around his chin instead. The cold wasn't so bad as long as he could be out of the wind.

Breathing out a chilly cloud of vapor, he drifted off, pondering the destruction he was about to bring down around Ephraim Swan.

But his dreams were of Dixie.

A long narrow building housed the town's only eating place besides the Oxblood. It bore a crude placard, probably made by the same sign-painting outlaw that had hung the one outside the bar, though it didn't show quite as much imagination. In bold white letters it proclaimed: THE CAFÉ

Frank got a table with his back to the unpainted wooden wall, and ordered eggs from a dark-eyed lady with long gray hair who looked like she'd been up all night. The woman grunted.

"Want bread?" she said, staring at him as if it didn't matter what he said, he was getting bread whether he liked it or not.

"Sure."

She poured him some coffee in a chipped cup, and waddled off about the time Tyler Beaumont showed up and sat down across from him.

"This seat taken?" the young Ranger asked.

"Nope, not till now." Frank sipped his coffee and rubbed the sleep out of his eyes. There were a few other early risers in the place. Outlaws were, for the most part, a lazy bunch who preferred to carouse late at night and sleep late in the day.

"Thought you might be savin' it for pretty little Suzette."

"That'll be the day."

Two grizzled men wearing long, dark frock coats stepped in and slammed the door behind them. They took a table near the stove.

"Clay Bonner," Beaumont whispered. "I know you've heard of him."

Frank nodded. "The Arizona gunslick."

The young Ranger looked over the top of his coffee at the new arrivals. "He's got a reputation for being quick but hot-tempered."

Frank grinned. "So do I, partner."

"Hey, Nugget!" the man with Bonner yelled. "You two sweet on each other? There ain't no banks in this town to rob so what's all the whisperin' about?"

"How you feelin' this mornin', Frank?" Beaumont said under his breath.

"Well enough, I guess."

"Hey! My friend asked you a question." Bonner glared at them.

"That he did," Frank said, sliding away from the table to give himself some room in case he needed to maneuver. "But it was a stupid question, so I didn't see any need to answer it. What we talk about is our business."

"How about I make it my business?" Bonner's chair tipped over and hit the ground as he got to his feet.

A lone man threw open the door and surveyed the room. Cold wind whipped in and tugged at the tail of his duster.

"Sit down, Bonner," the newcomer said, his voice cool and hard as hammered steel.

Bonner complied.

When the man shut the door and took a step into the dim room, it was easier to make out his features. He was tall and lean with a dark brow and deep-set eyes that peered out over a nose that hooked like the beak of an eagle. A black mustache curled up in large handlebars on either side of his face.

The gray-haired waitress brought him a cup of coffee. "Good to see you back," she said, absent her characteristic mumbling grunt.

"Just got in."

The waitress immediately slinked away as if she might get hit if she hung around too long.

The man gave a curt nod and looked around the room, pausing for a time to give Frank a thorough once-over. He picked up the coffee and pulled up a chair next to Tyler Beaumont.

"Who's your new friend, Johnny?" He spoke to the other man, but continued to stare at Frank.

"Name's Joshua Bean." Frank nodded. "And you are?"

"I'd like you to meet Tandy Beltran," Beaumont said. "He's the peacekeeper in this little burg."

"Law?"

Beltran drank a long warm up from his coffee and sniffed. The cold had given him a runny nose. "You might say that.

Swan's law. I make certain things don't get out of hand. When they do, I can generally end them quickly."

Frank looked at the grim determination of the man's craggy face. "I got no trouble believin' that."

"Good." Beltran put down his coffee and leaned back in the flimsy chair. Frank noticed he didn't care a bit that his back was to the door. Pretty cocky. "Now what's all this I hear about you causing so much trouble last night. Nobody's talked about anything else since I hit town an hour ago. What'd you say your name was?"

"Joshua Bean."

Beltran shook his head. "Never heard of you. If you're fast and mean enough to beat Big Un, then I damn sure should have heard of you."

Frank shrugged. "I'm not from around here."

"Where then?"

"Here and there."

A broad smile crossed Beltran's face under his huge mustache, but his eyes still glowed with malice. "I'm a good judge of character, Bean—or whatever your name is. I believe you're hidin' something behind that scruffy look and shaggy beard. If I had my way, we'd kill you now and sort all this out after you was dead—but the boss wants to meet you."

Frank tried not to appear too eager. "I'm just trying to mind my own business. I don't want to make any trouble."

"Whatever you say, Bean. But Swan wants to see you anyhow. He says he wants to lay eyes on anyone who can best Big Un at a hand-to-hand fight."

"When?"

"This afternoon. He's been on the trail a while. And he's got some business with Velda to take care of." Beltran gave a leering grin. "I'll come get you when it's time."

The enforcer pushed away from the table and stood. "Be ready," he said as he walked to the door. "I'm still trying to convince him to let me kill you."

"Don't try too hard," Frank said, returning the man's stare.

"You might bite off a bigger hunk of meat than you want to chew."

Beltran scoffed and disappeared into the cold. Bonner and his friend followed him out.

"You're crazy, you know that. You're already dead if you meet Swan on his own terms. You said he knows you."

"No." Frank shook his head. "I doubt he'll recognize me with all the weight I've lost behind this beard and long hair. Besides," he said, changing the subject, "who's the crazy one? Sounds to me like you got a little trouble brewin' of your own if you're sweet on Swan's woman."

"Velda can't help it if he picked her. He moves between the women here as soon as he gets tired of them. When he runs out of choices, he goes for some more. If they don't come on their own, he forces 'em."

"You really are sweet on her, aren't you, Tyler?"

"She's had a rough life, Frank. It ain't all her fault she turned out to be a whore." Beaumont took a deep breath. "If I live through this evening, I aim to take her with me—give her a decent home."

"Good for you," Frank said, hoping things turned out better for the young couple than they had for him. Then he realized what the young Ranger had said. "What do you mean if you live through this evening?"

"It's going to happen today," Beaumont said. "Sometime late this afternoon, three groups of Rangers will ride in from the flint hills and level this rotten town." He took a long yellow scarf out of his pocket. "If you live through your meeting with Swan, tie this around your neck."

"Yellow?" Frank took the scarf.

"Like the Rose of Texas. It'll let all the other Rangers know you're on our side."

"Anybody else I should know about here? I'd hate to shoot one of the good guys."

"There's a couple of us here. You'll know us by our scarves."

"Probably better I didn't know, just in case," Frank said.

"I'm serious about not meeting Swan in his own place." The gray-haired waitress came out to clear off the other table, and the Ranger stopped talking until she left again. Even then, he spoke in quieter tones.

"First off," he said. "they won't let you take a gun in to meet him. You'll be completely defenseless."

"Don't you remember Big Un? I can handle myself."

Beaumont gave an emphatic shake of his head. "It won't be like it was with Big Un. No one will stand around and watch. He's surrounded all the time by his own men—men he knows he can trust. And they have all got guns."

"Well, there you go then." Frank smiled. "My problems are solved."

"How's that?"

"You said it yourself. There'll be guns everywhere. When the time comes, I should have no trouble getting to one."

"I hate to be the one to break this to you, Morgan, but Beltran is fast. He's every bit as fast as you. Besides that, you're plumb wore out."

"We all meet our match someday, Tyler." Frank sighed. "I reckon I'm long overdue."

"You come here to die, Frank?"

"No, but if it's my time, I'll play whatever cards are dealt me. I've got a job to do—just like you."

"You must have really loved that woman." The young Ranger grinned.

"I did at that," Frank said. "I did at that."

Chapter 35

The sun was low on the western horizon, beneath a long glowing line of orange clouds. Frank lay on his bunk and rested, looking out the single pane of the dirty window in his little shack. He'd searched around and found enough wood out back to start a decent fire in the squat woodstove. The seal around the door was gone, and the old thing looked as if someone had dragged it outside and used it for target practice, there were so many holes in it. The wood went quickly, and he had to stoke the fire often to keep the place warm.

He reasoned that a good fire would loosen him up for what was bound to be a hellacious battle. One way or another, Frank knew he'd have to fight—either to get to Swan or to get away after he killed him.

It was a funny notion, but Frank didn't mind the thought of dying as long as he didn't have to die cold.

Young Ranger Beaumont had gone off after noon to prepare for the planned assault. Frank figured he'd gone to meet with the other spies who were in place, and didn't bother him. He also figured the lovesick boy was going to try and find Velda and console her after Swan was finished with her.

The tension of waiting for Beltran kept him from getting any decent rest, and he propped up his feet and broke out the Bible again by the open stove door.

He didn't have to wait long.

At a quarter past five, the enforcer's gruff voice came

through a crack in the front door. Frank had heard the heavy footsteps, and was already up with his boots on.

"You talk him into lettin' you kill me yet?" Frank asked after he removed the chair from in front of the door and opened it a crack. He held his Colt pointed at Beltran's belt buckle.

"Put that away, Bean. If I was gonna kill you, you'd been dead already." The man turned, ignoring the pistol, and walked down the street, expecting Frank to follow. He was definitely sure of himself.

Frank slipped the gun back in its holster and followed.

It was supper time and most of the town's inhabitants were gathered in either the Oxblood or the Café. With everyone bunched up like that, it would be a good time for an attack. The young Ranger had done his spying job well.

Frank listened to the laughter carrying out of the buildings lit by yellow lantern light into the darkening streets. He wondered where Tyler Beaumont had run off to. He was a good boy, solid, just like his father.

"Stop right here, Bean," Beltran ordered when they came up abreast of the old church. Paint peeled from the termite-eaten wood on the sagging building, but at least it had once been painted.

"What's next?" Frank faced the dark man.

"What's next is you hand over your gun and step inside." Frank pulled out the Colt.

"Easy now," Beltran grumbled, his hand on his own gun.

Frank smiled. "I'm only doin' what you asked." He handed the Colt butt-first to the other man.

"The knife as well." Beltran pointed with Frank's own gun. "You don't go in with any kind of weapon."

Frank removed his bowie knife and threw it in the dirt. It hit with a thud, sticking a few feet away from the enforcer's boot.

"Don't be cute," Beltran said. "I may yet get to kill you tonight. Now step on in."

Inside, the old church had been gutted and turned into a dilapidated storehouse for Swan's loot. Assorted rifles by the dozens lined one wall and a brass Gatling gun sat on a wooden tripod just inside the front door. Stacks of strongboxes containing hidden treasures—families' life savings, cattle-drive payrolls—cluttered the rest of the former sanctuary. A half-dozen Mexican saddles trimmed in silver hung on stands in front of a door that led to another room in the back—the room that held Ephraim Swan.

Beltran stopped just inside the church and pulled the door shut. It was cool inside and Frank guessed they didn't even try to heat the large room. "Stand there by the wall so I can search you."

"You've gotta be joking."

"Nope," Beltran sneered. "It's my job to keep the man safe. I still think killin' you is the best way to do that, but he's determined to meet you. Says he's gonna offer you a job if you're as good as everyone says you are."

Beltran pushed him against the wall and ran a rough hand up and down both legs and up his sides. Frank winced as the hands crossed his wounds and tender scars, but gritted his teeth so the man didn't notice he was hurting.

"Satisfied?" Frank said after the search was over.

"Just barely," the dark man said. "Now, let's get moving. I don't want to keep the boss waiting."

Frank was disappointed to find not Ephraim Swan, but Velda sitting on a long cushioned sofa in the back room. She wore a flimsy silk gown that showed more of her than Frank really wanted to see, and he immediately felt sorry for Tyler Beaumont. She smiled widely, twirling her brunette hair with a finger.

"He'll be right back," she said. "He had to take care of some business. It's good to see you, Joshua." She licked her lips and gave Frank a sly smile that made him feel as naked as she was. "You look down. Shoulda taken Suzette up on her offer."

Beltran scoffed at that. "Suzette and this skinny runt?"

"Hey, Tandy, you didn't see this fella," Velda grinned. "It got Suzette all in a lather, I'm tellin' you. It was her idea."

The door creaked open and Swan walked in. His wool shirt was untucked, and leather suspenders hung loose from the buttons on his britches. His gun belt hung on a wooden peg on the wall behind Velda.

Frank clenched his teeth when he saw the man, and tried not to think of Dixie. He saw her ring on the leather string around Swan's thick neck, and kept his eyes on the ground.

Swan was used to a certain amount of deference, and made no mention of the fact that Frank didn't look him in the eye.

"I've heard a lot about you, Mr. Bean," he said, slapping Velda on the rump so she'd slide over. He flopped down beside her and rested his hand where he'd swatted her. "I've gotta say, you're not what I pictured for a man who beat my giant."

"I reckon I was lucky," Frank said. He kept his voice low and slouched to add to his disguise.

Swan shook his head. "Lucky twice. First with Big Un, then with Hal. Hal was no Clay Bonner, but he wasn't slow either." The outlaw leader looked at Frank and shook his head. "No, I don't believe in that kind of luck." He leaned forward. "Have we met before somewhere?"

Frank shook his head. "Not that I know of." Swan was working his brain, trying to place his face. Frank needed to change the subject. "Your man here says you might have a job for me."

Swan nodded slowly, rubbing his face. His white eyebrow knotted and relaxed as he thought. "I might. Beltran wants me to kill you. Says there's no way I can ever trust you." He motioned Frank closer with a curled finger. He whispered, although his enforcer was only a few feet away and could hear every word. Swan's eyes glowed as if he'd been drinking. "I don't think that's what it is, though. You know what I think? I think the man's afraid you might muscle him out of his job."

"Horse shit!" Beltran spit. "This two-bit scarecrow couldn't whip me if I was drunk and asleep!"

"We'll see," Swan said. "But first we have to see if he's trustworthy." He suddenly leaned back again beside a stoic Velda. "Can you take orders, Bean?"

"Sure. I suppose it depends on the orders. If you want me to kill Beltran, I'd be happy to."

The dark man stiffened and Swan chuckled. Velda giggled until Beltran gave her a cold stare.

"I like your style. If it was up to me, I'd hire you right now." He swatted the girl on the rump again. This time hard enough to make her flinch and bring tears to her eyes. "Hell, what am I thinking? It *is* up to me. You're hired, Bean."

"That's it?" Frank stood and blinked in disbelief. This was all too easy.

Swan pursed his lips and sighed. "Not quite. You do need to have a little test to check the measure of your loyalty." He nodded at Beltran, who disappeared through the door behind him without another word. "Do you want to work for me, Bean?"

"I do," Frank said, judging the distance he would have to cover to get at Swan's gun now that Beltran was out of the room. He wondered if Velda would be a friend or an enemy when he made his move. Another man he could have trampled underfoot, but this woman looked to be just another in a long line of Swan's victims.

Frank took a half step toward the gun belt before the door flew open and Beltran dragged in a tightly bound Tyler Beaumont.

The young Ranger had been beaten severely. Large black and blue circles puffed out under swollen eyes. Dried blood crusted below his nose and cracked lips. A rawhide gag ran between his teeth and around his head. His hat was missing, and his shirt was torn almost completely off his body. His hands were tied behind his back, and one boot was gone.

Frank could see he struggled to remain conscious, to look death in the face when it came to him. Someone had sold him out. Beaumont's eyes widened when he saw Velda sitting on the couch beside Swan, and he hung his head.

"How well do you know Johnny Nugget?" Swan lit a cigar and waved the match at the wounded pile of flesh.

Frank steeled his emotions and shrugged. "Never saw him before I rode into town. He seemed like a good enough old boy. What did he do to make you mad at him?"

"You're a bad judge of character in this case, Bean. I been told that Nugget here is more than meets the eye."

"How's that?" Frank cast a quick glance at Beltran. The man grinned at Beaumont cruelly. Beaumont's wounds were at least an hour old, and Frank knew this was the man that had given them to him. You just made my list, he thought to himself.

"I hear the little bastard is a Texas Ranger," Swan spit, leaning back so he could snatch the pistol out of the holster on the wall behind him. "He's here to spy on us. All of us."

Velda hid her face, and Frank couldn't tell how she felt about the circumstances. One thing was sure, Tyler was young. If he was sleeping with her, he'd likely let something slip. Maybe the fool girl had thought it would get her some advantage to play the rat and tell the Ranger's secret.

Swan's eyes narrowed into tiny slits as he studied Frank's reaction. "We can't have that goin' on around here. Can we, Bean?"

Frank sighed. He knew what was coming and tried to form a quick plan of action. "No," he said. "I reckon we can't have that."

"Glad you feel that way." Swan grabbed the pistol by the barrel and handed it to Frank. "Go ahead and shoot him then. It'll take care of two problems at once. I can see if you follow orders and I'll be rid of the stinkin' lawman to boot."

Frank took the pistol. He pointed it at the Ranger's belly, then cocked it.

Tyler looked up at him, his swollen eyes wide and blood-shot. His mouth worked back and forth around the stiff gag, but he said nothing. He nodded almost imperceptibly to Frank, then looked at Velda and closed his eye—resigned to his fate.

"You want him to die quick or suffer?" Frank said, look-ing over his shoulder at Swan. There was a glint of regret in Velda's brown eyes.

The outlaw chuckled. "I do like your style. No, I just want him dead."

"Don't!" Velda screamed.

Swan and Beltran both laughed.

Without another pause, Frank pointed the pistol at Ranger Beaumont's head and pulled the trigger.

Chapter 36

Frank was almost positive the gun would be empty, but when the hammer snapped and nothing happened to the boy's head, he let out an audible sigh of relief.

As careful as Swan was not to let anyone in with a weapon, it didn't make any sense to him to give anyone a loaded gun just to test their mettle. If Frank would have followed his inclination instead of his instincts and turned the gun on the outlaw, there was no question that Beltran would have blown a hole in him as quick as he could pull the trigger.

"Good for you, Bean. You passed." The outlaw gave Velda another resounding swat on the thigh. "You, on the other hand, seem to care a lot more about this damn spy than you do about me."

The girl shook her head. "That ain't true. I just didn't want his brains splattered all over the pillows." Velda regained some of her steel, but Frank could still make out a look of pity in her eye when she snuck a glance at Beaumont.

Swan blew a smoke ring with his cigar. "We'll see about that," he said. He waved his hand at Beltran. "Get him out of here."

"What do you want me to do with him?" Beltran asked. There was a cruel twist in his lips under his curled mustache.

"Whatever you want. Just make sure he ends up dead." He turned to Frank. "Me and Bean have some things to talk over. Don't we, Bean?"

"Whatever you say, Wilson," Frank said, wincing as the words came out of his mouth.

"What did you say?" Swan sat up straighter and slid to the edge of the couch. He chewed on his cigar and stared at Frank.

Frank had slipped up and he knew it. He had to make his move now.

Beltran was bent over the wounded Ranger, the wooden grip on his revolver less than two steps away.

"You called me Wilson . . . I know you," Swan railed, jumping to his feet. "You're . . . Frank Morgan!"

The mention of the infamous gunfighter's name caused Beltran to look up at his boss with a start, but it was too late.

Frank closed the gap between himself and the dark outlaw in the blink of an eye. He knew he had to take care of the mustachioed killer first, or risk being shot in the back while he worked out a way to kill Ephraim Swan.

Beaumont looked up and saw what was happening in time to throw the full weight of his body into Beltran's legs. Frank was able to snatch the man's pistol out of his holster as they both fell in a tangled pile on top of Tyler Beaumont.

Beltran proved to be a strong and agile adversary. He drove two rapid-fire blows crashing into Frank's injured ribs.

The gunfighter flinched, trying to get his wind back while he fought the searing pain that shot down his right arm. He struggled to get to his feet. The pistol was heavy in his grasp and he felt it start to slip. By some miracle he was able to hang on to it.

Beltran's big hand snaked out and wrapped around Frank's right wrist, pushing the gun away from him. He gave it a stout yank and both men fell back to the ground.

Frank expected Swan to shoot him at any moment. His strength was failing. He knew he couldn't hold on to the gun forever.

A sudden thud rocked both men. For an instant, Frank thought it was the Ranger. Then he saw Velda, her flimsy gown gathered up at her hips, rear back and kick Beltran again in the head.

The outlaw's eyes went wide and his grip loosened enough for Frank to pull his arm free. Beltran was only momentarily stunned and moved toward Frank again, a deadly look of determination in his dark eyes.

The gunfighter shoved the revolver toward the only target that wouldn't endanger the Ranger, and shot Beltran through the neck.

His spine shattered, the outlaw went instantly rigid. He sputtered and gurgled, trying to talk, but his voice box had been torn away, leaving behind only a mass of blood and gore.

Frank realized he was no longer a threat and rolled quickly to get a shot at Swan.

The outlaw leader had vanished.

Velda still hovered over the wounded outlaw, her gown hiked up over pale but powerful thighs, ready to kick him again.

Frank grabbed his own knife back from the dying outlaw's belt and cut Beaumont's hands free before he climbed wearily to his feet.

"I misjudged you, young lady," he said to Velda, remembering how he'd thought she had told the Ranger's secret.

The words jarred her out of her stupor. She let the hem of her gown drop and flew against Frank in a hysterical rage.

"You were going to shoot Johnny, you lousy, mean, wicked son of a bitch." She beat against his chest with both hands, tears and spit flying as she railed. "You would have killed him, you bastard. I thought you were his friend."

The wounded Ranger gathered up his shrieking girlfriend while Frank looked on in dismay. Beltran's pistol still hung from his hand.

"It's all right," Tyler said over and over while he patted the girl's back to calm her down. "He knew the gun wouldn't be loaded. He showed it to me before he pulled the trigger."

The girl sniffed and looked up at him. "Really?" She looked back at Frank. "You were sure?"

Frank shrugged, wincing at the pain the action caused his shoulder. "I had a pretty good idea."

"Didn't you see him cock it when he pointed it at me? That way I could look right down every hole in the cylinder and let him know he was right." Beaumont gave Velda's shoulders a squeeze. "He wouldn't have shot me. Would you, Frank?"

Frank didn't say anything for a moment. Tyler looked at him.

"Would you?"

Finally the gunfighter chuckled. "Of course not. I could see in your eyes the gun wasn't loaded. If it would have been otherwise, I'd have shot Swan. Now let's do what we came for and go after the murderous son of a bitch."

The Ranger looked around the room for another weapon. War cries and gunfire rang out outside the church. "Don't forget to put on your yellow rags," he said. "Sounds like my friends just showed up."

"How they gonna see anything in the dark?" Frank pulled the yellow bandanna out of his pocket.

"Good point." Beaumont grinned. "I'll have to talk to the captain about that if we don't all get shot."

Velda gave him a worried look. Beaumont patted her on the behind—much softer that the way Swan had done it.

"It's all right, sweetie," he said. "That's why we picked yellow. Easier to see at night." The Ranger looked back at Frank and his eyes grew wide. "Frank, you're hurt bad."

Frank looked down and saw blood dripping off the barrel of the pistol in his hand. Old wounds had ripped loose, torn open in the fight with Beltran. A red stain colored his entire right side. Blood dripped steadily down his arm, covered his hand, and flowed off the front sight of the gun, gathering in a growing pool at his feet.

He shook his head.

"I'm fine," he said. "If you'd be so kind as to help me wrap one of Swan's fine silk sheets around my chest to stop this leak I've developed, I've got some unfinished business to tend to."

Velda grabbed up a sheet she'd been lying on and wrapped it snugly around Frank's chest. She sniffed, wiping tears out of her eyes as she tore a little shred of cloth off the end with her teeth so she could tie it.

Frank lifted his hands above his head with a groan as she pulled the fabric tight. It hurt to bring his arms up, but the pressure stemmed the flow of blood and helped to push back some of the pain.

"Many thanks." He winced as he lowered his arms.

Velda looked up at him and began to cry again. Her eyes were wide with fear and regret. "I swear I thought you were gonna kill Johnny or I never would have gone wild on you like that." Her voice caught in her throat, and the pitch rose as she worked herself into a full bawl. "I'da never hit you if I knew you was on his side and hurt so bad."

Frank stretched to get the sheet adjusted right, and shook his head to calm the lady. "I'm fine." He looked around the cramped room. "You could help me by tellin' me where Swan is likely to go."

"Why don't you let us take care of this?" The young Ranger rubbed at his jaw, where the gag had been, and blinked his swollen eyes.

"Hell, boy." Frank grinned. "Beltran whomped you good. You're hurt as bad as I am. You got two dozen outlaws to go arrest in this town. I say, fine, have at 'em. Just stay out of my way when it comes to Swan."

Velda dried her eyes on the sleeve of her gown and looked out the back door. "I know where he mighta gone."

Both men turned to look at her at the same time.

"Ephraim is really scared of his own shadow. He's a big talker when he's got his army around—and don't get me wrong, he's hellacious good with a gun—but he's always talkin' about this person or that being out to get him. He keeps hideout guns everywhere and two horses all the time—one in the livery and another in the little barn at the other edge of town in back of the old laundry they use as an opium den. He said if he needed to scoot from town in a hurry, he had to be able to ride out from either direction."

Frank bit his lip and clenched the pistol in hand tight enough to start up the bleeding again. The church was more or less halfway in between the two horses. Swan could be heading for either one. Frank wanted to be the one to take the ruthless outlaw, he owed Dixie that. He couldn't let him get away.

Whatever he did, Frank knew he needed to do it fast. He slipped his coat back on over the bandages, gritting his teeth as the tight skin over his old wounds stretched almost to the breaking point. Gun in hand, he opened the door to the outer sanctuary to see if anyone was standing guard. No one. The attacking Rangers from Company F were doing a good job of keeping the town's occupants busy.

He jammed Beltran's pistol into his waistband on his left side, and took his own gun belt off the peg just outside the front door and strapped it on.

"Looks like this is going to be a toss-up," he said as he checked the rounds in his Peacemaker. "I go one way and you go the other. I want to be the one to kill the bastard, but I want him dead more than that."

The Ranger nodded. He'd found a box of rounds for a Winchester carbine from Swan's gun collection against the wall, and was jamming cartridges into the tube. "Fair enough. You call the shots. Which one you want to take—the livery or the smokehouse?"

Shots rang out just outside the door. The men and Velda all ducked as stray bullets pierced the old wooden boards that formed the wall. A gruff voice yelled out: "Texas Rangers. Throw it down!" A crying moan followed more quick shots.

Beaumont had a grim look on his face. He sat Velda down between a stack of heavy boxes and the inner wall and gave her the loaded rifle. He grabbed up another from a nearby crate and began to load it for himself. The air outside seemed alive with gunfire and screaming, and he crouched low while he slid the shells home. "They're not giving much quarter out there."

"Would you?" Frank took a deep breath and made his decision. "I'll take the livery stable. At least I have a horse there and can go after him if he's slipped away. With all the shootin' he may be dead already, but I doubt it. As slimy as he is, I imagine he's working his way through belly-to-the-ground like the snake that he is."

He looked at Velda, who'd stopped trembling or crying now that she had a rifle in her hands. "Me and Tyler are going to go now. After we get up to the front door, you blow out the lights before we open it."

"You'll be all right in the dark here, darlin'," the Ranger said. "It'll be safer."

Velda nodded and the two men trotted to the door. She blew Tyler a kiss, then doused the lights.

Frank checked to be certain he still had the yellow scarf tied conspicuously around his neck, before stepping into the darkness. A sudden thought struck him as surely as any bullet. He gave Tyler a solemn look in the threshold of the doorway.

"You got one thing to remember, Beaumont. Someone sold you out to these outlaws. It wasn't Velda and it wasn't me. If I was you, I'd want to go find out who before someone else gets killed. There's a wild card out there who we can't trust, and there's a chance they're wearin' one of your yellow rags."

Chapter 37

It was just light enough to make out the bodies of three dead outlaws on the street in front of the old church. Frank looked at a smiling Beaumont and shook his head. The Rangers of Company F meant business, and everyone without a yellow scarf would do well to stay out of their way.

The bright rag scarves seemed to glow in the low light. It helped Frank's nerves to know he wasn't as likely to be gunned down by the raiding Rangers, but the bright cloth sure did turn him into an easy target.

He pulled his coat collar up against the cold and to partially cover the colorful bandanna. That would have to do. He bade good luck to the tough little Ranger and moved off to look for Swan.

Frank rounded the corner on the street leading to the livery at a trot, and ran straight into the wilted blonde, Suzette. She wore a wool coat that looked two sizes too big for her, and carried a carpetbag full of extra clothes.

They hit hard enough that it knocked the slight woman to the ground.

She jumped to her feet and began to brush herself off with an indignant air, visible even in the heavy shadows.

"Watch where you're goin' you stupid . . . " She stopped when she recognized Frank as the man who'd rescued her from a bad night with Big Un, the greasy giant.

Her voice melted from ice to warm honey in a matter of seconds, and she leaned in close, rubbing against the gunfighter's body. "I didn't know it was you, sweetness. You better come with me. There's Texas Ranger bastards crawlin' all over this place."

Frank shrugged her off, hoping she didn't know the significance of the yellow scarf around his neck. "I can see that," he grunted.

Three rapid-fire shots rang out across the street, and a man with a pistol stumbled out of the Oxblood saloon. He stumbled, fired once into the ground, then fell. The saloon was on fire, and the flames sprang to life in no time on the dry wood. In a matter of moments it was light enough for Morgan to make out the dead man's face as the gunman Clay Bonner.

Suzette grabbed at Frank's hand. Hers was cold and clammy, like snakeskin. "Let's hightail it off this street, sugar. I still owe you a free sparkin', and I want to see both of us get out of this so you can collect." She looked up and down the street, her dark eyes darting back and forth. "There's a whole bunch of the badge-totin' vermin out behind the Oxblood and the Café. They're settin' fire to everything. I know where there's at least one horse out behind the old laundry. We could ride double and sneak out of here before anyone knew we was gone. What do you say? I could use a strong man like you to look after me."

Just then, the mean-eyed bartender stumbled screaming out of his hiding place in the Oxblood. The man's clothes were on fire, but he didn't have enough sense to fall down and roll. He made it twenty yards down the street, lighting the way like a huge lantern as he went, before he succumbed to the flames and fell smoldering in the middle of the deserted road.

Suzette pulled Frank into a nearby side alley to get them out of the line of fire.

"That stubby little bastard Johnny Nugget is behind this," she spit. "With any luck Ephraim put a bullet in his head before he had to run off. Don't see what Velda saw in that sawed-off runt."

Frank grabbed the skinny woman by the arm and yanked her off the ground. The action sent fiery darts shooting up his arm, but he was too mad to care.

"Ooooow," she yelped, her eyes blazing in the reflected light of the burning saloon. She'd been hurt before and was used to rough treatment. "You're hurting me."

Frank held her fast and gave her light body a little shake to let her know he was serious. "Where's Swan right now?"

"He's leaving. Why should you care? He owe you money?" She gave a crazy little laugh despite the pressure Frank put on her upper arm.

"You might say that." Frank assumed that since Suzette was on her way to the hidden horse behind the old laundry, she had seen Swan going toward the livery. But he wanted to be certain.

"I mean it, Suzette. Tell me if you know where he is."

"At the livery. I saw him slip in the back way just before you knocked me outta my drawers."

Frank released his grip and let her slip back to her feet. "What's got into you?" she whined, and put down her carpetbag to rub the sore spot on her arm.

Frank let out a deep breath and shook his head. He couldn't just let her walk away. Young Tyler Beaumont had already proven he had a weak spot for the womenfolk. He was not likely to recognize her as his spy—a slipup that was bound to get him killed.

Frank looked at the livery a block and a half away. If Swan hadn't left yet, he was sure to be out of there soon. He had enough of a head start.

He changed his tactic on the woman. She'd obviously lived and survived long enough in this town that intimidation wouldn't work well on her. She would respond best to deceit.

"It's dangerous out here," he said. He helped her straighten her rumpled coat. "You got a gun or some kind of weapon?"

Suzette softened immediately. She was used to people like Swan who alternately hit her and kissed her. "I do, sugar."

She reached into her carpetbag and took out a four-shot pepperbox. Not the most accurate gun in the world, but capable of killing the stout young Texas Ranger at close range.

"Anything with more power than that little toy?" Frank wanted to be sure.

The woman smiled and mewed like a cat. "We women got things that are ten times more powerful than that to help us get our way, lover boy."

Horses nickered in the livery. Morgan didn't have time for any more of this.

He'd made it this far in life without shooting too many women, but this little tramp was fast moving toward her place on the short list. He snatched the pepperbox from her and emptied the shells out onto the street.

"What?" Her look of dismay turned into the glare of a sheep-killing dog. "You sorry bastard. You're one of them. I should have seen it."

"Shut up, Suzette."

"And to think, I was dumb enough to offer you a sure-enough no-charge sparkin'. I don't do that for anyone, least of all no sorry badge-totin' puke."

She'd slipped the pearl-handled knife out of her coat before he'd noticed it. As soon as she finished speaking she slashed out with blind fury.

Frank ducked to the side as the sharp blade whizzed past his chest. As mean as she was, once Frank knew Suzette had the knife, she was no match for him, and it actually made his decision about what to do with her all the easier.

She lunged for him again, intent on burying the blade in Frank's belly. He stepped nimbly to one side and whipped his Colt from the holster in one fluid motion. As she stumbled past, he gave her a stout whack across the back of the head.

The skinny blonde staggered forward a step. The pearl-handled knife fell from her grasp and she collapsed facedown in the dirt with a loud oompf.

* * *

Frank was moving toward the livery again before Suzette hit the ground. He'd hit her hard, hard enough to hear a bone crunch. A blow to the back of the head like that could kill a person, especially a skinny-necked little woman like her, but he didn't have time to worry about that. He couldn't very well let her just trot on down the street and kill Beaumont.

At least this way, there was a chance she'd survive long enough for the Texas Rangers to arrest her and cart her off to prison. Before she'd pulled the knife, Frank had been thinking about shooting her.

Half the town was on fire by the time he reached the livery. By design, the huge barn was set off a ways from the rest of the buildings in town so it wouldn't burn with all the livestock in the likely event the rest of the town went up in flames.

Frank stood by to the side of the livery's entry for a full minute, listening. The huge double doors, made to get coaches in and out, were cracked a bit, and he stepped up close to peer inside.

At first, he saw nothing but shadows. Horses shuffled and stomped their feet, no doubt smelling the surrounding fires. It was difficult to get a full view of the huge enclosure through the tiny crack, but as he stepped to one side, Frank could just make out the flicker of a lantern in one of the back stalls at the end of the structure.

Sporadic shooting still peppered the night as groups of Company F moved from shack to shack, ridding the town of Ephraim Swan's outlaws.

Frank looked around the front of the livery trying to figure out how to rid the town of Ephraim Swan. He thought about taking the outlaw as he rode out on his horse, but that was too risky. The shooting was everywhere, and there was no way to tell whether Swan would come out the front or the back.

Frank took a deep breath and drew his Peacemaker. The wound on his side was bleeding again. He could feel the warm stickiness of the blood as it soaked through the sheet around his upper body. He was getting weaker by the minute, so he'd have to see this through quickly.

When it came right down to it, there was really only one way Frank knew to confront a situation—and that was head-on.

Chapter 38

Frank waited for the sound of gunfire from behind the livery before slipping inside, hoping it would draw Swan's attention in the other direction. The gunfighter stepped to the side as soon as he entered and looked down the two rows of stalls, ready to shoot. It was over sixty feet down the narrow alley. Swan's lanky thoroughbred stood saddled in a pool of lantern light in the back stall. The outlaw was nowhere in sight.

Frank heard the rustle in the straw to his right just in time to drop to his knees and miss a shot directed at his head. Another quick shot sent him diving into the stall with his own startled black gelding.

"Step out and face me, Swan," Frank panted from behind the thick timbers that divided the stalls. His words were met by another volley of gunfire that kicked up splinters of wood and caused the horse to rear behind him in the stall. Frank rolled to one side to avoid the iron-shod hooves. "Take it easy, boy, or I'll have to shoot you myself." He spoke in low tones in an effort to calm the white-eyed animal.

"I'm gonna kill you, Morgan." Swan's voice trembled as he spoke.

"You already had four chances in the last thirty seconds. I say you're doin' a damn poor job of it." Frank cast his eyes around the barn looking for a way to draw the killer out into the open. "Come on. Let's end this now, man-to-man like it ought to be. I'll even give you time to reload."

Frank heard brass hitting the floor as Swan dumped his empties. He used the precious seconds to roll under the stall dividers and into a new vantage point three stalls down. On his knees now, he found an oval knothole in the thick pine board. From this new location, he had a half view of the left side of Swan's body. The outlaw's gun hand was hidden, but his left clutched a wooden divider to steady himself. Even from the distance away, Frank could see his knuckles were white.

He smiled at the little ironies of life as he took careful aim and blew off three fingers on the outlaw's left hand.

Swan screamed out in pain and fell out of sight behind the stall divider.

"You got something that belongs to me, Swan."

"I got money, Morgan. Loads of it. Let me slip out of here and I'll tell you where it all is hid."

Frank could hear the strain in the man's voice from his new injury, but he was having troubles of his own. Blood had run down his arm again, and his gun hand was a slippery mess. The recoil of his last shot had almost sent the Peacemaker flying out of his grasp. He transferred the pistol to his left hand and tried to wipe his palm on the hay, but the more he cleaned, the more blood flowed down his arm and dripped from his wrist and elbow.

He was already beginning to see stars. "Help me, Dixie," he whispered. "I can't lose him now when I'm so close."

"What do you say?" the outlaw called from the shadows. "You want to be a rich man?"

"I was just wonderin', Swan." Frank leaned against the boards. His loss of blood was making him short of breath. "Did my poor wife beg you like you're beggin' me?"

The outlaw was silent, but the mention of Dixie sent a surge of renewed energy through Frank's body. Even with the shot of vigor, he knew he might pass out at any moment.

"Might as well go down fighting," he mumbled to himself. He took a deep breath and pulled himself to his feet. Swan still hid behind the wooden stall divider.

"Sorry, Dix. I'm tired," Frank said loud enough for the outlaw to hear. He held the Peacemaker low against his waist, tight to his body to give him added support, and began to walk toward Swan's hiding spot, firing as he went.

"Come out and face me, you child-killin' son of a bitch," Frank said between shots. His soft voice pierced as surely as a bullet. He advanced unmolested until he stood in the middle of the alleyway, cocking and pulling the trigger on his empty Colt.

The sound of an empty gun finally drew Swan out of hiding. He stumbled out, a sneer on his face, his own pistol pointed directly at Frank's chest. He had his injured hand tucked into his waistband.

"You want me to face you, do you?" The smug bravado had crept back into the outlaw's voice. He nodded his head, glancing for a moment at the bloody ooze that dribbled down onto the hay from Frank's dangling gun hand. "I spend all this time thinking you were already dead, and it turns out I wasn't far off the mark."

A cruel smile crossed his lips, and his white eyebrow shot up in amusement. "You were askin' about your wife, Morgan. Wanted to know what it was like before I rubbed her out . . ."

Frank stood silently before the maniacal killer, panting and saying nothing.

"I'll tell you one thing: she was a sight to behold. Didn't even care what happened to her, just spit and screamed like a wild cat, trying to get us to leave you alone." Swan chuckled and spat on the ground. "You asked about her last few moments—if she begged for mercy before I cut off . . ."

Though his right hand hung useless and dripping blood, Frank's left hand moved with a speed even he'd never known. He snaked Beltran's pistol from his belt and before Swan even knew what was happening shot him between the eyes.

"Yeah, about that," Frank whispered. "I decided I really don't care to know."

Frank staggered, stepping forward to keep from falling. The room closed in around him and he began to sway on his feet. He was vaguely aware of the outlaw's body thudding to the ground before he sat back on the hay himself. He looked through the dimming haze at the bloody mess of his right arm. Just as he'd feared; he had a bleeder. A broken rib must have sawed through an artery. He'd seen people with bleeders before and knew there wasn't much hope.

He used what little strength he had left to try and focus on Swan. The outlaw lay in that peculiar folded-leg twist of a man who was dead before he hit the ground.

Sighing, Frank leaned back on a pile of bedding straw and chuckled softly in spite of the pain. He'd always figured on going out on some muddy street or filthy saloon floor, Compared to that, this was Heaven. Didn't really matter though. Dying was dying, no matter where it occurred.

Dixie's killer was dead, so he could rest now. The gun slipped out of his hand and he stared up at the wooden rafters. It was surprisingly bright up there, and he though he could hear his wife's voice.

He managed a weak smile. "Dixie," he whispered—and drifted off into unconciousness.

Epilogue

Two days later, Tyler Beaumont, Texas Ranger, sat beside Velda on a short couch at the end of Frank Morgan's bed. The wounded gunfighter was as comfortable as they could make him, considering what he'd been through.

Ranger Company F had only lost two men during the raid, but both were friends of his and that was two men too many. Beaumont was determined not to make it three.

Velda gave the young lawman's hand a squeeze. She wore a simple lavender dress and her hair was freshly washed. Anyone who saw her would never have guessed what she'd been doing when Beaumont met her. There was a tear in her eye. "You think he'll make it?"

Beaumont shook his head and gave a weary groan. "The doc says it's all up to him now. He's lost an awful lot of blood and a body only has so much of that to spare." He looked down at the weeping girl. "But I'm afraid it's more than that. With his wife gone—her murder avenged—I don't think Mr. Morgan gives a hoot in hell if he lives or dies. And right now, he has to *want* to live. He has to fight."

"If he fights, he could still pull through?"

Beaumont shrugged. "It's not a sure thing, but that's his only chance." Frank Morgan had saved his life and the ranger knew what he had to do. He stood and looked at the sleeping gunfighter's failing body.

"Morgan," the young man whispered. "I aim to find you something worth fighting for. The rest . . . well, that's up to you."

THE EAGLES SERIES BY
WILLIAM W. JOHNSTONE

THE MOUNTAIN MAN SERIES BY
WILLIAM W. JOHNSTONE